SPIDER, SPIDER

This is an uncorrected bound proof
copy, not for sale or quotation.
Please contact the publisher
for further information.

SPIDER, SPIDER

L. C. WINTER

DUCKWORTH

First published in the United Kingdom by Duckworth in 2026

Duckworth, an imprint of Duckworth Books Ltd
1 Golden Court, Richmond, TW9 1EU, United Kingdom
www.duckworthbooks.co.uk

Copyright © L. C. Winter, 2026

All rights reserved. No part of this publication may be reproduced, stored in a retrieval system, or transmitted, in any form or by any means electronic, mechanical, photocopying, recording or otherwise, without the prior permission of the publisher.

The right of L. C. Winter to be identified as the Author of this Work has been asserted by her in accordance with the Copyright, Designs and Patents Act 1988.

A catalogue record for this book is available from the British Library

Printed and bound in Great Britain by Clays Ltd, Elcograf S.p.A.

The authorised representative in the EEA is Easy Access System Europe, Mustamäe tee 50, 10621 Tallinn, Estonia.

Hardback ISBN: 9780715655825
eISBN: 9780715655832

PART I

Chapter One
Antagonist

In Spider's hand was a thin fragment of bone. She ran her thumb along its smooth face and then across the carving on the other side.

'Antagonist,' she hissed into the dark.

The word came back to her, rustling on the leaves of the plants she surrounded herself with.

Antagonist. It was carved into the bone, sharp ridges under her fingers.

The last time she had drawn this word from her clicking hoard of oracle sticks was nine years ago, and she had long since given up any hope of drawing it again. She ceased to breathe for a moment. She stared at it for a long time; the night outside the window deepened and quieted while she gazed at it, lost in a past vision. Finally, she slipped from vision to sleep.

When she awoke, she was still seated in her armchair, the bone in her hand and a penetrating pain in her head, as the silver light of a wet London morning seared into her eyes.

She staggered to her bedroom, rang the bell and suffered mute as Patience, the only other inmate of this twisted old house, thrust a tray holding porridge and a newspaper in front of her.

'My bottle, Patience.'

'Not yet, ma'am. I know you don't want to look at anything, not when you're in pain, but you need to see this.'

Spider slung the spoon into the porridge and pushed it aside with a groan.

'It's Darner,' Patience said flatly and Spider peeled open an eye.

Patience stabbed a finger at the paper. 'There.'

It was an advertisement, of sorts.

The people of this district are advised that Mr Jacob Darner, the Reverend Prophet of the Charitable Brethren, will preach to the benefit of their souls at three o'clock in the afternoon on Sunday the 8th of November 1857, from the steps of the Brethren Hall. The Prophet welcomes all who value their souls and recommends them to come and listen!

She sat up straight. The pain from her head ran like boiling water down her neck and across her shoulders, and she forced her clenched teeth open, hacking up the words as though they were phlegm. 'Him at last. He's back.'

'It's this afternoon,' Patience said, calmly. 'I could go for you, confirm it's him. I've seen your pictures.' Her eye strayed towards a framed sketch. The glass was broken, the picture barely visible through dark smears of dried blood across the surface of the glass. A bunch of dried monkshood flowers, grey with dust and ready to crumble at a touch, lay in front of the picture.

'No!' Spider swept the bowl of porridge to the floor with a crash, the tray clattering after it. 'He's mine. This is mine.'

Patience stepped back. 'Yes, ma'am, of course. In that case you need to rest. Try to calm yourself.' She pulled the curtains closed.

After Patience had cleared away the mess and hidden the last of the light, Spider settled herself in the dark. She made her breath come slow and steady; she made herself think.

Spider had to go out there. Soon. She had to see him with her own eyes. Could it be him? The curtains were drawn against any seepage of light but she could not shut out the fragments of street noise that made their way around and over the house, and into her darkened room. The sound of horses' hooves stabbed like fine pins in the orbit of her eye and whenever the church bells rang the hour, she squeezed her skull with her hands and bowed over with the pain.

It was tempting just to send Patience, but then she wouldn't really know if it were him or not. She would only have a distant report, the opinion of another and, while Patience could be trusted, she could also be mistaken.

The hired carriage was shabby and smelt of mice. It was the only one of its sort that could be had in this quarter of London at such short notice. The extra pay, both for the driver's silence and for bearing with much inconvenience, had been handled by Patience. It waited across the road from Brethren Hall. Spider was drawing attention to herself, she knew, but in this moment she did not care much. Heavily veiled, she sat back in the shadows. Since no one knew her, she would not be recognised but the people would be wondering who was in the carriage, why was it stopped here.

Passers-by peered at the windows, while carters, cabmen and draymen shouted in irritation at the obstruction. A policeman needed to be mollified.

Spider stared, waiting for the large double doors to open. In a previous life, Brethren Hall had been a fine cloth exchange and its architecture reflected the deep wells of money that had built it, some of it Blackwell money, coming from Spider's long-dead relatives. Silks and muslins and cottons moving through and creating money by their friction until they slowed and stopped. Wide stone steps led up to a studded double door beneath a domed tower, whose louvres suggested the presence of at least one bell. It had been sold, changed, broken. It was used as a church for a while and in Spider's distant memory of her childhood it had been a second-hand clothes market. Recently the Charitable Brethren had bought it and the words 'Brethren Hall' were now carved in steady letters above the entrance, the freshly carved stone clean among the soot-stained brick of the district.

The air in the carriage was both cold and thick. Spider rubbed her hands together. Waiting was excruciating, though the pain in her temple and eye was now reduced to an unpleasant pulsing. There was a thickness in her throat that might become nausea without much encouragement. She pulled out a small silk bag of dried herbs, pressed it to her nose and breathed through it, taking in the scents of mint and lavender, the pungency of valerian.

Bells began to ring and everyone passing in the street looked up at the Hall. The great doors opened slowly. Spider slid along the seat to be closer to the window, arranging her veil so that its folds did not obscure her view. Figures began to mill about in the doorway and then to stream out onto the steps. A line of women arranged themselves on either side of the door, all identically dressed in simple dark brown dresses and white caps, their silhouettes uniform with not a hair out of place among them. Then, two lines of men stood behind the women in plain collarless brown suits and a stream of children formed the last line in front of the women, each wearing a miniature version of the adults' dull identical clothes. The bell stopped and they all folded their hands as if in prayer. All their faces were closed and plain, wearing a half-smile, eyes set on some distant point away from the staring faces of the people around them.

One of the older children, thin and slight, reached out and touched the young girl in front of her and was immediately nudged by the woman behind her.

By this time a crowd had gathered to watch. Outside Spider's carriage a man said, 'I ain't got time for this nonsense.' Someone jeered.

A man appeared in the doorway at the top of the steps. Spider held her breath and gripped the edge of her seat. She felt as though the carriage tilted and shifted around her. She must not faint. Tall and thin, dressed in black but for his white cravat, he held the eye and still had the air of a puritan witch hunter of old, a right and duty of judgement assumed. The vertical hollows in his cheeks had only become deeper over the years and his eyes ranged over his audience, pouncing from one person to another.

It was him.

He opened his arms wide and began to speak. The power of his voice held the audience frozen; even the bustling, hurried people stopped and turned towards him. Deep and reverberating, there was a dark honey in it even as he simply announced himself to the world.

She didn't wait to listen; she didn't want to hear what he had to say to the people. The pain blossomed in her temple and she pulled in a breath, her bag of herbs tight against her face. She hammered her other fist against the roof of the carriage and with a jerk and a shout the carriage rolled away. She watched Darner's figure, burning in her eyes as if it was an ember, until the carriage had turned away and she could no longer see.

It was him.

It was him.

She had much to do. But first, something for the pain.

Leaves rustled and crunched under Spider's knees. She pulled away the ivy creepers that had, year on year, worked their way across this corner; her fingers scrabbled around the edge of floorboard that ought to move but did not.

A blade hovered into the edge of her vision. She glanced up to find Patience standing beside her looking down with concern, holding out the knife.

'Are you quite well, ma'am?'

Spider snatched the knife and didn't answer. Ridiculous question. Being quite well was something that applied to other people out in the world. She worked the knife between the crack in the floorboards and finally succeeded in levering up the first board with a small gasp of satisfaction.

Corbeau the crow, her old friend, hopped out from behind Patience and advanced on the interesting hole in the floor. He cocked his head to one side. He pecked at the floorboard and then dodged aside as Spider dropped the next board beside it with a clatter. Once three boards had been cast aside a sizeable space was revealed. Spider threw back a dusty scrap of fabric to reveal an old orange crate, crammed full of bottles and jars. Spider lifted out the crate and carefully placed it beside the hole.

'Put it on the table,' she told Patience.

'The table is full, ma'am.'

Spider raised her head, a movement that caused a web of pain to radiate from her right temple. The table was covered in small animal bones. A project, a pastime, nothing of great importance, not now. She got to her feet and in her hurry, stood on the edge of her skirt. She stumbled and Patience put a hand out.

'I think you should rest, ma'am,' Patience said.

'No. No, not until – not until after. I need to think. Then I can rest for a little while. But not long. I can't let him get away from me again.'

She swept all the small bones to one side. They had been carefully arranged by type and size but she could re-do that later. After. Patience picked up the crate of bottles with the small groan of someone whose back has a comment to make and put it on the table. Spider waved her towards the door and Patience rolled her eyes.

'I'll come with tea and a slice of seed cake in…' she glanced at the clock, '…about half an hour. And I'll bring your bottle. I can see you're ignoring the pain.'

Spider didn't speak, just waved her hand again and the door closed behind Patience. Corbeau hopped onto the windowsill and shuffled his feathers.

Spider ran her fingers over the tops of the bottles. She had not taken them out in some time. Some would require replacing, but perhaps she could manage with what was here. Would they have decayed? Perhaps they would even be more potent. The minerals would be fine in all likelihood. The arsenic would still just be arsenic. She lifted a small ceramic pot and opened the lid with a gentle chink. A beautiful blood-red powder lay within and clung to the sides of the pot. *Cinnabar.* She placed it back in the tray. A substance she had acquired more out of interest than any potential use it might have, but the colour always drew her and she was pleased to see the powder had remained dry. Damp was always a threat in this house and she might struggle to replace some of her materials without drawing attention in such a short amount of time. This collection had been the work of several years.

Arsenic. She held up the bottle and shook it. There was plenty left. Enough to kill half the district. She did not want to kill half the district. Just one man.

Aconitum.

Digitalis.

Papaver somniferum.

She peered into a small bamboo pot that contained a dark paste, now dried out. *Curare.*

She was a little unsure of the botanical preparations. She held up the bottles to the light and sniffed at one or two. The ones preserved in alcohol seemed to have survived. Such a shame she had no available test subjects.

The dried herbs and mushrooms had lost their pungency which was only to be expected. The wormwood was grey dust in its jar. Almost certainly useless now, but since she wanted to kill a man it was hardly important anyway. If this became a long task, she might have to wait for spring to bring fresh growth in her favourite plants, the green of new life extending its fingers up through the decaying remains of the past.

She took out three black bottles from the back of the tray. Her deaths. She sniffed the first. The label said 'quiet'. It smelt clean and still, despite all this time, faintly of lavender. It was a lie of course, the label. No death could ever really be quiet, especially a death brought in on a poison. One's breath must cease, one's heart must be brought to stillness. Neither could ever be entirely a peaceful proposition. But nevertheless, there are degrees.

Purge, the next bottle said, and when she uncorked it, a stink uncoiled into the room. She wrinkled her nose and tried to pour the substance out, but nothing except more of the unpleasant smell emerged. A pigsty next to an overflowing sewer. She hurriedly stuffed the cork back into the bottle and put it to one side.

A smile tugged the corner of Spider's mouth and she picked up the last bottle. *Nightmares*. She sniffed the bitter contents and then poured it into a small glass. She swirled the dark brown fluid. No mould. No unexpected stink. It would be a risk to use it; making something fresh would be more certain. But still, as she poured it back into its dark glass home, she felt more alive than she had in years. An opportunity she thought lost had been found and she had the tools at hand to make use of it.

Corbeau went to peck at the chinking bottles and she held out her hand. 'No, my dear, this is not for you.' He shuffled his feet and hopped out onto the window ledge with an offended air.

'Wait,' she said, and he paused, eye cocked over his shoulder. She took a dead mouse from her pocket and dangled it by the tail. Corbeau cocked his head, as if considering the question of the mouse. 'Fresh from the kitchen trap,' Spider said, and laid it on the edge of the table. She stroked his back lightly. He lifted the mouse and watched her, sceptical. Spider moved the tray of bottles to one side and took her oracle sticks from her pocket. Twenty-eight words to define her days. The crow tore at his mouse with a satisfied air and waited.

She went around the room lighting a few candles and turned the oil lamp down to a dim orange glow. With a soft clattering, she mixed up the sticks so that they lay in a mess of angles.

'The first. Pick.'

Corbeau eyed the heap of sticks before darting forwards and picking one. She placed it in front of her deliberately without looking at the word it bore.

'The second. Pick.'

This time the crow indicated his choice by pecking the stick so that it span. She laid this across the other stick at a particular angle. And so on, the third, fourth until eight oracle sticks lay arranged in front of her in an eight-pointed star.

She stared down at the arrangement, a little distracted by Corbeau's avid enjoyment of his gift. She waved a hand in dismissal and he hopped to the windowsill before disappearing out into the night. She closed the window and, muttering to herself, she began to take the star apart, arranging the sticks in a line but still avoiding letting her eyes fall on the words. Then she began to read, starting with the ones that had been at the bottom layer of the star.

She muttered to herself. '*Despair* at the bottom of things. It so often is. And then *Antagonist* again, influencing the past. *Darkness* leads me on. Does it? A strange thing – surely light leads, not darkness.'

The door swung open and Patience came in balancing a tray. She silently put it on a side table and waited, listening.

'Next *Justice* and then when we turn to obstacles, we find *Ally*.

Incomprehensible. Is that not incomprehensible, Patience? I hope it does not mean you.'

Patience said nothing, but smiled thinly.

'And our outside influences are *Love*. Love!' She waved the stick in the air. 'I don't think that has ever come out for me. That stick lurks at the bottom of my pocket perpetually. I have often wondered what even drove me to carve it. Love. At the crisis,' she turned over her penultimate stick, '*Death*. And the outcome of all—' The blank one, the stick with no word on it, the one that kept its counsel, left things open. She stared at it.

'So strange.' She kept staring and felt behind herself for her chair, lowered herself into it slowly, her mind swirling. Blank. Blankness, and love where it is never expected and an ally that's an obstacle.

She turned to Patience who had brought tea, her special seed cake and the laudanum.

Spider ignored the sustenance and reached for the small bottle. The dreams would help. They would elucidate by some sideways route. She would follow their tendrils through to him, she would find him, reach him and finally, after all these years, she would kill him.

Chapter Two
Escape

Thwack!

The birch came down hard against the small pink palms and the girl gave an inward gasp.

Nancy Ratcliffe stood to one side, fury raging upwards from her heels to the top of her head. Her little sister, nicknamed Pigeon, was so small and the man holding the birch leaning over her was a solid wall of anger. With Pigeon's gasp of pain, Nancy's own anger burst. She snatched at the yard rule leaning by the blackboard.

The man with the birch, Mr Bevel, was too occupied to notice. He grabbed her sister's hands from her armpits where instinct had thrust them.

'Hold them up!' he commanded with a snarl.

Nancy took two steps forwards and swung the ruler. It hit him – *smack!* – across the side of his face and he staggered sideways before snatching out with his left hand and grasping the rule. He turned on Nancy, face distorted with rage, and tugged. She clung on and he brought back his arm and struck her in the face with the birch, once and twice. Her face stung but she held tight, fingers burning on the wood of the yardstick.

Nancy's little sister launched herself at Bevel's muscular legs and bit him just above the knee. He gave a great yell and swiped at her with the birch, still holding on to the yard as Nancy tugged at it. Nancy's face was raw where the end of the birch had caught her cheek.

'Bloody criminals!' he shouted, his face red, neck bulging against his collar.

The other children huddled at the back of the room, staring wide-eyed in fear except for Robbie Johnson who watched with glee. 'Go on, Mr Bevel, wallop 'em!' he shouted.

The door of the classroom slammed open and the austere form of Mr Darner stalked in filling the room with his presence. 'What in God's name is going on here?' He grabbed the back of Nancy's dress and pulled her away. The yard rule clattered to the ground. Bevel gave Pigeon an extra smack with the birch and pulled her off, slinging her backwards to crash into a chair. She cried out.

The small classroom of the Charitable Brethren of Christ fell silent and all the children in their identical clothes shuffled their feet. Nancy wiped a trickle of blood from her chin where the end of the birch had caught her skin.

'I'm sorry, Prophet.' Mr Bevel wrenched Pigeon to her feet by reaching down, clasping her narrow little wrist and, hauling her upwards. 'I did not intend to disturb the peace of our Hall. I was merely punishing this one,' he gave Pigeon's arm a shake, 'when that harpy attacked me with the yard rule.' He pointed at Nancy with the birch.

'What is she doing in the classroom in the first place?' Darner asked. 'She ought to be with the women.'

'I got her in to watch. Thought it would be,' he sucked his teeth as he sought for the word, 'instructional for her, to see what she's bringing her sister to with her bad influence.'

Darner nodded. 'Not an unreasonable course of action, Mr Bevel.'

'Thank you, Prophet. God knows I dislike punishing the children—'

Nancy snorted. 'God knows when you lie, Bevel.' She spat the words, narrowing her eyes. The children at the back of the room gave a suppressed gasp and huddled closer together.

Bevel, redder in the face than ever, closed his eyes for a moment as if praying for self-control. His right hand opened and closed on temptation. He continued with a louder voice, 'But it's necessary as you know and I felt I might kill two birds with one stone, as it were.'

Nancy gradually became aware that Darner was watching her, his eyes dark with malevolence

'You,' Darner said, 'are a thorn in our side. You need to be taught a proper lesson; the humiliations are clearly not enough.'

The humiliations: a weekly ritual whereby a member of the Brethren lay face down on the floor in front of the others and was berated for their sins by Mr Darner. It was supposed to be two or three different Brethren every week; no one is free of sin, all took their turn, except the Prophet himself, of course. But lately Nancy had been there almost every week, her nose full of the dust on the platform, the deep tones of Darner's powerful voice beating the air above her, rising in indignation and anger, vibrating with disgust and passion, carrying the congregation with him in condemnation of her smallest offences.

Darner snatched at her and pulled her towards the door, his long, thin fingers wrapped around her forearm like a manacle, shifting painfully on the thin bone and tendon under her skin. He turned to Bevel. 'You deal with the sister and then meet me in the belfry.'

As Nancy was dragged from the room into the Hall's main entrance, she heard a *thwack!* and a cry from Pigeon. She struggled. 'Don't you dare—'

Darner put his hand across her mouth and pulled her into him so that she was an inch from his face. Pressed close against her he smelt of incense and old books and sweat. 'Out! Out of this witch, you devil!' He shook her. The great doors were closed, the space echoing. Members of the Brethren were gathering, watching, whispering.

Another *thwack* came from the room behind them and she tugged away but could not loosen his grip. His eyes bored into hers. There was triumph in them as she struggled against his imprisoning hold. 'Mrs Aldridge!' he called to one of the Brethren women, who bobbed in a small curtsey. 'Lend me your cross.' She pulled out the wooden cross that the Brethren always wore and glanced at her friends, unsure. 'We're going to expel the demon from this young woman and a cross worn by a righteous woman will be of great assistance. Come.'

Nancy struggled but it was futile. He was a tall, wiry man and she was small and thin, thirteen and not well grown.

'Tie it around her forehead. Tightly.'

Mrs Aldridge's hands shook as she took her cross and bound it against Nancy's forehead. Darner kept his tight grip on Nancy. 'Tighter,' he growled. She retied it, the cord cutting into Nancy's skin, the wood of the cross pressing against her skull. From the corner of her eye, Nancy could see her father in the group of Brethren, eyes wide and a hand across his mouth, his handkerchief clutched in his fingers. A tight hand on his shoulder prevented him from stepping forwards; Mr Herbert, quiet and correct, keeping Darner's peace for him, as always.

Nancy struggled and Darner kept his hand across her mouth. 'The cross will be a reminder during your ordeal,' he said to Nancy. 'It may help to drive the devil out. I deem he has a good home in you.'

Nancy licked his hand.

He drew back his palm and slapped her on the cheek. 'Devil witch.' He pulled her towards the stairs that led to the belfry.

'Pigeon!' she called as another *thwack* sounded across the entrance.

'You will pray alone in the bell tower, Miss Ratcliffe. You will pray as the bell tolls for your soul and you will come down to us, purged, with the glory of God ringing in your ears.' He punctuated each syllable of the last four words with a shake of her arm.

He pulled the bell tower door open just as Bevel emerged from the school room. A snatch of crying escaped before he closed the door firmly behind him.

'Pigeon!' Nancy called again and Bevel gave his bark of a laugh.

Darner half-dragged Nancy up the stairs, tugging her along so that she fell at almost every step. Her stumbling angered him and yet every time she nearly had her feet properly under her, he would tug again and she would fall. This was worse than she had expected. There was a deep trembling fury in Darner she had never seen before, as if he were waiting for an excuse. An excuse to do something worse. Everything in her reared away from it and fear swirled, mixing with the anger in her guts.

'If you'd just damn well let me stand, we'll get along!' she burst out in frustration when she fell yet again.

With a whip-like turn, he brought his hand around to hit her, a numbing slap to the jaw. Her head smacked into the wall beside her and she shouted in pain.

'Never use that language in my hearing again, demon witch. Two hundred years ago we knew what to do with sinners like you.' His breath was rank in her face. 'Fire or the rope, heathen slut. Fire or the rope, that's where you'll end.'

She stumbled again and he pulled her arm hard. She felt a painful tug in her shoulder and cried out. He was going to pull her arm out of its socket, but then they were up into the belfry. The pair of great bells hung there silent, the hole beneath them wide and empty.

He took some twine from his pocket and quickly tied her hands together in a praying gesture, the string tight against her wrists, and then tied the other end of the string to the joist closest to the bells.

He bent down towards her and pushed the cross pendant hard against her skull. 'Pray. Repent. There will be nothing else to do for an hour. They will read you a sermon you won't forget.'

His feet hurried down the stairs.

Nancy's jaw throbbed, hot and painful where he had hit her, she opened her mouth and quickly closed it again because it hurt. A thumping pain travelled up to her forehead where it had hit the wall. She writhed, trying to find a comfortable position on the hard unfinished floor but there was no good way to lie. She crouched awkwardly, watching the bells and the rope and the mechanism, fear growing inside her, swallowing her rage.

'Pigeon!' she bellowed into the air. 'I want my sister! I want Polly!' She used her sister's real name for once. The Brethren refused to respond to any reference to the girl's nickname. 'If you've hurt her, I'll—'

The bells began to move. She froze. The wheels on either side of the great bells began to swing back and forth, just a little. Back and forth, but there was no sound as yet. The first sound, when it came, was a gentle touch: a chime like a water drop on her head. Then the cascade began.

It came up through the floorboards at her knees, through the bruises forming on her legs and forearm, and in her ears – a clear domineering tone, so that her brain was vibrating. It crashed from the walls, down onto her and through her hands. The pain in her head and jaw rang in time with it.

She tried to twist out of the knot at her wrist so that she could put her hands over her ears but could not. Her teeth hummed. Her very bones seemed to be roaring. The pain of the cross on her forehead beat with the swinging bells. She lay down on her side and pushed one ear into the rough wood, trying to bring her hands to the other ear. The whole floor thrummed.

She watched them as the wheels spun, the sound becoming a sea washing around her, threatening to drown her, pulling her down and crushing her lungs.

Come on Nancy, she thought, *It's only sound. Breathe!* And she made herself inhale, in and out, feeling her heartbeat lose itself in the shaking bells' torrent of sound. She watched, back and forth, swing and swing, and back.

With each of the bronze bells' clapper strikes, she felt the volume of her hate increase. She wished that the movement of the bell would work itself loose so that they would fall and crush Bevel and Darner's bones. She knew they were down there, hauling the ropes, putting their malevolence into every drag of the bells' weight. She watched the motion and wished. The bells heaved back and forth, wood and metal and stone sounding. With each hefting circle of motion, the whole mechanism tugged against its moorings and she could feel the tower beneath her shifting with it. Darner's new bells were bigger than the old one they replaced – new fastenings on old beams. She squeezed her eyes shut, folding in against the sound.

She began to focus her attention on one particular bolt. She could feel the heft of the bells' swing pulling against this bolt, and she wished and wished that it would snap, break, shear off. She felt the twist of it in her mind and then it shifted with a jerk that took her a moment to realise was real. But the bells were already slowing, dropping a great echoing silence through the tower.

The ringing in her head was so loud that it was almost as if the bells had not stopped. Only their stillness proved to her that they had. Darner seemed to appear suddenly. She hadn't heard him on the stairs. He loosened her hands, spoke to her but she couldn't hear him. His mouth moved and she was bewildered. Why couldn't she hear him? The bells' sound echoed through her mind and her ears. He marched her down the stairs.

The sound of ringing surrounded her and down in the entrance-way her father waited, his face grey and frightened, Pigeon clinging to his legs. His voice made only a distant murmur but Nancy knew the words his mouth had formed as surely as if she'd heard them.

'Why can't you be good, Nancy? I just need you to be good.' The words finished in a coughing fit as he turned away, body shaking.

Darner ripped the cross from her forehead and then strode away. He may have said something but she didn't hear it. She ignored her father and bent down to look at Pigeon. There was a bruise on her cheekbone and when she gently unfurled her sister's palms, there were red weals across them, blood oozing through the damaged skin. Pigeon folded her hands and shoved them into her pockets, saying something that Nancy couldn't hear clearly enough to understand. Their father hurried them away.

In the loud silence they went down to the basement where the dormitories were. Her father's trembling fingers tucked her into bed as if she were a child, a hot dry hand on her forehead for a moment and then it was gone, snatched away as if he regretted the gesture. Nancy felt the breath on her cheek, the words small and distant, only just audible through the hum in her ears. 'I don't know what to do, Nancy. I think he won't abide you no more. I've just seen him and he's in a rage like I've never seen.'

Fear swept through Nancy. Her jaw throbbed and she remembered Darner's eyes. There'd been something deep and frightening in his gaze, in the tightly held rage when he'd gripped her arm, a sense that he might unleash it, that he might find a reason, and then he'd kill her. He wanted it badly and it wasn't safe to stay, not now. She had to get out and find somewhere for all of them.

She flung back the blankets and climbed out of bed. 'I'm going.' Her own words were dim and bowl shaped in her ears.

'You can't go. Out on the streets—' He broke into a coughing fit, trying to speak through it. 'I brought you here to keep you from the streets.'

He'd said this before: they'd joined the Brethren two years ago to get her away from the streets. He didn't want their poverty to drive her to crime or prostitution.

'I'll be careful, Dad.'

He looked back over his shoulder at the door, resignation on his face. 'Look for Lil, she'll help you find your way. You remember Lil? Mum's cousin?' He slipped his hand into hers and squeezed it.

Nancy nodded. She remembered. Old Lil had been their friend after their mother fled the city and returned to the Yorkshire village of her childhood, leaving them behind. Nancy's mother had been trying to escape herself and her weaknesses, and the city's grime. That time before had been a time of hunger, haunted by the tang of cheap gin and fear of the cholera that had periodically swept the district. But Nancy had never forgotten Lil's kindness: the shared food and hand-me-down clothes, a gentle hand on her arm.

'But what about Pigeon? Bevel beat her.'

Their father reached an arm out and curled it around Pigeon, hugging the small girl to himself. 'I'll look after Polly.'

Nancy looked at him, despairing. 'But you can't stop them. You don't even try!'

Tears welled up in her father's eyes and she looked away. 'Me and Polly will keep ourselves out of trouble.' He stopped hard against the unspoken words that it would be easier to do so without Nancy there, the maker of trouble. She who provoked.

Nancy looked at Pigeon. 'I'm going,' she stated, her voice still round and swollen sounding.

When Pigeon spoke, it was as though she were very far away and underwater. 'No!' The shape of Pigeon's mouth was enough to tell her what she'd said. 'You can't leave Dad.' Pigeon stamped her foot.

'Look, I'll come for you and Dad soon.' Nancy dropped to her knees and addressed her sister. 'I'll find somewhere out there for us so we can be together again.'

Pigeon looked dubious and above her their father shook his head and opened his mouth to say something, but started to cough instead. He took out the handkerchief spotted with old blood stains and leant against a bed as his whole body shook.

'I promise I'll come back for you.' She kissed the top of Pigeon's head. 'I love you, little Pidge,' she whispered. Pigeon burst into tears.

Nancy gripped her father's hand, looked into his eyes, which were still watering from the coughing fit. 'Take care, Dad.'

He took Pigeon's hand. He turned to go and paused, his back still and rigid for a moment, a minute, two minutes. Nancy wondered if he were saying something but then he left without looking at her. Nancy was alone.

She laid her shawl out in front of her and piled everything she owned on top of it before tying it into a small parcel. Perhaps silence would always be this ringing noise from now on; she wondered if she would ever sleep again? She limped to the window, hauled herself up and out of it, glanced back and then turned away into the streets.

Chapter Three
Ally

The beggar slumped in tattered clothes. Her hand, thin and long-fingered, rested cupped and open, hoping for a coin to fall in it. It remained empty. She was sitting in the doorway of an empty shop opposite Brethren Hall and under her bedraggled hat an eye watched the street and the entrance to the Hall. A crow perched on the roofline of the Hall, hunched and watchful.

Spider waited. The rhythm of the day, of the Hall, began to reveal itself. Delivery boys, policemen's beats, shops opening, the early trade in the pubs. In the Hall itself, a line of people came for an early service and left, bells ringing at the start of the service and then later for some length.

Her eye was caught by something down the side passage that ran around behind the Hall. Two arms emerged from a window at ground level; there must be a basement. Then the torso of a girl emerged and, with some wriggling and shuffling, the rest of her. She was thin and slight, dressed in the female costume of the Brethren: drab and simple. A dark plait had fallen from under her neat white cap. She picked up a small bundle. Then she looked up and down the side passage and walked quickly, turning away from the Hall as soon as she was on the road.

She stopped, looked back and then around her as if getting her bearings. A lost lamb from Darner's flock. At this distance it was hard to see clearly but Spider thought her face was bruised, raw.

She might be of interest. She might know things.

Spider pulled herself to her feet and set off after the girl, leaning on a stick with an exaggerated hobble. She bumped into a wide-skirted old woman accompanied by a young man. The matron flapped at her with disgust. 'Get away from me. Ugh, beggars.'

'They ought to be rounded up.' The young man stepped forwards scowling and pushed Spider away.

Spider nearly lost her balance and, recovering, lashed out with her stick and hissed a curse at them. The Brethren girl slipped around a corner into a narrow street, skirts swirling in haste. Spider hurried to keep up.

This side street was busy at its entrance. Men lounged outside a pub. Several small shops had their doors open, their customers and owners doing most of their business in the street itself, the small shops too crowded with goods for comfort. Spider sidled through the crowd. A slip of brown in the distance, a flash of the white cap. She was going to lose the girl. She pushed through, barely noticing if she bumped into people or the muttering and scowling which followed her.

The street, which narrowed into a sooty-walled alley, had several arches and turnings. The girl's face flashed back as she looked over her shoulder and then she was gone.

Spider was trembling as she hurried up the alley and through the arch she thought the girl had gone through. It led to a dilapidated court. A few curious faces turned to her.

'Did you see a girl?'

The people looked at each other, shook their heads. Lying maybe, covering for the girl. Spider took a step into the space.

'Go on, get out of here,' one of the women said, rising to her feet and Spider turned to go. There were doors into houses but she couldn't see another way for the girl to leave the yard.

Back in the alley she tried a neighbouring arch but it led to another even narrower passage blocked with a metal gate bearing a heavy padlock. She was about to turn and leave when she realised where the gate led: onto the Brethren's own back courtyard. It held a couple of privies, a stable with a donkey and an open area with an unlit brazier. Still, the girl wasn't here. Spider had lost her.

Back on the main street Spider, hunched over and wrapped in her tattered shawl again, looked up at the Brethren Hall. It twisted and shifted away from her and she reached out and held onto a wall. The sense of his presence bloomed out from the building like the spores of some malignant fungal growth. She felt it touch her and the hatred rose within her at its presence. She had to get to him. The sense of disappointment at losing the girl slipped into the background. She had to clear him away from the world and make him pay.

Leaning into the wall she slowly shuffled up the passage beside the Hall. Around the back of the building she could see the edges and corners of the outbuildings she'd seen through the gate. There was a row of low windows near ground level. Most were of obscured glass but one showed a half-basement decked out with rows of beds. Two of the Brethren's plain dresses hung on hooks and she guessed this was where the girl children and single women slept. The Brethren escapee, the intriguing girl, had scrambled out from one of these windows.

A man, thin to the point of emaciation, was sitting on one of the beds, his shoulders bowed over a small girl who was hugging him, her face buried in his shirt. He held his hands together over her head as if in prayer, his lips moving slightly. As Spider watched, he shifted one hand from its prayer position and stroked the girl's hair gently. His hands shook.

A shadow fell across them and a moment later Darner was there, standing behind the man who twisted around to see him, neck straining up. Darner placed a hand on his shoulder, seeming reassuring, but the man's shoulder cringed away beneath it.

Darner. It really was him. She could not have been mistaken when she saw him on the steps but this new sight of him made her head spin with the real flesh-and-blood of his presence. The man was here, only a few streets from her home. Spider's breath caught in her throat and she put her forehead against the cold brick to steady it. When she looked back, no one inside the room had moved.

Darner looked around the room slowly, almost theatrically, before saying something Spider could not hear but she guessed he was asking about the girl who had left because, in answer, the thin man's shoulders dipped further and he gestured towards the window. Spider slid backwards out of view, turned and shuffled back down the passage.

Behind her she heard the window open.

'You!'

His voice. His commanding intonation with the sense that it came from a being of greater stature than simply the body of the man. The memory of it brought a rushing sound into her ears. Water, smooth tiles and pain, her spent breath hard in her throat. She bent against the wall and breathed out slowly, then turned back towards him, keeping her face bowed and the shawl over her head. He had opened the window and was leaning out.

'Me, sir?' she asked, frail and trembling only partly in pretence. Her breath came in small, tightly sewn packages without enough air.

'Did you see a girl come along here?' His voice was hard and commanding, each word a stone.

'No, sir, I only just got here a few minutes ago.'

'When did she go?' He asked over his shoulder into the room. A murmured answer and Darner said, 'You'll do a mighty penance for this, Ratcliffe. Your weakness is a failure in God's eyes, but we will redeem you.' There was more apologetic-sounding mumbling and then Darner turned back to Spider. 'What are you doing here, anyway?' he asked, sharp and suspicious.

'Just looking for a corner to rest in.'

'Well, look elsewhere,' he commanded harshly and then seemed to recall himself. The great saviour. The charitable prophet of a rising sect. 'Unless you want to join our group in search of salvation, of course. Open service times are posted on the main doors and all are welcome.' With that he was gone, the window slammed shut.

A fear fluttered through her that her memories would weaken her, but she breathed hard and allowed them to build and harden inside her. Details she had almost forgotten gathering again to cement her hatred, to fuel what must come. It was a relief but with it came the pain in her head and she shivered with the intensity of it.

'Madam?'

Spider's head was bowed against the swirling pain; she gathered herself for the effort of taking herself home. But here was Patience, approaching uncertainly. Spider grasped her arm.

'Home, Patience.'

Her mind ran ahead to the house, the dark and the calm but then back, back to the girl. Who was she? And why had she been running from the Brethren? And why did Darner want her so badly?

Chapter Four
Beginnings, 1832

At the grand age of four years old, the little girl was better travelled than many an old man, having come from the other side of the world. She began to cry.

Sara's mother, Eliza, stared at the large green door in front of them, having pulled the bell. After shifting on her feet irritably for a few moments she darted forward and pulled it again. Behind them the horses of their cab stamped, as irritated by the wait as she was.

This time the door creaked open. Not a well-dressed servant. Not a servant at all, but the man of the house. Bent-shouldered, grey and sharp-eyed, like a dissatisfied heron. His blue eyes assessed Eliza, her pile of belongings and then, finally, the girl. She shrank away.

'Sister,' he said turning his attention back to her mother.

'Brother,' she replied.

'And what am I supposed to infer from your presence? Has he abandoned you?'

'No.'

'Delightful.' The man gave an unpleasant smile. 'You! You have abandoned him!' He turned his eyes on the girl. 'And a squalling child too. All the way from India.'

'We decided it would be for the best if I came back to England. He decided.'

The man eyed her and his lip quirked in amusement. 'He got sick of you, did he? Adventures not so enticing after all? Business in India not booming?'

'It was not the situation he expected. His plans...' Her voice trailed away and then she said. 'He was not always well.'

'And what can you possibly want from me?'

'A little brotherly charity, that is all.'

'All? All?' he shouted.

Passers-by looked on with interest or shook their heads in disapproval. The cab driver cleared his throat significantly.

'You want me to take you in with your brat, after you ran off like some street drab?'

'We were perfectly respectably married and you know it. Just as you know her name is Sara.' She placed her hand on the small girl's shoulder and Sara felt it tremble. 'He'll send money to support our costs. All we need from you is a roof and that you are not short of, I know.' She cast an eye over the building.

Several people had stopped on the pavement unashamedly watching the spectacle. The man on the doorstep shot a venomous look at a sour-mouthed woman who was whispering to her neighbour.

'We should talk about this indoors.'

'Perhaps. Perhaps, yes.' He stood back and then bellowed into the house, 'Bristow! Where are you? I'm opening my own door like a peasant.'

In the distance, another door slammed and footsteps hurried, getting closer until a flustered young man burst out of a side door and was directed to bring in the boxes.

'And, Jeremiah, would you mind?' Eliza indicated the driver.

'How much?' Jeremiah Blackwell asked the driver, and when he replied snarled as if a fortune had been requested. Money was passed, Jeremiah to Bristow, Bristow to the driver and then the carriage rattled away.

'Welcome back to Hangcorner House, Eliza.' Jeremiah bowed ironically as his sister passed in through the big door, ushering Sara along ahead of her. 'I'm sure it's a disappointment after dreams of Indian palaces and elephant rides but reality so often is.'

The door closed with a bang and as she walked into the echoing hall, Sara started to cry again and slumped down to her knees on the cold tile.

'Put them together in the turret room.' Blackwell addressed a taut housekeeper who had appeared from somewhere in the depths of the house. 'They'll be out of the way there.'

'It'll need preparation, sir. We haven't used it for years.' She eyed Sara as though she were a potential contaminant. Sara sniffed and resisted the urge to wipe her face on her sleeve.

'The room is empty, isn't it? I haven't said you can use it for storage.' His voice echoed off the tiles, hard and uncompromising.

'Yes, sir, but there's always dust and the chimney. The windows will need cleaning. I think the bed lacks a mattress. And the child will need a bed. Curtains. Linens.'

Jeremiah Blackwell waved a hand dismissively. 'Get it done, Mrs Nichols. They can sleep in the same bed. Use anything you need from other rooms. It just needs to be functional; it doesn't need to be pretty.'

'Yes, sir,' the housekeeper turned to leave. 'I'll ensure the rooftop greenhouse is closed up.'

Eliza's head jerked up at the mention of the greenhouse, a flicker of warmth across her face but then it was gone, hidden.

Sara was still sitting down. It was all so big and cold and frightening; there was this man, her uncle, made of edges and chill laughter that she couldn't comprehend and her mother was distant and stiff with pain.

Her lip wobbled with her tears and she gazed up at a snarling tiger's head that hung high on the wall.

'Do you like it, little Sara?' Jeremiah said, bending over her, a mockery of baby tones on his lips. 'Your papa sent me that beast. Since he took your mama off my hands, one beast for another – maybe I should send it back now, eh?'

'Leave her alone, Jeremiah.' Eliza took Sara's hand and pulled her to her feet and lifted her up into her arms. 'Come on,' she said, speaking to the housekeeper.

'Sister,' Jeremiah rapped out, interrupting their departure. 'Why have you come home?'

Eliza turned back to him in the doorway. 'This is not our home, Jeremiah. Our home is with my husband. But he no longer wants me there, or so he says. He promises to join us next year, two at most.'

'Ha!' He gave a bark of laughter. 'I have some sympathy for the man at last. At least you've managed to fall on your feet by returning here. You always did know how to manage things to your advantage.'

'If that were truly so, dear brother, do you think I'd be back here?' She swept the gloomy hall with her eyes, before her gaze came to rest on him sardonically. 'I never wanted to see this place again. I had hopes for a golden life. All I can wish for now is the return of my husband.'

'I told you, Eliza, I told you all his dreams of glory out there in the Empire were nonsense.'

'We were unlucky.'

'Unlucky!' He scoffed. 'He got sick of your whining and sent you home. I bet you clung to him.' He put on a high pitched voice. '"But I love you, Clarence, please don't send me away." No fear! He couldn't wait to send the impediment back on the boat home.'

Eliza looked at him with a blank, closed face. 'No one has ever loved you Jeremiah, not even liked you I imagine. But me? I hate you.'

For the first year or so after their arrival, Sara continued to trail along in her mother's wake. Her mother occupied herself by growing exotic plants in the rooftop greenhouse, looking out on wet London skies, enveloped in the scent of jasmine and stroking the soft hair of the creature clinging to her skirts. One-half of her attention was always on the lookout for post that never came and the other half on sending away for seeds that would not sprout.

She would ask Bristow: 'Is there a letter from India?'

There was never a letter from India and Jeremiah took to mocking her over it.

'Dear sister, my heartfelt sympathies, but it seems your devoted husband has not written again. He does know your address? Of course he does, since you eloped together from this house, running away to your exciting eastern sunrise. What can he mean by it?'

Her jaw would clench tight and when he was gone, she would cry angry tears. 'I tried! I did.' Sara would stand beside her, unsure of what to do, wide-eyed and afraid. Experience taught there was no right thing to do: to embrace, speak or also cry – all wrong. Later her mother would sob apologies into her hair.

Once they were in their second year and Eliza had ceased to ask after letters (she had gone through a phase of furious writing herself, letters pouring from her hands in streams), Sara took to entertaining herself and making toys out of anything she might find. She would take them to Eliza, displaying them proudly and receive a ghostly smile. Hiding became a favourite game; hide and seek requires two but just plain hiding can be done alone.

Jeremiah found her an annoyance. The servants felt sorry for her. Her mother got colder and sadder and quieter. She took to medicines and wine; sometimes there was a warm miasma of brandy that recalled the distant presence of her father.

Sara once heard the housekeeper say, as she folded table linen with one of the maids, 'Poor little mite,' with a shard of warmth in her voice, but then she said, briskly, 'Of course she's a proper nuisance, stealing things and borrowing things. She'd planted one of her mother's strange plants in a corner of the dining room last week, what a mess! And she was in that case of Indian knives yesterday.'

'Like a magpie,' the maid said.

'More like a spider. The way she scuttles and wraps things in her hankie to take them away gives me the creeps. She likes the strangest things. She had one of the old master's stuffed birds last week. I tell you, her mother—' But Sara never found out what it was about her mother because at that moment the housekeeper opened the cupboard in which she was hiding and all hell broke loose.

Quiet and lonely, listening and watching, Sara grew in the crooked old house and she grew silent and a little crooked herself.

The raven on top of the bookshelves glared down at Sara. With its glossy feathers and glass eye, it was the best thing about her uncle's study. Sara, a few years older now, swung her legs, both to entertain herself a little and also to keep warm as the room was cold. A long window let in the bright silent light of a snowy morning. It lit the collections of insects that lined the walls. Not her uncle's obsession but her grandfather's, their little labels faded and near illegible, the insects' legs stiff and pointed like wires; dust made of the scales from butterfly wings lay at the bottom of each frame. Insects and books and her uncle's dry voice raised in irritation: that was what his study meant to her. That and the stuffed raven.

Her mother and uncle were arguing and the servants were keeping well out of the way as usual. They were arguing about the cold and the cost of upkeep, his refusal to allow her fuel to heat any room but their bedrooms and certainly not the greenhouse. Her mother sat opposite Jeremiah. Her fingers were twitching and working in her skirts. A sullen fire lurked in the grate but threw out no light and little heat. Still, Eliza shuffled her chair towards it and held her hands out hopefully. Sara tucked her own fingers under her thighs and wiggled her toes as she swung her feet.

'I can never get warm in this house,' Eliza said. 'No wonder I lose nearly all of my plants every winter.'

Jeremiah Blackwell ignored her last jibe and changed the subject. 'I have news of Mr Atherton.'

Eliza looked up quickly. 'Why? What has it to do with you? And since when?'

'What has it to do with me?' he spat. 'Everything! Since your care seems to have devolved to me. I tried to sort this out years ago when you first arrived from India, but I had no success in communicating with your husband. Letters lost. Boats sunk. But last year we finally re-established contact—'

'But why hasn't he written to me?' Eliza asked, shifting forwards in her seat. 'I've been writing and writing, and just waiting her to hear. Years with nothing. He was supposed to be in England by now!'

Jeremiah ignored her outburst. 'When he finally bothered to reach me, he did send me some money to compensate for your upkeep and we had been discussing the future.'

'Is he coming here soon? To England? Has he found a successful venture at last?'

Something about her uncle's tone made Sara watch him warily. He wasn't meeting his sister's eye. 'No, Eliza. Listen to me. He set up a trust for your and Sara's future.'

'A trust? I don't understand.'

'I am to be trustee.' Satisfaction in his voice.

'But surely I—'

'It is done,' he said firmly. 'And today I received further news. He is dead.'

Eliza, pale to the lips, stared at her brother as if she didn't understand what he had said. 'What did you... sorry, I don't...' she trailed away. 'Dead?'

'Dead, my dear.' He looked at his hands. 'I am sorry.'

Sara stopped swinging her legs. Her father was dead. She examined this curious fact. She didn't remember her father except as a deep voice, sometimes raised, a trail of smoke and brandy, a height and heft. Her earliest real memories were the swaying deck of a boat, endless weeks of salt-tinged misery on the journey from India.

'Look on the bright side of it,' Jeremiah said drily. 'This means you can look for another husband, another home.' He waved a hand suggesting out-there-ness, leaving. 'You can go, find a new father for your girl. Make a raft of new brats. In all honesty, it seems best all round.'

'But I don't want another husband. I wanted him! To come here and be with us again. A family.' She stood and began to pace, eyes moving around as if looking for an explanation, an answer. 'He said he would come. How did he die?'

Jeremiah shrugged. 'Illness. His lawyer wrote to me, not a man given to elaboration apparently.'

'But he was so healthy.'

'The last time you saw him was over four years ago, Eliza. And when you arrived here you said he was not well.'

'I meant in his mind. All the disappointment and failures affected him, but in his body he was always a fit, strong man.'

'A man's health can change dramatically in four years, especially in India.'

Sara watched. Her father had always been a sort of gap and one that Eliza kept promising would be filled soon. But the words had become hollower as time went on, until Sara understood that they were merely words that her mother used now and again to assuage his absence.

Her mother sat down again and was sobbing into a handkerchief, bent over her lap. Jeremiah Blackwell looked on, waiting for her to stop.

Sara gazed at the window, letting her mind slip sideways but listening to the words all the same. Her uncle started talking again, about trusts and funerals and inheritances, ignoring the fact his sister was crying. Sara thought trusting was something you did. Trust people. Trust God. A shadow, a bird, flickered across the window and was gone. So, what was a trust? Something to do with money. And now they were shouting.

Her husband's money should come to her; how dare he, Jeremiah, conspire against her to deprive her of what was rightfully hers; she would be speaking to a lawyer, she was sure her darling would never have done this to her. She stood in front of his desk, fists at her sides, her hands trembling.

'You are welcome to try, dear sister, but I can assure you, you will have no success.'

'No doubt when you die, it will all go to Cousin Franklin, who we've never even met, and I'll be destitute.'

On the argument went. Betrayal, money, mourning, funerals, lawyers. Eliza was crying and Sara could tell (the exact nature of her mother's tears being vital to her) that now they were coming more from anger and frustration than sadness. She hunkered down in the chair and carefully examined the feathers on the stuffed raven. Slick and delicately curved over the shoulders, short and spiky around the face.

'I'm sorry, Eliza, but you'll have to live with it. Your husband made me trustee because he didn't trust you to be wise with the money. You'll behave like a responsible woman and that's all there is to it.' He held up a hand to shush her as she showed signs of being ready to burst. 'I will not let you starve and unlike your precious Atherton I will not abandon you. But you must live in my house by my rules, until and unless you find yourself another husband. Am I clear?'

Eliza strode from the room and slammed the door behind her. One of the cases of insects beside Sara fell off the wall with a crash, glass scattering across the rug. Half the insects disintegrated into dust with the impact and the others, pins still in them and awkwardly stiff, lay like an abandoned game of jacks, waiting to be snatched up. Sara knelt in the dust of dead insects, and began gathering them gently.

After this came long days of a dead silence: her mother in bed staring at the ceiling (alone now, Sara no longer shared her bed) as if she might burn down the roof with her eyes, or huddled in a darkened room moaning because of the pain in her head. Interspersed between, at unpredictable intervals, were peaks of tension in which her mother raged at her uncle. She threw things and threatened things and tore things, and Jeremiah Blackwell started to mutter about getting a doctor, about sending her away.

The servants hurried about, their eyes down, whispered together in corners, started to leave for other households and weren't replaced.

Sara was all but forgotten.

After a while Eliza stopped raging and dwelt perpetually in silence and darkness. Sara would creep into the room at bedtime and kiss her mother's fingers, which would twitch, reach out, fall back to the coverlet.

Sara was still all but forgotten.

She moved through the house like unnoticed vermin along the back passages and narrow stairs. She gathered small items in collections: shiny things, soft things, dead things. She had a jar full of discarded spider moults, translucent, their empty legs curled. She made friends with the crows, much to the annoyance of the remaining servants. She coaxed the most vigorous plants from the greenhouse to reach up and out until there were rotten passion fruit in the gutters and the pale stars of jasmine in the corners of the turret room.

The house abutted onto the warehouse of Jeremiah's business and its yard, and Sara found ways into the warehouse. She would sit and watch the carts come in and out, loading and unloading, ropes creaking. The men ignored her; she was just another scuttling thing with little beady eyes.

One day Sara came across her mother sitting on a chair in in the middle of the greenhouse, staring at nothing, jasmine tendrils around her feet. She knelt before her and took her hands. Her mother's eyes turned to her then drifted out of focus again.

'There's nothing, Sara, nothing at all.'

There's me, Sara thought but her mouth was stone and would not move.

'Our love, our wild hopes and dreams, all gone and the world turns out to be made of ash, all the light is an illusion. Even you.' Eliza brought her eyes onto her daughter. 'Even you are too far away.'

Sara bowed her face against her mother's knees and cried until she slept. She woke alone and cold, her forehead against the seat of the chair as if her mother had disintegrated and blown away on a breeze.

Sara had a small bed below the spiral staircase that led to the turret room where her mother slept. She hung her found items under the stairs so that they dangled above her in the half-light and she could watch them turn, her mind spinning and twisting away with them. One of the spiders from a display with its pin still through it, a feather, a shard of cobalt blue glass; items of different colours and textures and meanings in her mind. Under her bed there were piles of soil; she wanted to see what would grow in the dark.

One night she fell asleep to the gentle sound of sobbing coming from upstairs. She awoke to light footsteps on the stairs – her mother coming down, step by step. She lay quietly, listening and wondering where her mother might be going.

In the dark, her hanging objects were tiny points of light, beyond them the swish of her mother's nightdress and the white blur of it. She shuffled down into her bed slightly, hoping her mother would not notice her.

Eliza stood by the window. Sara always left the curtain open. From here she knew her mother could see the roofs and chimneys of surrounding houses, a few windows visible. Maybe a candle would be burning in one, a chimney sending a narrow trail of smoke into the air, the silhouettes of pigeons on the roofline shuffling irritably. Finally, Eliza's dark shape shifted, turned, the curve of her cheek, the line of her neck all that was visible. Sara held her breath – *please don't come and speak to me.*

In the distance a church bell rang three times, echoed by more distant bells.

'Still time,' Eliza breathed then she spoke more loudly, 'Sara? Are you awake?'

'Yes, Mama,' Sara whispered.

Eliza stepped towards Sara, her arms reaching out, ducking her head to come under the stairs and then she cried out and flapped her hands. There was a jangling and clattering. 'What?' Eliza cried out again.

'It's just my things, Mama, just my pretty things.'

Sara jumped up and pulled threads away from her mother, freeing her.

Eliza staggered back, her silhouette against the window. She rubbed a hand through her hair. The door opened and slammed shut. Sara got back into bed and listened to the dark. The sound of steps of bare feet went away down the passage and then the quiet came back. Sara thought her mother's feet must have been very cold.

When she woke later, there was a faint greyness to the sky. She flung back the bedclothes and crept up the spiral stairs. The bedroom was empty. Out in the passage she thought about where her mother could have gone. She could have descended to the pantry and the kitchens by the back staircase, but they would all be a-stir by now and her mother would not be there. Further down, more passages, more stairs. The warehouse door was ajar. Her heart gave a sideways jerk. She slipped through.

The warehouse was dimly lit by thin rays of morning light coming through the high windows above the big main doors, and the criss-cross stairs formed hashed lines of shadow. A cart stood empty in the centre of the space, waiting to be loaded for the first shipment of the day. The men would be here soon, with their big laughs and loud voices. She looked around. Her mother was nowhere to be seen. And then she looked up.

White layers of nightgown, spinning, spinning, spinning, like her small pretty things span on their strings. Dirty bleeding feet from the bottom of the gown, small hands at the side and a tilted face that span out of her view and turned. A creak from the rope and then it turned back. Behind her there was a clatter of hobnail boots in the yard, a cheerful shout of 'Morning!', a grunt in response. The outer door swung open and let in a wash of the dim morning light.

The pale nightgown gleamed in the brightness and her mother swung slightly. The wooden crane stood out just above her, a gibbet from which she hung.

Behind Sara there was a crash as one of the men dropped something and someone exclaimed, a blasphemy ripping into the still air. Then strong hands picked her up and swept her away from the view of her mother turning and swinging. Turning and swinging.

Chapter Five
Strength

Nancy was cold in the shadow of the doorway. The narrow strip of sunlight she was standing in was shifting into shade, sliding down the wall and across the pavement. Lil was off somewhere with an illicit tray of apples to sell and Nancy had come out to see whether people would pay for a song.

It was a bright day for the time of year, which would mean a hard frost that night. The clear blue sky was a bad omen for anyone who might be left without a place to spend the night; for everyone else, the sun was a reason to smile and half the city seemed to be out and about with their sweethearts, turning their grey faces to the light. Calculating on tugging their heartstrings, Nancy was singing the more romantic music hall songs: sailors lost at sea, soldiers missed on a battlefield, their loves pining at home. She had laid her shawl in front of her and arranged two battered bunches of dried lavender and a small pile of precious matchboxes for sale. They gave her an excuse; she wasn't begging, not really, just selling and singing to keep her own spirits up. Her thin voice had no great strength to it, but it was sweet enough. It wove through the people and a halfpenny chinked in the shawl.

Nancy's stomach grumbled, but she'd earnt enough that they would have something to eat and somewhere to sleep that night, so it didn't much worry her. 'I'll show you the ropes, Nance,' Lil had said. 'Don't you worry, my love, you'll be all right with me. We'll see what we can come up with for your dad.' Lil's definition of 'all right' seemed to be 'alive'. She was bent and aged beyond her years, and looked like a walking heap of old clothes but had bright beady eyes and a perpetual grin. This was because buying and selling second-hand clothes was one of her favourite ways of turning a penny and nothing would stop Lil investing her last five pence in a ragged shawl if she thought she could flog it for half a shilling tomorrow. Lil knew all the places to stay: which were decent, which to avoid, and which might give her a cheap bed. She had found Nancy a hatpin to keep about herself 'in case' and Nancy slid it into the seam of her dress. So far Nancy had only slept out that very first night. Tucked in the corner of a stairwell, she hadn't really slept at all, merely waited for morning, listening to the dark and tensing at every footstep.

Nancy rearranged the matchboxes on her shawl and counted her takings. A shiny sixpence and a bunch of coppers. She rubbed the sixpence for luck and put it back on the shawl to draw its brothers.

On the way here she had stopped to look at a toy shop. She put her fingertips against the glass; the shining objects on the other side wavered as she looked, as if they might disappear, but it was just the uneven glass making them bow and twist. There was a monkey between two sticks and, when you squeezed the sticks, it would jump and spin; she knew because she'd seen a boy playing with one, and the one in this shop was so prettily painted, the sticks decorated to look like the trunks of palm trees. Pigeon would love it. She swore to herself that one day she'd take her sister there and she'd buy something for her with her own money.

Suddenly a hand had emerged into the window display and she jumped, it was followed by the head of the proprietor, a bent old man with spectacles. He smiled and nodded at her, and picked up an elaborate music box. He wound it carefully, with an air of demonstrating to Nancy, although he must have picked it out for the shadowy form of a customer behind him, and when he finished winding, the music box started to move and twirl; it represented a carousel at a fairground, little tin people riding little tin horses, jerking up and down. It danced and gleamed, gold paint on red curtain swags. One of the horses was a unicorn with a silver horn and another wasn't a horse at all, but a lion turning and jumping, red mouth wide in a roar. The man in the window winked at her and then drew out of the window with the box, leaving it empty and silent. Nancy had taken one more look at the monkey and turned away to find a good pitch. Near the music hall, but not too near, just on the edge of its magic.

As the afternoon drew on, a crow strutted up and down the railings of the building opposite, peering at her with impatience as she began singing the last verse of what she had decided would be her last song.

A yell came from up the street, a shout of anger and a high-pitched laugh in response. Someone shouted 'Oi!' and she leant out of the doorway to see what was going on. A clatter of footsteps and a rush and there was a laughing face right in her own. She was shoved back hard and pinned against the door behind her. The boy whooped – dirt and a mess of brown hair and the smell of him. Behind him, his mate bent down and scooped up her shawl. She tried to brace herself on the door behind her, but the one holding her launched himself off her shoulders and the two boys leapt away and ran up the street.

Nancy crumpled to the floor, the breath knocked out of her. The bunches of lavender were strewn across the road and trampled by a donkey and cart – a faint echo of their smell immediately swallowed by muck. The matchboxes were trodden on by a passing costermonger who didn't even notice.

The boys were away, their backs darting among the traffic. She stared after them, anger and humiliation tearing through her, ears humming. They'd taken her money and almost all of her matches had either gone with them or were destroyed in the road. It was too much. After everything else she wanted them to die, to bleed; they had no right to do this to her. Tears leaked from her eyes, hot and angry. She picked up a single match lying on the floor and heat rushed up her body – imagining it their backs, she snapped it viciously. 'Kill them,' she muttered. A tightness moved up her chest to her throat and she swallowed it down. If only she really could kill them and all the others who just rolled over her as if she were nothing: Darner, Bevel, all the petty tyrants of life. But these boys were in her sights now.

She walked in the direction they had gone, looking for any of her belongings that might have fallen from the snatched shawl. In her pocket she held her last bundle of matches and as she walked, she snapped them one by one. Their backs, their arms, their legs, Darner's long fingers – one by one, *snap, snap, snap*. She dwelt on all the things that had been done to her; Mother leaving, being forced to join the Brethren, sermon after sermon, Bevel's beatings, being unable to protect her sister, the bell ringing in her ears and, finally, her last few things stolen.

At one point she saw a gleam, bent and picked up a farthing. She could have cursed the pretty wren and almost flung it from her but a moment of sanity caught her. A farthing was a farthing after all and on its way to being a penny. She kept walking, seeing signs of the boys' passage. A flustered woman. A man shouting. Another man replacing scattered apples in a basket. *Snap, snap, snap*, the crackle of a ribcage crushed.

A great clatter of hooves and shouts came from around a corner. She followed the sound onto a busy road. A drayman was struggling to keep one of his horses calm and a man tried to catch the giant horse's head as it lunged and kicked, the drayman shouting, 'I told 'em not to use her, I told 'em she's unreliable, too hot for this job! Careful there!' The enormous hooves crashed down, sparks striking from the cobbles. The other horse of the pair sidled and shifted, eyes wide. Unable to move away from its rearing mate, it was on the brink of panic itself.

A lumpen shape lay in the road beyond, awkward and unfamiliar in its bent parts, two figures or one, it was unclear. A man driving a carriage with a horse, fine and twitching with a black gloss, said, 'I'm getting out of here,' and set off at a barely controlled pace.

A woman stood on the pavement, hand rubbing her forehead, shawl forgotten and trailing beside her.

'What happened?' Nancy asked her.

'They just ran out, hooting and shouting like idiots. Just ran out. Should have had plenty of time, spooked the horse and then sort of stumbled over each other, fell right under the hooves, one went under the actual wheels.' She winced as she said this. A death sentence to go under a dray's wheels.

Two workmen stood across the road eyeing the fallen boys. Together they dashed in, bent low, the horse strained away from them and the wheels of the dray dragged a little before catching on a cobble edge. They gathered up the bodies and a strange, vicious joy shot up inside Nancy. It was the boys. They had been punished for what they had done to her. *Snap.* She snapped the last matchstick in her pocket, thin and splintered. Done.

An awful scream came from one of the boys and the men laid them on the pavement away from the horses. The huge beast was gradually calming, its bridle caught by a man who murmured at it gently. The boys were laid on the coats of the men who had pulled them from the road and another lad ran off, sent for a doctor. One of the men shook his head, grim and final, and Nancy edged closer to see.

The face that had grinned gleefully in hers only a few minutes ago was now grey, his breathing straining with effort. His eyes were wild and unseeing. As she watched he fought for air, then coughed up blood. It swelled and spilled from his mouth, dark and glistening. Then a silence bubbled up around him and he was gone. The bright laughing face, the boy who had thought it was a lark to steal the only things between her and the workhouse or the whorehouse, had paid for it. It was exhilarating; she clenched her fists, nails biting into her palms.

'See?' she whispered to herself. 'No one steals from me. No one.'

She tightened her lips against any more escaping words.

The other boy was red-faced and started making a strange animal-like noise, a lowing wail. A man ran up carrying a bag: the doctor. He looked at the first boy and with a set mouth said, 'Well, there's nothing I can do there.'

'There was a—' the man who spoke was pale-faced. He paused to swallow, '—a horrible cracking sound. The wheel—'

The doctor shook his head and moved across to the other boy. 'How about this one?' He knelt down and started to take a closer look.

The feeling of the wood snapping in her fingers.

'By God,' he said more to himself than anyone else.

'Right under the horse's hooves,' one of the men who had pulled the boys out of the road said.

'I can see that,' the doctor said. 'Crushed left leg, fractured arm, fractured skull and that's just from a quick look. I'll find more, I think, once we get these clothes off. Do we know who they belong to? Parents?'

'No idea; they came out of nowhere,' another man said.

'They was causing a racket all along the road,' a woman said in confirmation, shaking her head. 'Silly boys.'

'They stole my money,' Nancy said to her.

'Well, I'm not surprised. But no one deserves that sort of end.' She nodded at the dead boy.

Rough wood, pushing it, bending it, *snap*. Splinters of wood. Or was it bone? A shiver of guilt ran through her. 'No one deserves that,' the woman had said. Boys. Bright, silly, naughty boys – would they even have thought what it might mean to her to take her things? Of course not and again her anger swirled around the guilt, and she pushed it all down.

The boy was moaning now and, just for a moment, his eyes met Nancy's. His widened and then he grabbed the doctor's arm. 'Give it back!' he moaned.

The doctor shook him off, irritated. 'Calm down, boy, you'll only do yourself further injury.'

'Give it back,' he pointed a finger at Nancy, 'to her.' Tears and snot streamed down his face. He turned back to the doctor who glanced at Nancy, confused. 'Give it back to her.'

Nancy shrugged, but the woman next to her said, 'They took this girl's things, apparently.'

The boy cried out in pain again and then panted, 'In my jacket.'

The doctor slid his hand into the jacket and pulled out Nancy's wrapped-up shawl. The boy nodded violently and the doctor handed it to her. Most of the money and half the matchboxes were inside. The boy stared at Nancy, then he relaxed back onto the pavement.

Nancy looked down at the few grubby coins in her hand. It seemed such small payment for the death and pain around her. She closed her hand and shoved the coins and her guilt deep into her pocket. When she looked up a dark figure stood staring at her from across the road. Darner. Enraged disgust flared in his eyes. He raised his stick and pointed it at her as if handing down judgement, then the people closed in again, a cart went past and he was gone.

Chapter Six
Dreams

Spider lay on the floor of the greenhouse. The uncorked bottle stood on the tray beside her; a brownish smear dirtied the bright silver of the spoon. A green tendril of ivy lay across her outstretched arm as if it had grown there as she lay, despite the cold of winter.

The skull of a bird span through the edge of Spider's vision and spiralled, seemed to fly away from her but then, there it was again, spinning on the other side of its orbit. The rustle of leaves, the beat of wings, black wings, but that would be Corbeau, her friend, coming or going and the wind from his wings setting the mobile to spinning faster. It turned. A glass bottle, tiny, full of death. A hag stone, heavy at the heart of the mobile, a dried stem of foxglove. A spider balanced precariously on one of the limbs, alive; it lifted a leg; it had made a web from one corner of the mobile which now drifted, broken in the light air, the cold breeze from the window and Corbeau's passing. That meant something: the spider, its web's dissolution, its small weight tilting the balance down a little. She did not know what exactly, not yet.

Death was coming. She drew it closer, tugged on the strings of death in her mind. Death for whom? For him, certainly, but only for him? That was less clear.

Something scratched to her right and then Corbeau's head intruded into her vision. He looked down on her. Then she felt herself twisting again and she span into the crow's eye. He flew through the gaps in the broken glass across the rooftops, stopping to peck at a dead pigeon's flesh. But he was not hungry and so he flew again, wind in his feathers, over to Brethren Hall, and landed on the belfry. People bustled to and fro; he gave a raw scream and spread his wings. With bitterly cold winter air holding him, he flew back through the window, landing in the bare twisted mess of the passion flower, its leaves decaying across the floor.

She fell out of the crow's eye. Twisting and spinning, she dropped to the floor, a black glass bead rolled under an old yellow leaf and stopped. She put out her legs, eight of them and here was her body lying flat on the floor. She scuttled out and caught herself in her own hair, her twisted spider limbs writhing into her scalp until she was there, Spider, the person lying on her back again. She looked up as the mobile span above her, telling her of incoming death with the bitter taste of the concoction on her tongue and the ghost of her mother sobbing in the greenhouse.

Slowly she rolled on to her side, shook the ivy tendril away and got to her knees. She had to go, to move. There was watching to do.

Spider had an excellent view of the steps of the Brethren Hall and she was certain she couldn't be seen. Yellowed newspaper blocked the light from the window and she peered out through the gaps between the sheets, the dry sweetness of the paper in her nose. Cold air poured in through the glass window; Patience had made a feeble fire in the old grate.

Spider's only regret was that she couldn't see down the side passage the girl had run from and though she hadn't seen her again, the incident still caught her thoughts.

She had asked Patience to make enquiries about one of the narrow empty buildings opposite the Hall to give them somewhere dry to watch from.

The building had once been a shop and the bay window on the first floor offered a clear view of the Hall. The newspaper in the windows made the rooms dim and yellow-lit when the sun was bright, faded and dark the rest of the time. The floors were uneven and patches of plaster had fallen from the lathe. A candle on the mantelpiece was the only source of light after nightfall, while every shifting of weight made the floorboards creak like old voices speaking a forgotten language.

Patience had paid the rent up front, in cash. She told the house agent that she was going to tidy up the shop floor downstairs and start selling hats. He clearly thought she was mad, but that didn't change the fact that it was six months' rent in hand. He passed over the key and wished her well. Now Spider had her lair, ready on the first floor, above the old shop floor, which she could access by a side door without being seen.

With her eye at the window, Spider felt detached, a spirit hovering over the street. Those two men having an argument – over what, she wondered? She could hear their voices raised over the other sounds of the street but couldn't distinguish their words. That woman standing and waiting. What was she waiting for? A policeman walked up the street, rubbing his hands together in the chill, eyes wandering aimlessly. The waiting woman, seeing him, turned and walked away, head tucked.

Spider was already used to the regular intervals of the policemen's beats. Some of the men were watchful, observant; others walked with their outside mind shut off and wouldn't have spotted a pickpocket right in front of them. One stopped and peered in at the windows of the shop's ground floor, tried the door handle. Spider waited, half-expecting him to enter but he stood in the street and cast an eye over the front of the house. She paused, rigid. Stepping back would be worse than staying still, the flicker of movement would give her away. He gave the building one last look and walked on.

She pressed her herb bag to her face as she watched. Patience stood quiet by the back wall. 'Do you have a plan, ma'am?' she asked.

'Plan? No not yet.'

'What are you watching for?'

'I need a way to get closer to him.'

Patience looked doubtful, but Spider knew if she waited and watched for long enough, something would present itself. She had a feeling it already had: that girl. There was something about that girl.

As the room darkened around her, Spider fell into a trance; the people shifted up and down in the street below, the light turning away, fading through greys, some part of her mind remembering.

She awoke to alertness when behind her Patience shifted and coughed. She wanted to leave, Spider could tell, wanted to rest. She was just about to say that perhaps it was time to return to

Hangcorner House, when she paused. There was light spilling from the yard behind the Brethren Hall. Flickering light. A fire.

Spider gathered her shawls about herself and hurried down the stairs. The street was already quiet, light behind the windows of the pubs and houses, doors firmly shut against the bitter cold of the night. She slipped up the alleyway that led around behind the Hall and, at the far end, pressed herself into the dark corner by the gate.

The light she had seen was coming from the brazier in the centre of the yard. The adult Brethren were filing down the steps at the back of the Hall, muttering and hugging themselves against the chill. They drew into a circle around the heat, trying to get as close as possible to the fire. The orange light flickered across their faces. Two young men emerged from the Hall, carrying large metal buckets, struggling with the weight of them. One slopped a little water and a woman said, exasperated, 'Oh, do be careful, it'll freeze and someone will slip. The Prophet's entrusted you with this and the least you can do is not spill it all.' As she finished, he reached the bottom of the steps and stood to one side, putting his bucket by his feet with an air of relief.

Two men appeared in the Hall doorway. One was painfully thin, wearing only a shirt, trousers and shoes. He looked back over his shoulder as if unsure what to do, but was hurried down to the courtyard by the other. As the thin man came near the light Spider saw it was the man she had seen in the dormitory. Ratcliffe.

Then Darner was there, looking down on his flock as if from a pulpit.

'We are here, dear Brethren, to witness a penitence.' A shuffle went around the circle, looks exchanged. 'Our brother Nigel

Ratcliffe is in danger of being lost to us, of turning away from his faith.' The thin man started as if he had not expected to hear his name. A concerned muttering went around the circle of brethren.

Darner continued. 'Nigel Ratcliffe has demonstrated a concerning lack of faith of late; he was unable to rein in his daughter Nancy, which is his duty and, worst of all, he has lied to me and by doing so has deceived Our Lord.' He spoke quietly but the words were clear, the sense of disappointment, a trust betrayed hanging sad in the air.

'Lied? I haven't lied.' The thin man twisted his handkerchief in his fingers.

'You know where your daughter is—'

'That I don't, Prophet. I promise you—'

'If you do not know her exact location at this minute, if you truly tried, you would know how she might be found, with whom she would associate and you would tell me. Her location is unimportant. I could find her. In fact, I have seen her.'

Ratcliffe started. 'Is she—?'

Darner ignored the interruption. 'She is unimportant. She ought to be here and you are to blame for the fact that she is not. Your belief is feeble – in me and, worse, in God. Your faith is weak.' He paused as his flock shifted and glanced at each other. 'Tonight we will strengthen it. Together. We will pray with you and for you.'

Spider wanted to run. She remembered the man's voice and it echoed in her mind from the past, vibrated strangely through her. She wanted to go, but if she left her dark corner she would be seen. She pressed herself back against the wall.

The thin man began coughing, a plaintive hacking sound that shook his whole body.

'You will kneel here and pray, Ratcliffe, make your penance to God. It is a cold night and no doubt you will be grateful to God for every icy pang. Every pain represents an opportunity for you to redeem your sins. Kneel, Ratcliffe.'

The man stumbled forwards and knelt in front of the steps.

Spider held her breath close to herself, leaned into the wall.

'For the first prayer of your penance, we will pray with you. We who wish to see that you are redeemed and fit to rejoin us, we who support you in your efforts to make penance, we who love you.' Darner nodded at one of the young men with a bucket, the one who had carried his bucket neatly and without spilling. Nigel Ratcliffe knelt with his head bowed almost into his lap, his handkerchief to his lips as he tried to suppress another coughing fit.

The young man hefted the bucket and emptied it over Ratcliffe, who reared up with a great gasp and wordless cry. The Brethren members stepped back and one or two murmured. The water splashed around him and immediately began to freeze as it spread out over the cold stone.

'Our Father,' Darner began loudly, over the freezing man's shuddering breaths and the muttering of his Brethren, who immediately gathered themselves to join in with the rest of the prayer. Ratcliffe was pale and shivering violently but his blue lips still moved with the words of the prayer.

When they reached the end of the prayer, a smooth and loud 'Amen!' went up into the frigid sky and Darner nodded to the other young man with a bucket. Ratcliffe cringed, then collapsed onto the ground. But the young man walked past him; the water was for the brazier and with a great gushing hiss the fire was extinguished.

As the Brethren streamed back into the building, none of them reached out to the shivering man lying on the floor. As the last member went past him, Darner exchanged a look with the large man who had initially herded Ratcliffe outside, went in and closed the door behind himself.

Ratcliffe moaned on the floor and struggled onto his knees. 'Bevel,' he said, hoarsely addressing the large man. 'Mr Bevel. I'll do any amount of penance indoors. A week, a month. I can't…' his words faded away into the shivering of his mouth. 'I'll die out here. I'll do…' He began to cough and bent over, racked by it.

'You'll pray,' the large man said, flatly. Now Spider saw he held a truncheon in his right hand. He tapped his leg with it and glanced over his shoulder at the building. Only one high window looked out on to the yard, its thick curtains drawn.

Ratcliffe sobbed, his shivering audible through his tears.

'Pray!' instructed the man he had addressed as Bevel.

'Please, Lord God, have mercy! Please save me!'

'A proper prayer!' Bevel poked him with the end of the truncheon.

Suddenly, a thin ray of light stretched across the ground over the trembling man's bowed back. It stretched and widened. Spider looked around, hoping that someone would come and put an end to the dreadful scene. Bevel did not stir.

Darner had drawn back the curtains in the high window and was looking down on them, his silhouette harsh against the warm light of the room behind. Bevel glanced up and Darner gestured, a motion of blessing and encouragement.

'I'll die, Bevel,' Ratcliffe repeated. He didn't seem to have noticed the light or the watching figure.

'I think that's rather the point,' Bevel said and raised the truncheon. It fell with a crack across Ratcliffe's back. Ratcliffe curled upon himself, his arms crossed over his head and he whimpered as blow upon blow landed on his limbs and his side. His breathing caught in his throat and he coughed as he tried to breathe. At one point he tried to crawl away along the ground but Bevel just kicked him until he curled up again.

Spider, cold and still, watched with a growing understanding. After the first few blows her eyes locked on to Darner, watching the watcher. He stood, a look of satisfaction on his face. How long, she wondered, had it taken for him to acquire that skill? To hide the pleasure. He had already been practising when she first knew him.

'Please!' burst from Ratcliffe's lips and, glancing up, Bevel paused, responding to a gesture from Darner.

'Go,' he said and gave the man one last kick. Ratcliffe crawled off along the alleyway. Bevel and Darner exchanged a last look before Darner drew his curtains. The yard fell into darkness and Spider began stretching her fingers and toes. They were numb and she knew she'd stumble if she tried to stand. Bevel gave a little laugh to himself. His face flared orange as he lit his pipe. Then he walked off towards the street in the direction taken by Ratcliffe.

Chapter Seven
Memory

Sara held her eye to the crack in the back of the wardrobe. On the other side of the wall her uncle rummaged through his papers. He had mentioned to Bristow that he must check exactly how something was written in his copy of his will now that Sara was of age and so Sara had come to spy, to find where it was kept so that she might see what it contained.

Her uncle hunched in front of his bureau and extracted all the papers, placing them in neat piles around him. Albums, bundles of letters, ribbon-bound envelopes stacked up. At last he removed one last small tied bundle of letters which he tossed aside and, beneath it, the will. He opened it up, read it, lips moving slightly and then placed it back. He quickly piled everything back into the cupboard and got to his feet. As he left his room he was calling for Bristow to send for a cab to take him to the lawyers.

Once her uncle was out of the house there was little chance that Bristow would come up to his room. Whenever Mr Blackwell was out, the house relaxed slightly and the servants with it. She heard the front door slam and climbed out of the wardrobe.

The room next to her uncle's could have been a nice apartment, with a large window looking onto the street but they so rarely had guests; it was a generation since her family's business had accommodated trading partners and clients. Dwindling for fifty years it had been desultory even before Eliza's death and since that time Mr Blackwell's business had shrunk to a few decrepit investments returning just enough to keep a manservant, a maid and the housekeeper demoted to cook-housekeeper, much to her chagrin. The warehouse attached to the house lay silent and empty. So the second largest bedroom was simply storage for old furniture, chairs, a chest of drawers, a wardrobe containing Mr Blackwell's old suits and a spyhole into his room.

Sara slipped into her uncle's room. The lock on the bureau was small and simple and could be opened by almost any key that would fit in the hole – a fact she had discovered ten years ago when he had confiscated a toy from her and stored it there. She started removing the papers and just as she reached for the will she noticed the bundle of letters by her knee.

Mrs E Atherton

Letters for her mother. Strange paper.
She opened the top letter of the bundle feeling a fluttering under her ribcage.

Dear Eliza,
Your brother tells me that you still refuse to reply to me. Your stubbornness and coldness appal me; it is not what I would expect from my Eliza. When I think that I found you over

affectionate and too eager for my company! I understand your disappointment; I am disappointed in myself. If I could have had a little more courage and optimism, rather than allowing myself to be crushed by the first touch of failure we would not be apart. Since your departure with Sara I have found greater success – not with the main venture but with that little 'silly idea' of yours. Well, it is bearing fruit. Would you join me? Can you bear the long journey?
Please, your loving C.

Numbly, forgetting the will, Sara piled everything back in the cupboard as neatly as she could, arranging it so the missing packet of letters was not obvious. She locked the bureau and stumbled as she went back to her room. Her face was cold and she clutched the letters in tingling fingers. Her uncle had hidden her father's letters from her mother. Her uncle was to blame. It was true her mother had never been easy – a woman whose flame of temperament had flickered, dimmed or roared, varying by the hour. But here it was, undeniable. Her uncle had poisoned their lives.

Sara took out the doll she was making. It was made of linen and stuffed with rags and dried herbs. The sort of doll that would be scorned by children with broderie anglaise on their petticoats, but treasured by those with scraps of sacking wrapped around their feet. For Sara, it was a canvas; at twenty-one, she was far too old to play with it.

The doll had no features yet. An expanse of bland nothing-person, it hung limp in her hand. It was a few months since she had discovered her uncle's betrayal, but it was only yesterday that she had decided to make this doll. She was sitting in the rocking chair in the turret that sprouted from one awkward corner of the rear of the building. It had been designated Sara's turret after her mother's death, conveniently out of the way of everybody and everything that went on in the house.

Nobody had mentioned the greenhouse but she had continued to use it, turning it away from her mother's sweet-scented tropical plants (to which it had never been well suited, unheated and high up for the wind to find its way in) and towards her own preferences. The passion flower still sprawled, ungovernable and stinking when cut, but there were foxgloves, peonies and roses, lavender, poppy and monkshood, hemlock, and chrysanthemums so that to an innocent eye in summer it seemed liked a caged corner of an English garden torn from the side of a country cottage and set high on a London roof. The turret was her retreat; the greenhouse was her work.

'Give me that,' she said to Corbeau who had been sitting in the open window with some grey wool in his beak, stolen from her work basket. She snatched the wool.

The crow gave a disgruntled croak as he hopped down to the floor and began working at a gap between the floorboards with his beak.

With six quick stabs from her needle, she had given the doll a grey moustache. She went on to apply a ring of hair and some mutton chop sideburns.

'What are you doing, Corbeau?' she asked as she selected a scrap of white linen to be an undershirt.

He ignored her and kept at his task.

'Suit yourself.' Her hands shook very slightly as she made the undergarments, sewing directly on to the doll's linen. Enjoying the feeling of the needle slipping in and out of the fabric, the skin.

When she stopped to get the chill out of her fingertips by rubbing them together, she eyed the crow's industriousness with curiosity. He ignored her and kept working at his task, whatever it was.

Once the doll was clothed, she picked it up and looked in its face. Its expression was blank, despite the little black dot eyes and the pink line of a mouth.

'You're not finished, are you? There's something unmade and empty.' She rubbed a thumb across its face. 'Is it your eyes?'

She pulled out a bag of dried flowers, the blue of a clear night sky: the claw-shaped hooded flowers of Aconitum, last year's harvest of monkshood. She tore a fragment and folded it into a stitch or two, and then another. Each a slightly different colour, a slightly different shape but the doll now had cold blue eyes. She smiled and seated the doll against her work basket pleased with its new poisonous eyes.

The crow looked at it askance and slowly slid his beak sideways. Before he could do whatever action he was contemplating, Sara reached out and grasped him around his wings, so that he was trapped. He gave a caw of surprise and struggled faintly against the long thin fingers tight around his ribcage.

He reared his head back, eyes beady and made a stab at her wrist with his beak. She laughed as a trickle of blood ran down her hand and dripped onto the floor. She raised him up to her eyeline and asked, 'What am I missing?'

His small heart thrummed against her thumbs. 'Ah!' she said. 'Of course.'

He hopped out of her reach as soon as she released him, turned his back and began rearranging his feathers to his requirements, slicking them down with his beak, even where they weren't disturbed.

She extracted two walnut halves from her collection of useful things and started to look in the corners of the room. She emerged with her hands cupped around something that scrabbled inside her fingers. The panic of the small creature tickled her palm. She put the spider on the table and swiftly placed an empty glass over it. It ran around the inner circumference and then stopped, its front feet on the vertical surface of the glass, a prisoner, hands raised in supplication, prayers unheard.

Using the fang of her seam ripper, she plucked apart the stitches that ran up the doll's chest. The scraps of fabric she had filled it with spilled out like entrails. Then she took the walnut, trapped the spider inside it and bound it around with red thread, using elaborate knots. The panicked feet of the spider whispered against the inside of the walnut and she pushed it into the chest of the doll. She closed the slit with quick, neat stitches and sat the doll on the table in front of her.

'Welcome, Uncle,' she said.

Corbeau returned to digging at his floorboards and Sara watched with interest. He was lifting the corner of a board slightly as if it weren't nailed down. She knelt behind him and prised it up. One came up and then another and another. There was a cavity between the joists below, neatly lined with wooden sides. A useful space, it was empty but for a single spider which Corbeau claimed with a crunch. A place for illicit religious tracts or love letters, a place for the illegal or immoral. She felt a kinship with whoever had used it long ago. It would be very useful.

At breakfast her uncle was grey in the face. He pushed the congealing kedgeree around his plate, eating none; Jenny the maid took his plate away as full as when she'd placed it before him. His breath was drawn in and out with effort, his eyes wide and frightened. Sara asked if he were well, was there anything she could do, and he replied, bringing a remnant of brusqueness out especially for her, 'My health is none of your concern. If you've finished eating, go to your room.' Then he grasped his chest, a spasm of pain across his face as his fingers clawed at his heart.

She obeyed. Insofar as she left his presence, at least. She didn't go to her own room but to the neighbouring room and its spy hole.

Sara pushed the suits to one side and carefully lifted a plank away from the back of the wardrobe. Sara put her eye to the crack in the panelled wall behind it. The room on the other side of the wall had once been luxurious: velvet chairs, a gilt mirror, a large mahogany bedstead with thick tapestry curtains. Now, however, she could see the cloth backing of the velvet, the places where the gilt had tarnished, the dullness of the unpolished mahogany.

The door to the bedroom opened and her uncle staggered in, leaning on Bristow's arm, and followed by Mrs Nichols, the cook-housekeeper.

'Should I call a doctor, sir?' Bristow asked, concern on his face.

'No, I don't want the blasted doctor. I just need a little sleep.'

Bristow exchanged a concerned look with Mrs Nichols.

'Can I get you anything, sir?' she asked.

'No, you cannot. You can get out of my room!' This exclamation would usually have been delivered with a roar of rage, but it came out thin and petulant and, as the two servants hurried out, he whispered, 'By God, it twitches. Can't it stop?' He beat his hand weakly against the pale linen at his chest.

As the servants walked away down the corridor Sara overheard Bristow say to the housekeeper, 'I don't like it. I prefer it when he's loud.' Mrs Nichols grunted in agreement.

Sara stood in a window staring down on the street below. A cab was pulling up outside the house, with a jostle of hoof beats that was just audible from her vantage point.

A man in a good coat with a large bag stepped out and paid the driver. From here, his hat completely hid his face, but Sara knew who he was: the doctor. They had called for the doctor. She smiled.

She left the room and looked down to the entrance hall. The doctor handed his coat and hat to Bristow, glancing upwards. His gold-rimmed spectacles blinked up at her from the gloom of the hall. He hurried after the manservant.

Sara stood and considered for a moment, before drifting through the back ways of the house to the wardrobe and the crack in the wall. In the time she had been away her uncle's bedclothes had been rumpled, covers tossed aside; he was almost invisible, just a hand among the sheets, a nose and chin tilted upwards.

The doctor came in and her uncle lifted his head a little, before falling back again.

'Well then, Mr Blackwell, you seem to be in something of a state.' The doctor rummaged in his bag for a moment, then leant over the bed and began examining his patient. After listening and prodding, he took a few notes with a concerned face, then said, 'I want to talk to the staff and your family, just to eliminate a possibility.'

Sara stood back from the crack in the wall. If they wanted to speak to her, she couldn't be found in this room. She carefully replaced the plank in the back of the wardrobe and crept quickly into the hall. She had just rounded the corner to the stairs when the door to her uncle's room opened and the doctor's voice called for the housekeeper.

Back in her own room Sara stood, trembling, waiting. She eyed the floorboard that hid her bottles and the doll and, with an impulsive dart, knelt and removed it. Standing with her back to the door and with a *snick snick snick* of her seam ripper, she opened the doll's chest and removed the walnut. The spider inside moved its legs weakly when she tipped it out of the shell. She poked it with the seam ripper and it twitched. 'Go on,' she said, 'find a corner.'

Corbeau stood on the window sill outside and cawed to be let in, but she shooed him away. 'Now isn't the time,' she said. He flapped away, resentfully, to the nearby roofline and she could feel him glaring at her.

Footsteps approached her room. She shoved the doll back into the hole. The tiny bottles laid neatly in the bottom of the hole clinked: wormwood, tansy, poppy, rose, foxglove. She replaced the boards and turned as the door swung open. Mrs Nichols stood in the doorway with her usual look of repressed distaste. She cast her eyes across and around the room and seemed relieved to find the crow wasn't present.

'Miss Atherton, the doctor would like to see all of us in your uncle's room.'

'He can't possibly need me,' Sara said with a nervous smile.

'Everyone in the house, he said,' said Mrs Nichols, as she turned back out of the room, closing the door behind her.

Sara braced herself and hurried to obey the summons.

The door to her uncle's sickroom was propped open and as she walked in, Bristow was opening the window to relieve the dense stuffiness. A faint smell of vomit and soap hung in the air but she noticed that the sheets had been replaced and the bedding straightened. Her uncle sat propped up on a pile of pillows, his face grey and his usually strong gaze wandering about the room.

The doctor stood beside his patient and eyed them all. 'The whole household?' he asked with a faint air of incredulity.

'Yes, sir,' said Mrs Nichols, brushing a hand down her skirt and jangling the keys on her belt. 'The master prefers to keep a small household these days and Miss Atherton is the only other family living here. She's the master's niece.'

They stood in a row: Sara, Mrs Nichols, Mr Bristow and the little maid, Jenny, on the end, trembling, her brown eyes as wide as if she were about to be sent to slaughter. The doctor's eye fell on the girl and he seemed to take pity. 'Don't worry, child, I might not need you at all.'

The girl said, so quietly that she was almost inaudible, 'Thank you, sir, very kind of you, sir.'

'Well, Mrs Nichols, can you tell me what and when your master usually eats, and then, specifically, what he has eaten in the last day?'

She began telling him the routine of the household when it came to food and drink. For breakfast, the master sometimes ate porridge, sometimes bacon and toast, or kippers, sometimes kedgeree, depending on his mood. A good main meal in the middle of the day: usually roast meat and vegetables, followed by a pudding. Tea in the afternoon and a light supper before bed, usually a soup. She detailed the previous day's menu under the doctor's questions.

He nodded as he wrote it carefully in his book. 'And did the household gather for all these meals?'

'Only breakfast and the main meal. The others are taken in their rooms if they want them.'

'And on the day that Mr Blackwell fell ill, was there any deviation?'

'Not at all.'

'And drink. What does the master drink?'

'Coffee and tea, and wine with the main meal. Maybe a Madeira with supper, occasionally a brandy after.'

'And the other night?'

'Madeira but no brandy.'

A rasping sound came from the bed and the ill man raised his head slightly. He rasped out the word, 'Cordial.'

'Oh, yes,' said Mrs Nichols, with a glance at Sara. 'Miss Atherton always gives her uncle his cordial when she says good night.'

The doctor turned a searching look on her. 'Cordial?'

Sara's tongue was stuck to the roof of her mouth. She needed to speak; it would look very strange if she didn't. She peeled it away and was surprised when her voice emerged calm and normal. 'My uncle developed a liking for a certain cordial during his travels in his youth and so he has cases of it sent here. From Italy, I believe.' She glanced at her uncle, who was watching her. 'He finds that it assists his digestion.'

'And you give him this cordial? Every evening?'

'Yes. I come in at about nine o'clock to wish my uncle a good night, and I pour him a small glass at that table.' She pointed to the table at the far side of the room, on which stood a small tray and the bottle of cordial. 'He is usually seated by the fire and I put it next to him, wish him a good night's sleep and leave.'

The doctor strode across to the bottle, poured a small amount into a glass, sniffed it and grimaced. 'Well, I can't say I see the appeal. You did this as normal the other night?'

Sara nodded. 'Exactly as normal.'

'Humph.' The doctor stared at his patient. 'Does he drink it in front of you?'

'No, not usually. Sometimes he has the first sip, but no, he usually waits until I'm gone.'

'Right. Well, I think that's all I need from you.' He turned away and pulled a chair closer to the bed.

As they all left the room Sara wished that she could listen to whatever was going to happen next but she couldn't risk it. She took herself to the library within sight of the servants and settled down to stare at a book until several hours after the click of the front door latch and the cabbie's hoof beats had taken the doctor away.

Over the next month her uncle slowly recovered, his gaze steadied and his voice regained its strident tone. He moved from bed to chair, to shuffling around the house and from shuffling to walking. His skin lost its look of decaying stone and became pink again. She felt the strength returning to the eyes that turned on her as she poured cordial from the new bottle, the old one having disappeared with the doctor. The viscous liquid clung to the inside of the same small green glass he always used. He set it on the small table beside him, the firelight gleaming through it, and watched her leave the room.

The house felt unfamiliar, busy. Sara stopped and listened. There were creakings in places that were usually silent. Then the murmur of a curious voice with an unknown cadence, the wrong rhythm of a stranger's tread, a tension. This meant visitors. Invaders.

Having come in quietly through a side door she walked up the stairs hugging the wall so as to avoid the treads creaking. She moved quickly and silently, stopping to listen every so often. Male voices. Once she regained her room, she took out her freshly carved oracle sticks and spilled them across the table. Corbeau hopped in through the window, his head tilted to one side. Sara indicated the sticks. 'Choose,' she said and the crow chose.

She rubbed her fingers along the smooth bone feeling the ridges of the word on the other side before she turned it over.

Darkness.

There was a knock on the door. She hadn't heard the feet approaching.

Corbeau picked another stick and threw it on the floor.

'Come in,' said Sara as she gathered the majority of the sticks into one pocket. As the door opened, she bent and picked the crow's last choice from the floor.

'Mr Blackwell wants you,' Mrs Nichols pursed her lips, 'right away.' She cast her eye around the room, upper lip twitching. Her gaze rested for a moment on a carefully placed row of spider moults along the edge of a shelf and she made a barely audible sound of disgust before turning away.

Mrs Nichols held the door open for Sara and stood outside the door watching her as she walked away. Sara looked down at the oracle stick in her hands.

Antagonist.

Her uncle was seated behind his desk with a hard look on his face. Beside him stood a neat man in a suit, with glasses and an interested face. Was this the antagonist of whom she was warned? It seemed unlikely. He looked weak; his hands were gently folded and he wore a vague smile. He gave the slightest bow and did not meet her eyes.

'Sara,' her uncle began. 'Something disturbing has been found in your rooms.'

The door opened behind her and Mrs Nichols walked in with a tray. A spiralling sensation wound its way up Sara's back and she held herself tight; it would not do to sway on her feet or faint. Mrs Nichols placed the doll Sara had made on the green leather of the desk, and then one, two, three small glass bottles. Pretty glass bottles in blue and green that chinked pleasantly against each other as they were placed. But she knew what they were and where they had come from. Poppy, foxglove, wormwood. Almost all the contents of her little hiding place, except the letters from her father.

'Sara, your room was mine once.' Her uncle gave a cold smile.

Her stomach lurched. She ought to have known. If someone else made a hiding place, someone else knows it is there. Mrs Nichols met her eye, a triumphant laughing look and walked out of the room.

'I shouldn't have expected any better from my sister's brat. I took you in; it was my duty as a Christian and your uncle and yet here we are.' He scowled at the bottles and doll and leant back in his chair as if trying to increase the distance from them. 'This surprises me.' He gestured at the doll. 'What nonsensical savagery. I guess your mother was infested with such ideas. But this,' he picked up the jar labelled foxglove, 'this is attempted murder.'

Sara stared at the doll and the bottles. She wondered when they had been found, stolen from her. She had not looked at them since her uncle's recovery, had been thinking and planning, pausing before further experiments. She was briefly relieved that she hadn't yet harvested the monkshood this year.

'Well?' he asked.

'I didn't intend to harm anyone.'

He pressed his lips together. 'I'd like to see you slammed in jail to rot. Guilty of attempted murder.'

She took in the other man's face. One of the new police detectives? He did not look like her idea of a police detective. His eyes were restless but not as if they saw everything, rather as if they could not rest. He had brought a chemical smell into the room. She wrinkled her nose.

Antagonist.

'However, I don't wish the gossip, the scandal, the pity – or the bother – of a court case.' He turned to the man beside him. 'This is Doctor Whitehead. He runs an asylum in the home counties.'

'Asylum!'

'Please, my dear,' the doctor spoke with a soft, hurried voice, 'do not let the term frighten you. It means, after all, a refuge.'

She took a step back and the doctor coughed loudly.

Behind her the door opened and two men entered. The smaller of the two hung back a little and tried to smile reassuringly but any effect it might have had was swept away by the look of relish on his larger colleague's face.

'I won't—' Sara began.

'You don't have any choice in the matter,' the larger of the two men said, as they stepped forwards and grasped her by the arms.

'Get your hands off me!'

'Come now,' said the man who had already spoken, his strong hands round her wrist and upper arm.

She wrenched away and he jerked her back. 'Careful, you'll hurt yourself.' He squeezed his hand so tightly on her upper arm that she called out in pain. On the other side the smaller man made a noise of protest.

The doctor frowned at the big assistant. The man's grip loosened a little and he smiled and said, 'Now, now,' in a calm voice. It was not a reassuring smile. She tugged. His grip was looser but no less unbreakable.

'It's all right,' the smaller man said in a soft Midlands voice though it was clearly not all right.

Her uncle smiled sardonically. 'This is not where I expected to be all these years after I found your mother on my doorstep. Though I knew she'd bring me nothing but trouble.'

'Miss Atherton,' Doctor Whitehead came towards her, 'this will be so much easier for you if you come calmly. Do not work yourself into a crisis. Come now. Sullivan won't hurt you if you don't fight.' He gave the looming assistant a significant look.

'I will not!' She tugged at her arms and a look passed between the doctor and the kinder attendant.

The doctor sighed. 'I really had hoped to avoid the use of the jacket. It's so unseemly and the neighbours will tend to notice.' He turned to her uncle. 'Mr Blackwell, is there anything you can think of?'

'You can bring the van into the warehouse yard at the back of the building. It is no longer used and no one overlooks it.'

The doctor picked up a bag from behind her uncle's desk and drew out a garment. It was thick grey canvas with large buttons down the front and strangely long sleeves, ending in straps. Addressing Sara's uncle, he said, 'Now, under a regime of moral therapy as we run at Lansdowne, we avoid restraint as far as possible. Sadly, one can't always avoid it.' Mr Blackwell nodded and gestured: *go ahead*.

She tried to back away but the men held her. 'Don't you—' the larger man said and tightened his grip further, twisting it. She called out again with the pain.

'Don't hurt her,' the doctor snapped, with a flashing glance at the larger man, then seemed to regret his tone and said more gently, 'Please, Sullivan, remember the young lady is frightened and shocked.'

The doctor walked behind her with the garment. Her right arm was brought towards the sleeve by the smaller of the two attendants and she fought back, tried to pull away. Although the man was slight and seemed less inclined to deliberately hurt her, his grip was as unbreakable as Sullivan's.

Sullivan wrenched her other arm round, causing a tearing pain in her shoulder and she gasped as the sleeve was pulled up. With the large man's breath in her face, she felt her head spin.

'Watch her, Lambert,' said the doctor, and the smaller man gripped her by the back of the jacket, holding her steady. He made the kind of soothing noise a man might make to a fractious horse and indignation flared in Sara's chest.

With the pain in her shoulder, she could no longer exert much force with her right arm and the men quickly and easily wrapped her arms around her, buckling the straps behind her back.

The doctor shook his head. 'I just want you to know, my dear, that we would much rather not tie your legs, but if you try to kick, bite or scream we will tie your legs and gag you.'

'It's all right, Doctor,' said the larger man, 'she's pretty lightweight, one of us can carry her alone, won't be a problem at all for two. Carry her anywhere you like.' A slight insinuating sneer came into his voice but when she looked around at him, he was gazing blandly at his employer.

'Yes, I'm sure you can manage her, but I'd much rather she came willingly.' Dr Whitehead turned to Mr Blackwell. 'You have the certificate?'

Sara's uncle nodded and passed the doctor an envelope. 'And you'll ensure that you source the required signatures?'

'No difficulty at all, dear sir. I have men I call upon; they're quite used to it. Experienced, well-qualified colleagues. It's all above board.'

Sara tugged at the jacket and found she could barely move at all. The doctor noticed and turned his attention on her. 'Now, my dear, our aim is to rid you of these thoughts about witchcraft and poisoning. You must come to respect and appreciate your uncle's laudable assumption of a duty to care for you. To me, those seem the key tasks. To do this, we will have to work on your mind, to calm it. This will remove the delusions these thoughts are based upon. We hope that someday you will be able to return to the bosom of your family.'

Here he stopped and looked around at the gloomy room, taking in the lonely situation. He coughed and continued, 'To return to your home and live calmly, a sweet life of womanly goodness, perhaps even find yourself a husband and have a family of your own. Wouldn't that be nice? I imagine that, at present, the belief in such a future is beyond you, but I assure you that it is possible.' He smiled beneficently and gestured towards the door. 'Please lead on, Mr Blackwell, show us the way to this warehouse's yard.'

They were a strange procession. As they passed Mrs Nichols, she stood with her arms folded and, Sara thought, a secret enjoyment of the scene. Bristow stood behind her, his lips tight with a repressed smile. He prodded his colleague and muttered something.

Mr Blackwell snapped, 'See me in my study in about twenty minutes, both of you, and ask Jenny to join us.'

'Yes, sir,' Bristow said, pulling himself upright.

Out in the dusky yard, Mr Blackwell gestured to the double gates that led to the road and said, 'Through here.' He looked at her one last time and then headed back into the building without a word.

'I'll go in the van with her. Lambert and the doctor can sit up front with the driver,' Sullivan said. A small, cold weight settled in Sara's stomach. She didn't want to be alone with this man. She shook her head before she even knew she was doing it. He laughed.

There was an awkward pause and Lambert looked at the doctor who avoided his gaze.

'No, no,' the doctor said, bright and brisk. 'You sit up front. I'll go in the back and Lambert can join me.'

Sullivan shook his head and went off to fetch the van, loudly hawking a gobbet of spit onto the cobbles. She shrugged her shoulder against the ache that bloomed in it. At first the doctor, who had taken over holding that arm, held tight and interpreted her move as an attempt to escape.

'That brute pulled my shoulder,' she said.

'Hmm.' The doctor kept his grip firm, but allowed her to move the shoulder a little.

Sara considered screaming but realised that even if 'help' should come, a policeman perhaps, that help would only end by assisting the doctor and making another witness to her humiliation.

A clatter of hooves and wheels sounded along the road outside and a large black van drove in, pulled by two smart chestnuts. It resembled a police van with a grille at the window. Sullivan sat hunched beside the driver and scowled.

The doctor must have seen her go pale at the sight, because he said, 'Now, my dear, it looks intimidating, but worry not. I've done my best to make the asylum a warm and friendly place. We are a family, of sorts. We have our difficult uncles and our sullen youngsters, just as in everyday life. And, just as in everyday life, we care for them and try to reflect God's love for all.'

The van drew to a halt in front of them and Sullivan hopped down.

The doctor continued, 'You see, my wife is very involved with the women patients and the invalid care, a woman's touch. And we have an excellent chaplain, excellent. He takes very good care of our souls. Such good care. The Reverend Mr Darner is a man of real conviction and fire.'

Antagonist.

Sullivan flung the rear doors wide. Sara gave a last convulsive effort to escape their grip but, 'Oh no you don't,' said Sullivan and, gripping the back of the jacket, half-lifted and half-threw her into the van. The doctor and Lambert climbed in beside her and the doors slammed shut, leaving a small slice of blue-grey light falling through the grille onto Sara's face. She started to sob.

'Don't cry, my dear Miss Atherton, there's really nothing to worry about.' The doctor leant forwards, his head blocking the tiny fragment of light. 'You'll be in safe hands at Lansdowne Asylum.'

Chapter Eight
Darkness

Nancy's feet ached with cold. The puddles were still frozen hard and the bitter wind pinched at her cheeks. Two crows argued over a scrap of something that might have been old meat and might have been mud-caked pastry, their rough caws clanging off the icy air. She wanted to blow on her fingers, but then she'd have to put down the two hats she was trying to sell. Lil had bought them from a peddler, insisting they could be tidied up and sold for a profit, and now Nancy was standing on a street corner, turning them this way and that for a woman to examine.

'Yes, I'll have 'em. They'll do for my girls, just about.'

The woman haggled over the price and was just counting out the coins when Nancy spotted a familiar figure hurrying along. Lil waited impatiently until the woman had gone and grabbed Nancy's arm.

'What's up?' Nancy asked as she was propelled along the street.

'You'll see.'

As they dodged the carts and carriages on a main road, Nancy tried again.

'Where are we going?'

Old Lil made a flapping gesture with her hand which Nancy interpreted as shushing but she wouldn't be shushed. 'Come on, Lil.'

Lil stopped, exasperated. 'It's your dad. I came across him on the street.'

Nancy's guts sank. 'What?' There was nothing out here for them except dangers of various sorts. Her father's weak lungs. No work. 'I'm not ready for him yet. I was going to get us a start.'

'That's as maybe, but he's out and he ain't well.'

'Come on then!' said Nancy setting off in a hurry. 'This'll have something to do with Darner, I bet you.'

'Here,' said Lil, pulling her into an alleyway.

They took several turns through yards and under arches until Nancy wasn't quite sure where they were. They crossed a road Nancy recognised, one whose houses had been smart a century ago, but whose yellow brick was now blackened, their once-grand quarters split into many poor rooms, crammed with families. Then they took a street named after a garden in which nothing green had grown for fifty years, unless you counted the grass that sprouted in a dribbling gutter.

Finally, Lil tugged her into a cramped square surrounded by houses. It might once have been a mews, but now people were squeezed into every space. A donkey peered over a stable door; five grubby children were sitting against a wall, looking as though they'd been stacked there for convenience. Lil led her to a lean-to shed in the corner. Several pigeons shuffled along the roof. Lil pulled back the sacking hanging in the doorway.

Nancy hesitated. She could hear the sound of someone planing wood nearby.

Lil beckoned and still Nancy hesitated.

Two of the children watched listlessly. In the distance, someone shouted and another replied, the matter-of-fact hollering of men working. The donkey huffed.

Nancy stepped into the lean-to.

Her father was lying on the ground and she realised that no one was planing wood; the sound she could hear was his breathing, each rasping inhale a struggle, hauling air in, but never enough. Her father was grey-faced, a sheen of dampness across his skin, and even thinner than before. He was folded in around his own pain and didn't seem aware that anyone else was in the room. He was shivering and appeared to be naked under his filthy blankets.

'What happened to his clothes?' Nancy knelt beside him, feeling as though she'd left her innards in the courtyard behind her.

'They was wet.' Lil nodded to a man's shirt and trousers that hung from the rafters.

'Wet? It ain't rained.'

Lil shrugged.

An irregular moan came from her father which might have been an attempt to say 'Nancy', but it was lost in a coughing fit. Nancy took his hand. It was cold, trembling against her warm fingers.

'I don't think there's much hope for him,' Lil said.

'Why is he out here, though?' Nancy asked.

'Earlier, when your dad was a bit more alert, he said something about Darner kicking him out because of you. Because you were such a bad influence. It happened last night, I think.'

The previous night's frost had been iron hard, the air bitterly cold. They had stayed in a dosshouse where, after the beds had run out, the proprietor had sold spaces round the fire for half the cost of a bed; she'd claimed it was her Christian duty and that she couldn't see people freeze on a bad night. There had been fearful talk of snow as people held their fingers towards the warmth.

'Last night? And in wet clothes?'

Lil nodded glumly. 'Well, I've no idea how he got wet. That might have been some bastard's idea of a lark.'

'Couldn't Dad have pawned some of his tools? Sometimes he did that in the old days. Got a bed at least.'

'He didn't get any of his tools back. They belong to the Brethren now. Anyway, I found Nigel and got him in here.' She looked around at the derelict lean-to. 'I meant it for you and me, but I guess we'll all squeeze in.'

'Thanks, Lil.' Nancy reached out and grasped the woman's hand. 'Really.'

'I'm sorry, Nance. I don't think this is a good place for a man with bad lungs. It's perishing and the stench can't be healthful.'

She was right. Nancy could feel the damp air on her skin and a nearby heap of muck and rubbish was ripe enough that it tainted the air in the courtyard, even in the cold. There was no fire, no warmth.

'Where's Pigeon?' Nancy looked around as if she might have missed her sister curled in a corner. 'She wasn't out last night too?' A fear flared up in her that her sister had been with her father and he'd lost her in his sickness and his weakness and now she was alone somewhere in the frozen streets.

'No. She's still in there. With the Brethren.'

Her father's eyes were bright in his sunken face; they flickered at Pigeon's name, but then drifted out of focus. His thin hands grasped the blankets and Nancy had a brief memory of his old hands, the ones he had before. Before his cough had come. Large, firm hands moving a plane swift and sure, back and forth, making curls of wood that she would collect to use for her dolly's hair. Then another time, at Brethren Hall, when he built the steps for the stage, his pencil darting quick and neat across the wood, explaining what he was doing at every moment.

Nancy stood in the doorway, desperately trying to think of how she could help him but realising, with a slow pain, that there was very little they could do. The children by the donkey's stable were watching her. One of them jumped up, punched his neighbour on the arm, shouted, 'You're It!' and ran away. The others immediately sprinted off, the pigeons scattering into the air as well, in a rush of noise and movement. The child designated 'It' began chasing the others.

Lil looked out of the hut. 'Oi! Didn't I tell you to shut up? Sick people need peace and quiet.'

'Drunk people, more like,' said the oldest boy, standing square with his hands on his hips.

'No, sick,' said a girl, correcting the boy.

'Just keep it down, can't you?' Lil turned away.

The girl who'd been 'It' called to Nancy as she passed, 'Hey, Brethren girl. There was someone looking for you. I think it was you he meant.'

Nancy stopped and asked, 'Who?' Dread washed through her.

The girl shrugged. 'Big man. Brown suit, bowler hat.'

Nancy exchanged a look with Lil. Bevel. Working for Darner. And now they knew where she was. They must have followed her father. Fear swelled with the thought and she tried to dismiss it. She had her father to worry about.

'Nancy,' Lil said, a warning in her voice and Nancy saw that her father was jerking slightly as he coughed, as if trying to sit up. She hurried forwards and slid an arm around his shoulders. He took her other hand in his and she felt the weakness of it; something within her stretched taut. As they lifted him, lungs rasping and gurgling like a bellows full of river water, he fell sideways onto her, his mouth next to her ear, moist and ugly, the smell of his breath in her nose, his stubble against her cheek. She recoiled internally and guilt swelled up with her tears.

He began to cough, wet racking coughs, and the blanket fell down his body.

Nancy stared. Great purple weals were developing across his arms and chest, which was all she could see. Lil met her eyes, her mouth thin, and nodded.

'Someone…' Nancy's voice trailed away. She couldn't form the words.

'Some bastard beat him. I saw when I got his wet clothes off him.' She reached out and tugged the blankets closer about him.

Nancy tried to push down her rage at the thought. 'Can we get a fire? He needs to be warm.' She wrapped her arms around him in an attempt to give him her own body heat. His head sagged against her shoulder and she stroked it, as if he were a child. 'Do you think there might be a charity doctor? A nurse?' She fumbled in her pocket for the hat money.

Lil shook her head, refusing the money. 'I'll see what I can do.' She patted Nancy's hand and went out looking for fire and healing.

'I'm sorry, Dad,' Nancy muttered. Sorry for the feeling of revulsion and horror, sorry nothing could be enough to help, sorry she was small, weak and poor and sorry she could not convey him to a hospital with smooth sheets and kind nurses.

When Nancy awoke, she was lying pressed up against her father's back, trying to keep him warm. He coughed weakly, no longer trying to wipe away the bloody spittle that hung from his lips. Nancy leant across him to wipe it and he jerked his head away from her hand as if he couldn't tell who, or what, was touching him.

Lil was busy just inside the doorway. She'd found an old metal tray and some firewood. A thin trickle of smoke was drifting into the air from the wood.

'That Annie's given me a couple of burning coals to get it going. She owes me a favour.' Lil sniffed, pleased with herself and then blew on the wood. 'Once this is going, I'll see if there's any help to be had.'

Her father rolled back on the pile of blankets and straw, eyes gazing blankly at Nancy. She leant in and whispered, 'Come on, Dad, you've got to prove us wrong and get better.'

'Polly,' he managed to rasp. 'Promise?' And then he turned away on the blanket, eyes closed.

'I'll look after her.' Nancy said. 'Promise.' His hand gave the smallest of squeezes.

She closed her hand around the sensation of his hand in hers, hoping to keep it safe.

'I should never have left them, Lil,' she said, quietly.

'You weren't to know, Nance. You couldn't know what that evil bastard was going to do.'

'I should've known. I should've known he wouldn't let it rest.'

'Don't worry about it now. We'll worry about him once your dad is all right.'

Nancy gave a short laugh. 'I'll kill him, Lil. I will.'

'Just go to sleep, Nance,' Lil said and bent to blow on the fire again.

Nancy lay huddled up against her father's back, listening to his breathing, feeling the lumps of his spine move with the effort. Several times it paused and she sat up, concerned, only for him to start breathing again. Lil was still gone. She watched as the light faded outside.

When she woke in the dark for the last time, the fire had gone out; she could hear the bells again, echoing from her dreams and her father lay still in her arms.

The day began with finding a sheet to wrap his poor, thin body in; back to all the places Lil had tried in the night, this time for a shroud, not a healer. A stranger's charity brought it in the end; mended so often there seemed hardly enough of the original to make a handkerchief but it was clean and Nancy cried into it all the way back to his body, feeling at any moment that she might stumble into the chasm that had opened in her. Nancy folded it over the face that did not look like his own anymore and yet did – a crumpled and empty version of him. His face caught on ragged gasps hanging in her mind even when she was thinking of something else.

Over the next few days, they walked across the parish to find some kind of funeral for him, to find some note from some grey and disapproving official that affirmed they couldn't pay, to find some assurance that the anatomists wouldn't get him. She couldn't bear the thought of him being taken apart like an old cabinet. In the end they had no choice but to leave him in the hands of a little old man who indignantly declared that none in his care would be found under the anatomist's knife. Her father would be buried in the pauper grave with the other poor souls. He swore it, with his hand held over his heart, and Nancy had to trust him because she had no alternative.

Sleep was the only thing left to them. Nancy drifted in and out of consciousness, aware of Lil's bulk behind her; Lil's musty scent, built of other people's old clothes and her own odour mixed together, was comforting and had a warmth to it. A dog barked in the distance and, closer by, the donkey shuffled in its hay. On the street beyond the archway, a couple of men shouted, an argument rising and then failing to fully materialise, quieter men's voices tugging it apart and drifting off into the distance. Nancy snuggled into Lil and sank further down into sleep.

A little while later she woke as a hand shook her arm. She looked up into Mr Bevel's eyes. She scrambled backwards, bumping against Lil who woke with a snort.

'Hello, Nancy.'

The sudden brightness of a lantern made her blink. Over Bevel's shoulder she saw Mr Darner and Mr Herbert.

'What do you want?' Nancy asked.

'You need to come back to the Brethren,' Bevel said.

Behind him, Herbert said, 'You know that your father wanted you to stay in the Charitable Brethren and now he is no longer here to protect you, we have come to take you back.' He clutched his wooden cross with fervent fingers, as if touching it as he spoke would give his words conviction.

Darner smiled down at her, the lantern he held casting shadows on his face.

'Not on my bloody life,' Lil said, scrambling to her feet. She pushed Nancy behind her.

'And who are you?' Darner asked sneering down at Lil.

'A friend of Nancy's. A better friend than you'll ever be.'

'Nonsense. Just a petty agent of the devil's work.' With a crack, Darner struck Lil with his stick and she fell against the wall of the hovel, slumping heavily to the ground.

'Lil!' Nancy screamed and lunged towards her friend.

'Nancy.' Herbert reached out and grabbed her arm 'You can't live here. In this.' He looked around. 'Not when there's a clean bed, healthy food and a safe and honest life happy to welcome you just around the corner.' He smiled encouragingly.

'Leave me alone!' she tried to shake him off. Lil groaned and shifted, huddling against the wall. 'Lil!'

'I'm all right, Nance,' Lil muttered.

'Come back to us, Nancy,' Herbert said, trying for warmth in his voice and succeeding only in sounding greasy. 'You belong with your sister.'

'My sister belongs with me, not you. And safe! Was my dad safe when *he*,' she indicated Darner, 'kicked him out? In the frost, with no coat. Deliberate. It was murder.'

'I released him to rejoin you, ungrateful child. Since he could not bring you back to where you belong to receive your punishment. He was pathetically weak in his sin.'

The fact that in bitter moments she had secretly thought her father weak made her angrier still. 'You stole my father's tools! You left him destitute. And with the frost and his lungs you knew what the outcome would be.'

A smile caught the corner of Darner's mouth and he pushed it down. Behind him, their small fire flared up, as if new fuel had been thrown onto it, and she felt her rage go up with it. Until now, some corner of her had thought that it had been an accident; surely he had not intended that the expulsion onto the streets should kill her father. But now she saw. Darner had known and he had enjoyed it. She wondered if Darner had been the source of the bruises, if he had drenched her father's clothes before shutting him out in the hard cold.

The red light from the fire flickered across Darner's face and he waved away her comment. 'That is irrelevant. The fact is that when he joined us, your father made me your guardian in the event of his death.'

Nancy suddenly remembered the lawyer, Herbert, reading official-looking papers aloud, indicating where her father should sign. Behind Darner the flames began to lick up the side of the small hut.

'Good God, Nancy, look,' Lil said.

An ember spat and landed on Darner's coat. He patted it out. 'Come on, let's go.'

Mr Herbert tightened his grip on Nancy's arm. She jerked away but he managed to keep his grip. 'Come on, Nancy, be a good girl.'

Lil scrambled to her feet and lunged at Herbert. Bevel stepped forwards and punched her in the face – a simple, short blow that landed as if his fist were made of lead. She dropped, groaning and clutching her face.

Nancy screamed in rage and fear, broke free from Herbert, kicked out at Bevel and caught the back of his knee. He stumbled. She pulled out her hatpin and stabbed him in the arm. He let out a pained bellow and turned on her. In the low light, his face was shadowed and full of anger. His hand bunched into a fist. Nancy pulled back the pin to stab again.

Darner's voice dropped into the mess like a stone into deep water. 'Stop this.' Flames started to run across the floor along the rags.

'That little witch stabbed me!' Bevel said.

Nancy snarled, 'I'd kill you given half a chance.'

Bevel laughed and took a step towards her, but Herbert grabbed her arm again and stood between them.

'Enough,' Darner said. The others stilled. Lil began to roll over onto her knees and Darner kicked her. She pulled her arms over her face and whimpered.

'Leave her alone, you murdering bastard,' Nancy said and lunged towards him.

She was held with an effort by Herbert, who said, 'Mr Darner is trying to save you from a life on the streets, as your father wanted.'

Darner crushed a flaring ember with his toe and put his lantern down on the ground. 'Thanks to me, your father lived a good year or so longer than he would have otherwise. And if you hadn't left in such disgrace, he'd still be at Brethren Hall, alive. I have no doubt of it.'

Nancy couldn't answer this and instead spat on the ground in front of his feet. The ember he had stamped out flared up again and he stepped back.

'You left and I had to punish you for your insolence and ingratitude. We all know what you'd have fallen to if your father hadn't joined us and that's exactly where you'll end up if you don't come with us now. Earning your bread on your back. I'll find some further penance for your misbehaviour once we are back at the Hall, since even the death of your father does not seem to have chastened you.'

Nancy found that her ears were ringing with a crackling, singing sound. Lil looked up at her with red eyes, nose and face bloodied. With a small whoomphing sound, Darner's lantern burst into flames, burning tallow seeping out from it.

Nancy stretched out towards Lil, but Herbert pulled her back.

Bevel laughed again, a short, hard laugh like his punch. A dark wet patch was growing on his upper arm and sweat beaded on his lip.

'Let's go,' Darner shouted, hurrying out past the flames and Herbert began pulling her along. He had neither the brute bulk of Bevel nor the iron strength of Darner, but he was still more than a match for an underfed and grieving child. She staggered along beside him.

In the open air, the father of the family from the old stables was looking out, the light of the flames on his face. 'Fire!' he called back into the stable. 'Fire!' And suddenly the yard was full of five children and the man and his wife. 'Go to the pump!' he screamed and shoved a pail at his oldest child who sprinted out into the street. He moved towards the blazing lean-to. The flames were now battering at the brick wall at the back of the hut, stretching up towards the roof line of the larger building behind.

'Lil!' Nancy stretched back just as the older woman staggered out of the blazing ruin, followed in quick succession by Bevel, who shoved her to the floor.

'Oi!' shouted the father of the stable children, and rushed to Lil's side. In the confusion, Nancy wrenched her arm from Herbert and bolted. She reached the corner of the courtyard and scrambled up a pile of refuse onto the top of a wall. She turned back to see the lean-to collapse in on itself as the first bucket of water was thrown on the flames. Lil was being helped to her feet by the man from the stables. She looked up at Nancy, gesturing frantically for her to go. Darner followed Lil's gaze, then charged towards Nancy. She dropped to the other side of the wall and ran.

Chapter Nine
Fortune

The Prophet was shortly to give the next of his street sermons and Spider was waiting. The room that looked out on the steps of Brethren Hall had changed. Spider had hung her treasures around her, the things that helped her see, turning and changing so that she looked out through an oracle's lens. The shaft of light was cut and changed – reflected in a chunk of broken mirror, twisted into many colours through a chandelier pendant, seen straight and clear through the partial orbit of a shattered skull.

Down on the street, a few people stood around, waiting just as she did. Waiting for the sermon? Perhaps. Earlier she had overheard a man discount Darner as a religious nut, but then he said, 'The man can talk, I'll give him that.' Two policemen wandered up and positioned themselves near the steps, watching the crowd. Otherwise, the bustle of the street was going on as usual. Patience stepped up to one side of the window and, careful not to block Spider's view, peered out through a small tear in the paper.

A small child, back straight with the importance of her task, emerged from the pub on the alley corner holding a jug of beer in front of her, tongue peeking from the corner of her mouth.

A butcher, leaning in the door of his shop, called something to her and she redoubled her concentration. He laughed and turned indoors. Two women argued on the pavement and the girl edged around them carefully. They paused in their argument to watch her.

One of Spider's oracle lenses neatly caught a girl coming up the street. She moved between a group of people and a wall, looking towards the empty steps of the Brethren Hall. Spider caught her breath. It was the girl. The girl who had come out of the Brethren's own basement. She was dressed in rags rather than the brown Brethren gown, but the biggest change was the expression on her face. Taut and intense, her eyes were fixed on the door. Even from here Spider could tell the girl was trembling. With what? Fear? Excitement? Rage?

A bundled-up old woman limped after her. She grasped the girl's shoulder, giving it a small comforting shake. The girl patted the woman's hand and looked back at her.

Why were they here? Why now? It couldn't be coincidence. A chunk of red glass span across her vision and briefly washed the world outside with blood as the bell began to ring and the great doors at the top of the steps swung open.

The girl on the street below jerked towards them, but was held back by the older woman. As the members of the Charitable Brethren emerged from their Hall to line up on the steps, the girl and her friend started to move between the assembled crowd. Passers-by found themselves tangled up among those who had come to listen. The carts on the street stopped and started, people shouted. The policemen stepped forwards and put a stop to an argument and the traffic started to flow again, slowly.

The young woman and her friend made their way through the crowd, avoiding the gaze of the policemen. But Spider could see them and could hardly drag her eyes away to watch for Darner.

The bells came to a crescendo and then Darner emerged from the Hall. He waited for the last echo of the bells to fade before spreading his arms wide. 'Friends! I welcome you…'

He continued to talk, his deep, clear voice audible from her position, but Spider was distracted from his speech by a scuffle happening below her on the street. The girl now held a knife, bright in her fist, knuckles pale as the blade. Her face and her eyes strained forwards, every tendon in her stretched to reach the man at the top of the steps. The only thing holding her back was her friend, who was gripping her arm with one hand and gesturing madly with the other.

The girl was holding the knife down by her side. Spider could see it, but she doubted that anyone in the crowd could. The girl turned on her friend and shouted, audible from Spider's perch, even through the glass, 'I don't care!'

And then the friend stepped right up to the girl's face and whispered something in her ear. Something that made her collapse entirely.

The people immediately around them shifted around and away. A large cart stood between them and the policemen but as the girl sank to the ground in the road, the carter shouted out in alarm and the policemen started towards the disturbance. The girl's friend dragged her to her feet and Spider leant forwards.

She had to follow them. She had to know who these people were. The girl might be a help or, worse, she might reach Darner before Spider could. She recognised the girl's drive; it was like her own but untempered by time and patience. The girl might get there first, even if it meant a rope around her neck.

The friend's shawl fell back from her head as she scurried them both away and Patience exclaimed, 'Oh, it's Old Lil!'

Spider, half-risen from her chair paused. 'You know her?'

'I've seen her hawking old clothes in the streets around here. The shopkeepers are always chasing her away and complaining about her bothering people.'

The woman looked as though she'd taken a bad beating; her face was bruised and one eye was swollen shut.

'Would you know where to find her?' Spider asked.

'I expect I could find out,' Patience said stepping away from the window. 'I don't know the girl though.'

Spider smiled and settled back into her chair, and turned her eye back to Darner, wondering what he had done to raise the girl's ire. What might she know about him, how might she help? Spider put her eye to the orbit of a bird's skull and watched Darner talk. She didn't have to give chase, undignified, desperate. Patience would find them later.

Patience was crying. Quiet gasping little sobs as if she were trying not to be overheard, though she was alone and, as far as she was aware, Spider was at the other end of the house. Spider was not at the other end of the house. Spider was watching the tears drip from Patience's chin onto the freshly laundered sheets she was folding. Spider's eye was pressed to the keyhole of the door to the narrow passage between the walls of the laundry and kitchen. It led to the tight dusty stairs that twisted up and back towards her rooms.

It was puzzling and disturbing that Patience was crying. It was not unheard of for Patience to weep; she had sadnesses, as all people do. But to cry in the middle of the day and over the laundry, the clean sheets spotted with her sadness? That was strange.

Spider stood up in the dark and tapped her chin lightly. She hurried up the stairs at the end of the passage and into the dimly lit room at the top. She rummaged in her pocket for an oracle stick until one slipped between her fingers. She drew it.

Despair.

Why despair? Why was Patience despairing now, when it seemed that long-held pain might finally be resolved?

Spider shuffled back along the corridor, taking the conventional way to the servants' quarters and stood for a moment in the doorway of the laundry, waiting for Patience to notice her.

'Oh!' Patience started and jumped to her feet. She resumed folding the sheet.

'What's the matter, Patience?' Spider asked, stepping into the room.

'Nothing. Nothing. I'm fine.' Patience smoothed the sheet.

'You are not.'

'I was just thinking about my parents.'

Patience licked her lips and her eyes remained fixed on the sheets as she folded. A lie. Spider said nothing and Patience became a little flustered. She fumbled the sheet. Spider stepped forwards and took the corner so that it wouldn't land on the ground.

'Oh, ma'am, you can't do that. Please leave it to me.'

'I can fold a sheet, Patience.'

'Well, it's just—'

Spider held the sheet wide and Patience reluctantly followed her motions. They folded it in silence. As she laid it on the pile of folded sheets, Patience ran a hand across the smooth linen. Today was her ironing day. The laundry room was dry and warm after the thick steam of wash day. The smell of hot metal and hot fabric filled the old servants' quarters and the row of irons were sitting back in their usual place beside the stove.

'Nearly done,' Patience said, filling the silence. She rubbed her face.

'What's the matter?' Spider repeated the question.

'Nothing. Nothing. Please, ma'am. I'll take these up to the airing cupboard now, if you please.' She stepped towards the door but Spider was standing in the doorway.

'Not until you tell me why you're crying. It's not your family.'

Patience put the pile of washing down with a thump. 'Can't you tell with your visions and things?' She put her fists on her hips. 'Seeing. All the time seeing and yet blind.'

Spider was taken aback. 'I do not—' She started.

'No, I expect you don't. All this about oracles and about the past. All about what was done and making it right. What about the future? You'll bring yourself to the prison or the madhouse if you're not careful.' Spider opened her mouth to speak but Patience continued, 'Or worse!'

Worse? She could only mean the gallows. Spider felt her head spin and she pushed away the thought of her mother's pink heels protruding from the bottom of her nightgown, turning, turning. She gripped the door jamb.

'And taking that young girl with you perhaps. If you find her.' Patience dropped herself into the only chair in the laundry. 'Oh, I wish I'd never shown you that newspaper.'

Spider felt her skin crawling with Patience's worries and expectations. She brushed her arms, her chest tight.

'I can't help… I can't help it, Patience. I must.'

Patience looked up at her and sighed.

'I know.'

'He has to go. He needs to be cleared away and I need to be the one to do it.'

Patience nodded. 'I'm just worried where it'll end.'

'You're my beneficiary, you know.'

Patience shook her head, her mouth thin. 'That's not at all what I mean and you know it.'

'I know but—'

'It's a kind thought, ma'am,' Patience said warmly. 'But I'm not worried about myself.'

Spider nodded, her throat tight against the crawling feeling in it. 'I need the girl.'

Patience put her head on one side and thought, and when she spoke she was business-like.

'Do you think she'll help? The girl, I mean.'

'I don't know.' Spider's voice strengthened. 'But she's a factor and she needs to be under my control. I need to have her here.'

Patience stood and picked up her pile of linens. 'Well, ma'am, I'd better get on with my work if I'm to be busy this evening, looking for this Old Lil character. Don't you worry, I'll find the girl.'

Spider watched Patience bustle away up the corridor and leant against the wall, closed her eyes. There was a twisting pain in the side of her head, a small one for now and she breathed against it, willing it away; just now, she could not afford too many days hiding in the dark. Once the girl was here, she would be one step closer to Darner.

PART II

Chapter Ten
Creation

Sara stared at the whitewashed ceiling. Pale yellow light came in through the bars on the high window and brought a scent of lilacs with it. Somehow it gave the room the feeling of a hermit's retreat, calm and reverent.

Had she no memory of the journey, she might not have believed that this was an asylum. In the night, someone in the distance had been chanting in a high-pitched voice. It reinforced her sense of having been transported to a religious house, until murmured voices interrupted and the chanting became shouting. She hadn't been able to make out the words. Then she had slept and woken, slept and woken. Vague dream-shapes slid through the corners of her memory: stairs, cold metal on her feet and a sense of spinning.

She got out of bed and put on the neat, faded green dress that lay on the chair. It was simply cut and didn't fit her very well, designed for utility rather than style. The fact that it was green struck her as a symptom of Doctor Whitehead's ideas about making the asylum a pleasant place in which to heal. On the previous night's journey, there had been plenty of time for him to outline his philosophy of treatment. 'A convalescent home for the mind, my dear. We try to minimise such unpleasantness as restraint and meet our patients as equals.'

At the time, Sara was uncomfortably cocooned in the straightjacket, which made it hard to sit upright as the van drove over the bumps and swayings of the road. Her shoulder still aching from the assistant's rough handling, she stared at the dim circle of Whitehead's face in the dark with an expression of incredulity. He was not able to see it, apparently, and didn't appreciate the irony.

She sat on the edge of the bed in her new dress and considered the seriousness of her situation. Some people never got out of these places. But those people were, presumably, mad. She considered herself to be entirely sane, but had not been quite subtle enough in her actions – actions that were reasonable enough, but deemed unseemly by the world. For a rational person, it should not be impossible to be recognised as sane, once a suitable period of treatment had passed. That, or escape.

Her course of action, therefore, should not be to argue with those who perceived her as mad but to visibly 'improve' under the treatments over time – a couple of months perhaps. Quickly, but not so swiftly as to arouse suspicion. At the same time, she should seek to understand the routines of the place and the layout of the asylum in case she needed to use the more drastic method. Escape would mean she could never go back to Hangcorner House. To be deemed sane was the preferable route. She had just come to this conclusion when footsteps sounded outside the room and a key clanked into the lock.

Last night, the doctor had said, 'We will need to lock you in at first, my dear, I hope you understand. Once you settle in and accept that this is your home, I hope we will be able to dispense with such a caution and in fact we may move you to one of the women's dormitories. Of course, the outside doors are always locked anyway and there's the wall and the gatehouse...' His voice trailed away as if he'd lost the train of his argument and he patted her on the shoulder, smiling.

Now the door opened smoothly. An unfamiliar man stood in the doorway and looked at Sara intensely and for a long time in silence. There was something puritan about his stern, gaunt face with its long beard and his old-fashioned black clothes and white collar. She stepped back, fear creeping across her shoulders and wondered what this man wanted, examining her. Unmoving, a carved figure of judgement.

She glanced at the window as if that could offer any possibility of escape and as she looked back he stepped forwards and with his long legs he was up to her in a moment. He grasped her face and pulled it up to his so that she was on tiptoe. He stared into her eyes. His damp breath pushed itself across her face and she recoiled, but his fingers and arms were too strong. She clutched his forearms through his coat and it was like holding a skeleton made of iron. She couldn't move his arms at all and the way he held her jaw meant she could not open her mouth. He continued to grasp her face and stare at her. She struggled and glared back at him, silent and furious.

'You are the witch,' he said. His voice, sure and rich, carried such certainty that she almost felt herself drawn in by it. 'Dr Whitehead has told me about you and your...' he pulled his lips away from his teeth and spoke with distaste, 'deviance. Your attempt upon the life of the head of your household was a perversion of the natural order.' He tightened his grip on her and then pushed her away from him.

She staggered against the wall. He returned to the doorway and she rubbed the sides of her face, trying to remove the feeling of his cold, hard fingertips against her cheeks and to quash the feeling of helplessness that had risen in her and, worse, the squirming sense of shame that he had so easily conquered her.

'I am the chaplain of this place and I will not tolerate such blasphemy and sin. I will see that your taint is not allowed to infect the other poor souls resided here. I have the spiritual fate of every soul in this place held in my hand.' He lifted his open palm as if holding those souls up before her.

Sara, remembering her resolution to prove her sanity, suppressed a tremble that threatened to venture into her voice and said, 'I trust in God's judgement.'

The chaplain ignored her and continued. 'And he casts the unworthy into the fire.' He dropped his hand with a dismissive gesture, casting her away. 'You must pray or be lost! Pray on your knees until they bleed.' He focused on her intensely, his eyes wide and dark.

'Hello, hello, what's this?' said a voice in the doorway. Doctor Whitehead appeared behind the chaplain. 'Mr Darner, I really do prefer to be the one to greet our new inmates on their first morning in our humble abode.' He gave a small, light laugh. 'But no doubt you mean well.'

The chaplain looked down at the shorter man and there was a pause. After a moment he stepped back and said, 'Of course, Dr Whitehead, but while the asylum is your domain, I have an ultimate responsibility to God to seek to save all souls. Even those who seem unworthy.' He cast an eye over Sara, turned and strode from the room. As he left, the doctor watched him go and then met Sara's gaze with a bright smile.

'Well now, I hope you slept well, my dear?'

She had not, but that wasn't unusual for her and so she smiled and nodded. This was the man she would eventually have to convince of her sanity.

The doctor wittered on, repeating much of what he'd said to her the previous night. '…always looking to make our patient's lives more pleasant … services in the private chapel … useful work in the mornings. Treatments in the afternoons, or whenever we think they're necessary – time afterwards to be ready for dinner, you know. We do like everyone to come to table for dinner unless they really are too unwell. Can't heal the mind on an empty stomach, that's my wife's motto, and I have to say I quite agree. Oh, bless me, I am going on.'

In the distance a bell rang.

'Ah, there you go, the breakfast bell. I am so glad to see you're calm this morning. Please come along with me. I take all my meals in the refectory with the patients.' He held out his arm and she found herself being led through the corridors as he continued. When they entered the refectory, it was like looking at a distorted reflection of the few formal dinners she had attended – eyes turning towards her as she walked into a large room on a stranger's arm (it had always been a stranger), the smell of food drifting in from a kitchen somewhere.

The room had a polished parquet floor, a high ceiling and long windows through which she could see wide grass lawns and flowerbeds. She might have thought it had once been a ballroom if the doctor hadn't already told her that the buildings had been especially built to his own design.

The other female inhabitants of the asylum were dressed similarly to her and in four different shades: green like hers, blue, pink and lilac. The dresses all showed signs of fading and wear, but they were spotlessly clean. The men wore grey trousers, white shirts and jackets in a similar array of shades as the women's dresses, cut from the same fabric she guessed. The patients were separated by sex: the men seated at long tables to one side of the room, the women on the other.

'See how smart they all are!' the doctor said, beaming at everyone. 'My innovation. I chose cheerful colours for the dress and my wife agreed. It makes the laundry a little less easy than dressing you all in grey but the cheering effect of the sight is well worth it.'

He approached the nearest women's table and cleared his throat. Sara had a sudden feeling of dread. She pulled her arm away but he tightened his grip on it. 'May I have your attention, everyone?' Most of the faces turned to him. Someone further back stood up to see her clearly and a sweep of whispering ran around the room.

'This is our newest companion.' He patted her hand. 'This is Miss Atherton and I want you to give her a warm welcome.' There was a spatter of applause and cries of 'Welcome' broke out. Underneath the cheerful welcome, though, there was a tenseness. A few of the inmates looked at her with anxious eyes, shifting in their seats, and a man on the nearest table shouted, 'Never mind, love.'

The doctor indicated that she should sit between a dark-haired woman staring blankly at her plate and another who nodded at her but remained silent. As she sat down, she brushed against the dark-haired woman, who winced away from her, rubbing her arm as if Sara had hit her. Sara tried to apologise but the woman just shook her head and looked away.

'Don't mind her,' a woman across the table said. 'She's just barmy.'

A moment later a woman in an apron carried in a large pot and started ladling the contents into bowls which were distributed by nurses and a straight-backed woman in a nicely cut dress with smoothed hair. As she moved down the table, Sara could hear the inmates as the bowl was placed. 'Thank you, Mrs Whitehead.', 'Thank you, Mrs Whitehead.', 'Thank you, Mrs Whitehead.' The woman across the table groaned quietly. 'Porridge day,' she said. 'I hate porridge.'

Sara examined the face of the doctor's wife as she placed a bowl of porridge in front of her; her face was serious, her forehead creased. She met Sara's eyes. 'Welcome, Miss Atherton,' she said and Sara repeated the mantra of her fellow inmates: 'Thank you, Mrs Whitehead.'

A hush crept across the room and Sara looked up. Mr Darner had just entered and taken the empty seat to the left of Doctor Whitehead. Somehow he made it look as though he was sitting at the head of the high table, with Whitehead to the right of him. Someone dropped their spoon into their bowl with a clatter.

'We must pray before we eat,' Darner said, his voice carrying around the room. 'We must show gratitude for what we are given, must we not, Mr Brown?' he said, ice in his voice.

The man who had dropped his spoon muttered, 'Of course, Mr Darner.'

'Indeed.' His eyes scanned the assembled people and Sara suddenly knew who he was looking for. She resisted the urge to shrink down in her seat and when his eyes fell on her she braced for it.

He said grace, lingering long and richly over the words. The whole time, he had his eyes fixed on Sara's and she on his, determined not be cowed. It was not a prayer she recognised, seemingly one of Darner's own devising and it ended with the lines:

> You feed our bodies as you feed our minds,
> You keep our lives as you keep our souls,
> Blessed are we who bow before your bounty,
> Amen.

The word 'Amen' rippled around the tables and only then did Darner look away from Sara, turning his eyes to his food. She was not hungry but forced herself to eat a little of the dull meal. She didn't know what the day might bring and she did not want to be weak.

Sara found herself allocated to a small group of women, who were led along a well-lit white corridor. Sara found herself standing next to a cheerful girl who waved at her, then turned to look at a group who were going to a different day room. She said to Sara, 'They get to do sewing. We aren't allowed needles and scissors.' She swung her arms and smiled. 'I don't know why.'

The woman leading them away said drily, 'Last time you were given scissors, Miss Hawthorn, you cut a great hole in your dress.'

'Oh yes. So, I did.' She laughed, then looked sad. 'I wanted to make a dolly,' she confided to Sara. 'I could have done it too. At home I sewed a lot. Teeny tiny stitches. Pretty. But they won't let me have a needle.'

Sullivan was following the group. He met Sara's eye, nodded

and said, 'Good morning, miss.' She turned away and hurried forward so that another patient was between them.

Miss Hawthorn was still looking sad, but she brightened after a moment and asked the attendant who was leading them, 'Are we in the parrot room, Miss Gavins?'

The attendant did not answer but opened a door to the left. The girl clapped and laughed with pleasure, pushing forwards to be the first in the room. A bow window looked out at a garden that led down to green lawns. Beyond a high wall lay fields of wheat; Doctor Whitehead had told her that they belonged to the asylum and were farmed for its benefit.

Through the window she saw a group of five male patients with wheelbarrows being ushered along by Lambert, the attendant who had been present with Sullivan at her detention, and a man wearing a flat cap and a brown jacket – the gardener, perhaps. He directed the men to different areas of the garden and she watched as they began weeding the beds and the paths.

'Occupation,' Miss Gavins said to Sara. 'It is key to a moral regime at an asylum. Keep bodies occupied and the mind has less time for worries.'

Sara wasn't so sure about that; she could see that the nearest man to her was talking speedily to himself, lips moving, head shaking, but all the while he continued to pull the weeds.

'At the very least,' the attendant said, 'something is achieved.'

Behind her came a scream and Sara turned quickly. The attendant continued to stare out of the window. 'Never mind that, it's just Herman. I expect Miss Hawthorn has disturbed him.'

Sara noticed a cage standing next to the door. It housed a huge blue parrot, which Sullivan eyed with malice. Miss Hawthorn stood a careful distance away from the cage, but her fascination was making her lean in, eyes wide.

'Hello, Herman,' she whispered.

'HERMAN, HERMAN,' the parrot replied in a scream and Miss Hawthorn laughed.

'Stop that noise!' The attendant addressed the parrot. 'You know very well how to behave.'

The parrot lifted a foot and scratched its head in an imitation of a salute, 'Yes, Miss Gavins,' he said in a moderate voice. 'No, Miss Gavins. Gavins!'

Miss Gavins turned away and told the patients to take a seat at the table in the centre of the room.

'We're making rugs,' she explained. 'Once there are enough for each patient's room, they'll be distributed.'

'I don't see why we can't have them now. Why can't I have one of my finished ones?' said Miss Hawthorn, dragging herself away from the parrot and taking a seat.

'Because that wouldn't be fair. Equity of treatment, that's Dr Whitehead's guiding principle.'

'I've got one of your rugs already, Miss Hawthorn,' Sullivan said, leaning against the wall. 'By my bed. It's a bit rough, but it'll do.'

'They're supposed to be for the patients!' Miss Hawthorn said. Sullivan grinned.

Miss Hawthorn rubbed her eyes and tried to smile at her knees. 'Well, I'm glad you like it,' she said, sounding unsure.

Each patient was given a basket of rags, a latch hook and a half-finished rug, and most of them set to work. One woman silently glanced at her hook and then stared out of the window, eyes fixed on the middle distance, grasping her rags in white-knuckled hands.

Sara picked up her hook and, after a moment watching Miss Hawthorn's quick hands, started work on her rug. 'Why is there a parrot?' she asked.

'Doctor Whitehead thinks that living creatures and plants give the patients something to care for. And they brighten the place up.'

Sara eyed the parrot, who was staring back at her with a humorous air.

'Who looks after Herman?' she asked.

'Miss Dutton here.' Miss Gavins nodded at the quiet lady, who almost surfaced at the sound of her name but appeared to sink back into her reverie.

'I could do it,' Miss Hawthorn said. 'I'd like it. I help sometimes, don't I, Miss Dutton?'

Miss Dutton turned her head and, apparently with some effort, focused her eyes. 'Yes, dear. It's very hard. It tires me. My head hurts so.' She appealed to Miss Gavins. 'Could I have something for my head? Could you ask the doctor?'

'No more laudanum, Miss Dutton. You know what he said. You haven't added a single rag to your rug. Look. Miss Hawthorn has made three rugs already this year and though you have yet to finish a single one, all you want is your laudanum.'

Sullivan snorted with laughter and shook his head.

'It's all right,' Miss Hawthorn said brightly. 'I'll do her share and help with Herman. He bites sometimes,' she said to Sara. 'When he's in a bad mood. A bit like me!' She shouted with laughter at this observation and Miss Gavins gave her a nasty look from the corner of her eye. Miss Dutton gave a slumping sigh and returned to gazing out of the window.

The door opened and Sullivan jerked into a more alert stance. Miss Hawthorn stood up suddenly, dropping her rug and her hook. She backed away from the door, her mouth a wide gape of fear. She shook her head from side to side. Sara turned to see who had walked in. To her surprise, it was Doctor Whitehead, a benevolent smile on his face.

'Miss Gavins,' he said cheerily, 'I am afraid I must deprive you of one of your fair companions.'

'No, I won't, I won't, I won't!' yelled Miss Hawthorn, her voice rising into incoherence. She bent and picked up her hook and threw it at Doctor Whitehead. It fell far short and clattered at his feet.

'Dear Miss Hawthorn, I am not here for you.'

'You can't make me!' she shouted, having not taken in his words.

'My dear!' he said firmly. 'I'm *not* here for you. You may continue making your rug.' He bent, picked up the hook and held it out to the trembling girl. She stared at him and then darted forwards and snatched it.

Doctor Whitehead turned to Sara and said, 'Miss Atherton, I would like to begin your treatment today.'

'Treatment?' she asked taking a step back, alarmed by Miss Hawthorn's quivering fear.

'Yes, my dear, we are going to administer a course of hydrotherapy. Don't let Miss Hawthorn's reaction taint your expectations. It is not unpleasant.'

'Water,' whispered Miss Hawthorn, her eyes wide.

'Yes, just water,' Whitehead said with a note of impatience in his voice. 'Just water. Life-giving water. Nothing to be afraid of.'

'I think I'd much rather make rugs with Miss Gavins here.'

'Well, my dear, this is not a place where one has choices, as such. That is, in fact, rather the point of an asylum is it not? You come here and are relieved of the necessity of making choices until such time as you regain the capacity to do so for yourself.'

He stepped forwards and stretched an arm out towards her as if to usher her out of the room. She jabbed at him with her hook and he yelled out. He staggered back and stared at the new hole in his coat. Miss Gavins rose to her feet with an exclamation and Miss Hawthorn gave a shout of glee. The other patients backed away from the disturbance.

Doctor Whitehead picked at the hole in the tweed. 'No blood spilt or skin broken, no harm done. Except to the coat of course. Mrs Whitehead will be furious but it can't be helped.' He tutted, then nodded at Sullivan.

Sullivan stepped forwards and grabbed Sara's arm, she flailed at him and he grabbed the other, pulled her into his chest. She inhaled a noseful of stale sweat. She dropped the hook with a clatter and he gave a hoarse laugh. 'Gotcha now,' he said.

'That's enough, Sullivan, keep hold of her and come along.' Whitehead strode out without a backwards glance.

Sullivan tugged her towards the door and she felt her shoulder twinge where he had wrenched it the day before. He noticed the wince and pulled again. She pushed away with her feet and he growled, giving a bigger yank so that she stumbled forwards.

'That's it,' he said. 'Come along nicely now.'

They stopped outside a door with a sliding observation window in it. This corridor was tiled underfoot, unlike the ones in the main building which had wooden floors. The air was hard and unforgiving and every small sound bounced and echoed. In the distance, something clanked.

'I hear the boiler's running,' Doctor Whitehead observed.

'Started it at eight, saw to it myself. Knew you'd want it,' Sullivan answered and received an approving nod in answer.

Inside the white-tiled room, two female assistants were waiting next to a bath with water running into it. A high window of frosted glass let in a greyish light. To one side was a chair with restraints on the armrests and legs, fastened to the floor with a drain beneath.

'You're not wasting the heat?' Sullivan said to the women. Whitehead walked up and put a hand in the water.

'No, just getting the cold in first.'

The doctor turned a couple of taps and steaming water started to run into the bath. A pipe clanked loudly.

Sara tugged against Sullivan's grip.

'You'll stop that, miss. These nice ladies are going to put you in a special gown. You don't want me to do that, do you?' He grinned down at her and she pulled away. 'No, didn't think so. But if you give them any trouble, I'll have to help, won't I?'

One of the two women approached and Sullivan passed Sara's arms to her. The attendant held them slightly away from herself with an expression of disgust on her face as if Sara were covered in something foul. Sara resisted the urge to tear away from them all. Sullivan's threat made her feel nauseous and she held herself in as he nodded to the women and left the room. As the doctor followed Sullivan out, he spoke over his shoulder: 'Calmness is always the easiest path, dear, you'll see.' The door shut after him.

The other woman held a long white linen gown thrown over her arm and she looked in Sara's face, 'You really don't want Sullivan back in here, miss. I can promise you that, so behave yourself. In fact, I recommend you stay on the good side of him and his cronies as far as you can, and that's more advice than I should give.' The other woman nudged and shushed her. Together they removed Sara's asylum clothing, which seemed to have been designed with this purpose in mind.

When they put the gown on her, her limbs seemed stiff and immobile and, although she wasn't deliberately resisting, they struggled to get it over her arms. When she was finally clothed, the fabric was rough against her skin.

'All done?' Doctor Whitehead put his head around the door just as they were finishing. 'Jolly good. Now, my dear, we are going to use a very calming treatment today. You will lie in the warm water here. The water will be constantly refreshed as it cools so you will not become chilled, and you will find your mind calms. All the thoughts that have been fighting for your attention for so long will be stilled; it will probably take several treatments but I can assure you that you will come to look forward to the experience; most patients do.'

Sara thought of cheerful Miss Hawthorn and wondered if this was the treatment she dreaded, or whether her fear was something to do with the chair.

The doctor seemed to read her thought on her face and hurried on. 'I have taken this treatment myself when my mind is a little agitated and I can tell you, my dear, nothing beats it. We will check on you periodically so that any needs you might have can be managed, worry not. Come now, don't resist the ladies or I shall have to bring Mr Sullivan in to assist.'

A hammock hung within the bath and Sara could see that this was where she was supposed to lie. It might be wise to go along with this; it was not so very terrible to lie in warm water for a while and yet her instinct was to rebel. The warm water filled the room with steam and made the air less chill, but her limbs still didn't want to move and as she stepped up to the bath, she felt a resistance.

'Come on,' she muttered, and Doctor Whitehead caught the words.

'That's it, my girl, come on.'

She felt a flare of irritation at the words 'my girl'. He had no right to call her that, but she let it pass and allowed the assistants to help her into the warm water. It felt pleasant, though there was something gritty against the smooth enamel of the base of the bath, as if the taps had flushed out small particles of sand. She lay back into the water, felt her hair flow out from her head. Behind her the women were rummaging in a box and she raised herself up to see what it was. They hefted something large between them and then started to bring it towards the bath.

'Lie back, dear,' Whitehead said, his palm outstretched.

It was a canvas sheet and Sara suddenly realised what it was for. They were going to pin her into the bath, shut her into the water. Panic gripped her and she scrabbled to get her feet under herself. She rose, water cascading from her gown, soaking the skirts of the woman attendants, who shouted with annoyance. She pushed away at the canvas, shouting, 'No! You won't shut me in!'

The door opened and Sullivan came in. 'What's the problem?'

'Grab her!' the doctor called out as Sara attempted to jump out of the bath. Her feet slipped and she surged forwards, her leg caught in the hammock.

'Oh no, you don't,' said Sullivan and hauled her upright.

'Dear me, we're going to have to use the restraints. I do hate it so. It's much more calming if we can manage without.'

'I think you'll always have to use restraints with this one.' Sullivan shook her and took firm hold of one of her wrists.

'I don't want to go in that thing,' Sara said, forcing her words to be calm and firm.

'My dear, you will find it beneficial if you only give it a try,' Whitehead said.

'I do not want to be pinned down like an insect specimen,' she said loudly, trying to project the same authority as if she were demanding something from a servant.

Sullivan sniggered and she glared at him.

'Your face won't be covered. There is a hole in the canvas. See?' Whitehead held it up to demonstrate that there was, indeed, a hole for the patient's head.

'Do you wear that thing when you're trying this treatment?'

'Well, I... it's not really relevant for me.'

'So you just enjoy a long, warm bath now and again, and think it's the same as being tied down in it?' She laughed.

'Miss Atherton,' Sullivan said, 'Doctor Whitehead here has carefully determined the best treatment for you from his long years of experience with people of unsound mind. I suggest you listen to him. It will be easier than the alternative.'

'Alternative?' She looked at the man who had ceased his leering grins and now looked annoyed and bored.

'Force, Miss Atherton. Force.'

The doctor looked at Sullivan with distaste but said nothing.

Sara looked at the large man beside her. Could feel his tightening grip on her wrist which felt frail, made of small delicate bones. She wondered what Whitehead thought they were using now. The threat of force was force in itself. Wings fluttered feebly in her chest.

The earnest doctor still held the canvas, his waistcoat buttons visible through the hole for the patient's – her – head. Behind them both the attendants stood ready; they stood, watching and waiting, until they might be needed. The door was a long way away and beyond it were only cold corridors and more locked doors. She deflated.

'Good girl,' the doctor said, interpreting her expression as surrender.

'I'll get in calmly if he goes,' she said, indicating Sullivan.

Sullivan looked to the doctor who nodded. Sullivan passed her wrist to one of the women, who held it tightly. The other attendant came to her left side and they helped her to get back into the bath. The water level was a little lower now, the temperature a little cooler.

The assistant commented that they'd have to top it up and span a tap. Warm water started flowing into the bath behind her and Sara tried to relax. They strapped her wrists to the sides of the bath and then the sheet, smelling of canvas and old water, was laid over her and she was plunged into darkness. Her face emerged into the hole and the doctor looked on, bouncing a little on his toes, a relieved smile on his face.

There was a rattling and tugging on the canvas as they secured it around the bath.

'Now, we shan't abandon you. We'll pop in and check on you now and again, don't worry. Call out if you have a problem as the ladies will be nearby. Sullivan, too, if he's needed.'

She resolved only to call out if it was a desperate situation.

One of the assistants went to the window and closed the blinds, throwing the room into shadow and then the three of them left the room. The door closed behind them and she heard a key turn in the lock. *Why did they need to lock her in?* she wondered, her limbs half-floating, half-supported by the hammock and the restraints. It wasn't as if she could leave. She experimented with putting her feet down but the angle of the hammock meant this was impossible. What if the hammock broke? She would sink and drown before anyone could find her. For a moment, she was almost glad of the restraints; if it came to that she might be able to hold herself up by them. She tugged and found she could raise her chest a little, press it against the cold of the canvas cover.

Mumbling came from outside the door as the doctor spoke to his assistants, and then she heard footsteps on the tiled floor. The neat, self-satisfied *tap tap* of the doctor and then, after a few minutes of low voices, Sullivan's heavy tread and the assistants' more delicate ones dispersed in different directions.

The building was very quiet. Was she the only patient being treated in these rooms today? Something in the piping clanked and a little rush of warm water ran down her body. It stopped and a gurgle from the overflow echoed against the tiles. In the distance footsteps briefly came into earshot and then drifted out again. She hung in the slow warmth, feeling helpless. She briefly considered surrendering herself to it, in the hopes that it would work like her mobile or sleep to bring her visions. Then she thought of herself lying there, unable to see or hear if someone came into the room, and instead of relaxing into the warmth she lay with her ears alert for small noises and her fingers tight on her restraints.

Chapter Eleven
Guardian

Nancy pressed herself against the wall of the narrow alley down the side of the Brethren Hall. In the dusk, it was grey and empty. There was nowhere to hide. The rain came down in a determined pat-pat-pat. Somewhere, a gutter was overflowing with a dirty-sounding dribble.

At this time of the evening, the children would be in bed in the care of one of the young women. She heard the bell summoning the adults to prayer, and made her way to the dormitory windows. From the outside, all she could see were the low, narrow windows of frosted glass, except in one place, where a broken pane had been replaced with normal glass. Nancy had always chosen the bed close to it if she could, because she preferred to see out.

The dormitory was dark. No one was reading by candlelight. She wondered whether they were huddled around one of the older children, as they told one of the more gruesome Bible stories. This activity was frowned upon by the adults but the Brethren children could just about get away without serious punishment as long as the tale had Biblical origins. She bent and peered through the dim glass. No, the rows of beds showed little humps of sleeping figures.

Nancy tapped on the glass. The shape in the nearest bed stirred. Whoever it was threw back the covers and approached the window – not Pigeon but a girl Nancy recognised. The children in the other beds were moving, sitting up.

Nancy took out her long hatpin and worked it between the window and its frame. She knew the narrow windows had only a simple hook to hold them closed. She pushed back the hook with her pin; it took a couple of tries as the curved hook caught. But then she had it and levered open the window.

'Pigeon,' she called in a hoarse whisper.

'I'm here, Nancy,' came her sister's voice, thin in the dark. The small figure came towards the window and looked up at her.

'Get your things, Pigeon, I'm taking you out of here.'

Pigeon ran back to her bed.

'What's going on?' A voice came out of the dark. A taller figure came forwards. One of the older girls.

Pigeon ran back to the window with a small bundle, her dress hurriedly thrown on over her nightdress.

'You can't climb out of the window, Polly,' the older girl said.

'Come on, Pidge,' Nancy said and reached down for Pigeon's arms.

Lil's voice in her ear that morning had said, 'If you hang, Pigeon will never escape.' It had cut through her anger, her need to do something right then. Guilt and grief had swept through her. She had been going to abandon Pigeon, to break her most important promise to her father.

The older girl said, 'I'll shout for the grown-ups!'

'If you do, I'll curse your arms to shrivel away,' Nancy said, staring hard at the girl who gave a shriek and backed away.

Nancy grasped Pigeon's small wrists and began to lift. She found it was much harder than she had thought to lift her sister from this angle.

'Get a stool,' she said.

Pigeon passed up her small bundle which smelt of grubby linen and bread; Nancy guessed her sister had hidden away some of the bread rolls from dinner. She usually did. It was the only sign that she remembered the hunger from the time before they joined the Brethren. The girl who had woken Pigeon passed her a stool from beside her own bed.

'They're breaking the rules,' the older girl said, indignant.

'I'm not stopping Nancy Ratcliffe,' one girl said. 'She's scary. My mum says she's a witch.'

'We should shout for help.'

The other children all looked at each other doubtfully.

With the stool, Pigeon's head was level with the window.

'Hey, help! Kidnap!' the older girl shouted, alone.

Nancy grasped her sister under her arms. Pigeon kicked off the stool and Nancy began hauling her out of the window.

'Hey, help!' the girl shouted again and this time more of the children joined in. The girl dashed forwards and tried to grab Pigeon's legs but Pigeon shook her off, catching the girl across the face with her heel.

'Ow!' she cried and the rest of the children, seeing this, picked their side and shouted at the tops of their voices, 'Help! Kidnap!'

Nancy heard heavy footsteps in the corridor outside the dormitory and heaved Pigeon out into the damp alley.

A male voice cried, 'Oi!' and they looked up; it hadn't come from the room behind them. A silhouette stood at the far end of the building. As he started towards them, they scrambled to their feet and ran, splashing through the mud.

They dashed out into the main road and across it, narrowly avoiding a hansom whose cabbie swore loudly down at them, shaking his fist. The horse stamped its hooves and his red-faced driver frothed further as their pursuer also cut in front of him.

Nancy glanced over her shoulder and saw that the man behind them was Bevel. She put on an extra burst of speed, Pigeon's hand tight in hers, turning up a side street. They passed two women chatting on a doorstep and one of them called something after them. Bevel hurtled into the alley behind them and then Nancy heard a shout and risked another glance over her shoulder. Bevel was lying on the ground and one of the women was bending over him, exclaiming that she was sorry, she hadn't seen him, was he all right? The other woman flapped her hand to Nancy, urging her on.

Nancy and Pigeon darted into a narrow passage lined with gates. They ran past a couple, then Nancy grabbed a door handle with a brief prayer and they fell into a small yard. Pigeon went to slam the gate behind them, but Nancy pulled her back, then closed it carefully and quietly. In the corner of the yard stood a rank-smelling outhouse, and she pulled her sister into it as footsteps clattered along the passage outside.

Was the passage behind the yard a dead end? If it was, it wouldn't be long before Bevel realised that they had gone through one of the gates. If not, he might just think they had passed out at the end. In the distance, she heard a gate open and close. A few seconds later, a click as he tried a latch. Bevel was working his way back towards them, checking each yard. He would be bound to look in the outhouse. In the dim light, Nancy looked at Pigeon and put her fingers to her lips. She gently pushed the door open, reached down and picked up a handful of stones from the yard floor. A locked gate rattled from the next yard along. Nancy stood up silently and pulled the door of the outhouse closed behind her.

Pigeon's eyes were wide and scared and Nancy put her finger to her lips to calm her. Her sister put her own finger to her lips and seemed to hold her breath as the gate to the yard was opened. Nancy paused for a fraction of a second before giving a low grunt, as masculine as she could make it, and dropped the stones into the open pit. *Splat splat*, pause for another grunt, *splat*.

There was quiet as the man outside listened and then the gate opened and closed again, and footsteps made their way to the next gate. Pigeon giggled and stuffed her sleeve in her mouth to repress it. From the neighbouring yard came the sudden sound of a clattering chain and a dog baying with rage. Barking and snarling and swift footsteps before the gate slammed and the footsteps faded into the distance.

Pigeon giggled again and Nancy pressed her hand over her sister's face. They waited another minute or so before emerging into the relatively fresh air of the night. Pigeon gave an imitation of the grunts that Nancy had made and then Nancy couldn't help but join in her laughter. They bent over and Pigeon clutched Nancy's skirts, laughter sketching up into the sky above.

'Plop, plop, plop,' Pigeon said, and screamed with further hilarity.

A door in the house slammed open and a woman said, 'What in hell is going on out here? And who the bloody hell are you?'

Pigeon coughed her giggles under control and Nancy said, 'Sorry, missus, we'll go.'

'I think you'd better. Go on now.'

They hurtled out of the gate, scatterings of giggles still bubbling up in their throats.

By the time they reached the doss house, their mirth had subsided, leaving a gentle ache in their ribcages and bellies. They were cold, too, thanks to the rain. The kitchen was full and noisy and Mrs Osborn, the matron of the house, beckoned to them. 'You here without Lil tonight? And who's this?'

'My sister.'

'I thought so. Got an extra penny? You can stay in my rooms. Be safer.'

Nancy watched one of the men pull one of the women onto his knee. The woman pushed him away with a comment about what he could afford. He gave the sort of laugh that has a snarl in it, looked at the girls in the doorway and beckoned.

'Yes, your room sounds good,' Nancy said, making the decision. They could steal food if it came to it. Pigeon kept so close to her that it was hard to walk. For a moment, she wondered whether she had been right to take Pigeon away from the Brethren, where she was at least well fed, and then she remembered the red weals on her sister's hands and Bevel's swift fists.

The matron took them to a small room above the kitchen. Sound and light from below crept up through the gaps in the bare floorboards. A bed was pushed against one wall and a small cot against another. 'My Dotty slept there until a month ago,' she said. 'You can have it.'

'Who's Dotty?' Pigeon asked, talking around the thumb she had stuck in her mouth.

'My daughter,' Mrs Osborn said, shortly. 'She died of the consumption.'

'Oh,' said Nancy and eyed the bed. Would the girl's ghost make it difficult to sleep perhaps?

'It's all right,' the woman said. 'She's gone. You gonna pay me now? If you please.'

Nancy pulled out the handkerchief and slipped the coins out.

'Well, sleep tight,' she said. 'Ignore the noise from downstairs. I close up at eleven.'

When the door closed behind her, Nancy and Pigeon climbed into the cot. Nancy knew she had to tell Pigeon what had happened to their father, and she dreaded it.

'Do you know where Dad is?' Nancy asked, wondering if the girl had any idea at all about what had happened, or perhaps thought their father was still at the Hall.

Pigeon hid her face and spoke through her hands. 'Mr Darner said he's dead.'

'Did he?'

'He said he left me and then he died. He said he left me behind, like you did.' She took her hands away and looked at Nancy. Her lip wobbled and a tear seeped out of the corner of her eye.

'But I didn't. I came back for you.'

'Yes.' She brightened a little and then her face fell again. 'But Dad hasn't.'

Nancy hugged Pigeon. 'Mr Darner was right that he died. But he would have come back to you if he hadn't.'

'Mr Darner said he'd be burning in hell.' Pigeon's voice rose and trembled.

Nancy's anger flared. 'Darner's wrong.'

Pigeon looked dubious, as if she didn't regard Nancy as a higher guide to religious questions than Mr Darner. 'That's good,' she said, still doubtful, and then buried her face in Nancy's chest and started to cry quietly. The anger Nancy felt at Darner's harsh words to Pigeon, so needlessly cruel, made her fidgety. She wrapped her arms round her sister, until Pigeon's small sobs gradually became gentle breathing. When she was sure that Pigeon was asleep, she climbed out of the cot to pace, her thoughts racing over the things Darner and his Brethren had done. If she had her way, they'd all hang at Newgate.

She found her eyelids drooping and climbed back into the cot. She lay down facing the door, wary of who might enter. Pigeon cuddled up to her drowsily. She quickly sank into a shallow sleep; she kept bobbing to the surface when someone laughed in the room below, or a step sounded outside the door.

Eventually the noise reduced a little, as people took themselves to bed or banged the front door as they left. An argument arose between Mrs Osborn and a man who said he had no money tonight but was certain he could pay her in the morning. He didn't argue for long, just maintained that it was unfair, Bill always got credit, why couldn't he, he'd known her as long? When the matron said bluntly that was 'cause Bill really did always pay the next day and he never had in the whole ten years she'd known him, he said no more and the outer door slammed.

Still the house was not quiet. Distant conversations and a brief bustle of raised voices. In the room below, someone was clattering pans and moving around, occasionally speaking a word to someone else who mumbled a response. Then the knocking and swishing of a broom, 'Lift your feet, Meg,' and a last opening and closing of the door. A final bang as the bolt was shot home.

A little while later, the door to the room opened; then Mrs Osborn came in, bolted her door, quickly prepared for bed and was snoring only a moment after bundling herself in the blankets. Nancy watched this through half-closed eyes and, reassured by the bolt on the door, finally allowed herself to drift into deep sleep.

Nancy was woken by a grunt as Mrs Osborn threw back the bedclothes. It was still dark outside, and the candle she lit showed the water staining on the walls and the rot in the woodwork. A distant church bell declared it to be six in the morning. The proprietor gave herself a very superficial wash with a flannel and basin of water that stood on a dilapidated chest of drawers, then pulled on her clothes with an air of fatigue.

She glanced over at the girls' cot and hurried out of the room, taking the candle with her. Nancy waited until she heard the sound of the big bolt being drawn back on the main door downstairs. She nudged Pigeon awake.

Footsteps and clatterings were starting up across the house, alongside shouted admonishments from those who had no need to rise so early and wanted to be left to sleep. The pump by the back door creaked and gushed, and a kettle clanked onto the range top. Nancy took Pigeon's hand and led her downstairs. She peered around the kitchen door, thinking to take her leave from Mrs Osborn, but she was busy at the range and the leering man from the previous night was the only one who saw them. He winked. Nancy pulled Pigeon's hand and they were out into the street.

'What are we doing now?' Pigeon asked as she dodged a running stream of horse piss.

'Going to meet Lil.'

'Why didn't we go there last night?'

'Because the Brethren know her and they could come and find us.'

'Oh yeah.'

Lil had found a room for the night around the corner from the charcoal ruins of the old lean-to and that's where they found her, sucking her teeth at the sight of the charred ruin. Her bruises were multicoloured by now and people were giving her a wide berth.

'Did the Brethren find you?' Nancy asked.

Lil nodded and wiped a sleeve across her bleary eyes. 'Yup. I don't think they quite believed me when I said I didn't know where you was, but they didn't push too hard. What's your plan, Nance?' she asked.

'Get Darner, now Pigeon's safe.' She looked over to where Pigeon was shyly watching some children playing hopscotch.

'That it? And how are you going to get Darner without hanging for it?'

'I'll think of something.'

'And what about after?'

Nancy stuck her chin out. 'We'll go find Mum. I know she went back to Yorkshire. And when we've found her, I'll get a job somewhere. I'll look after us all.'

Lil lowered her voice, 'You know she went back 'cause she was in a right state with the drink. You do know that, don't you?'

'She went back to get better. She might be better.'

'Humph. Maybe, but getting out from under the drink isn't an easy job.' Lil hefted her bundle on her shoulder. It suddenly struck Nancy that Lil's pack was unusually large and she seemed to be wearing fewer layers of clothes than usual. Since she wore her stock, she hadn't lost any when she'd escaped from the fire, but it seemed to be gone nonetheless, replaced with a bag on her shoulders.

'What's this all about?' Nancy indicated the bags.

'It's about time I went tramping. I've had enough of town.'

'But you can't leave us!'

'That's why I was asking your plans. You could come with me. It's a hard life, but you'll be away from the Brethren. We could head to Yorkshire. Together. I've never been there. I'd like to see where my family came from. That way if you can't stay with your mum, you can stick with me.'

'I can't go yet!'

Lil sighed and then, shuffling a little, reluctantly said, 'Look, Nancy, the Brethren weren't the only people to come looking for you.' She put her hands on her hips and shook her head. 'This is barmy, that's what it is.' She looked at Nancy for a little while.

Nancy was surprised to see her eyes were wet with tears.

Lil forced some words out. 'Look, I said I'd tell you.' She rubbed her eyes. 'There's someone else who's just as crazy about Darner as you are. She'll help. Hates him as much as you do. She's got resources too: money and a house.'

Help. She might be able to get real help, someone clever, with money, work out a real plan that might leave her free. The hope took Nancy's breath away for a moment.

'But you can come with me instead. Please.' Lil held out her gnarled hand. 'Please come tramping, Nancy. Forget all this vengeance stuff, it's poison. I've got such a bad feeling about this.'

Nancy thought of the way her father would look down and smile when Nancy had been furious about something, and would reach out and gently touch her frowning eyebrows. 'My angry, stubborn little girl. Leave it be.'

But she couldn't leave it be, could never leave it be.

'Who is she? Where can I find her?'

Lil sighed and dropped her hand. 'Hangcorner House. It's the house at Hangcorner Yard. You know.'

'The empty witch house?'

'It's not empty.' Lil sniffed. 'Not empty at all.'

Nancy pushed the gate into the dark alley that led to Hangcorner Yard. It creaked open. Pigeon's hand in hers was sticky and they looked back at Lil.

'Go on,' Lil urged looking up and down the empty street and Nancy went on through to the cobbled yard. Lil closed the gate, wincing at the high whine of the rusted hinges.

From the front, the building looked like a respectable town house, but somewhere in the middle it shifted between house and warehouse. Large wooden double gates hung crooked at the entrance to the yard, leading to doors in the strange building that were big enough for a cart to go through. Nancy could see an abandoned wooden crane, faded old signage and empty stables. Weeds grew thick between the cobbles of the yard and thorned vines of bramble sprouted from cracks in the walls. Huge thistle seed heads lurked in corners, disintegrating into grey messes. Ivy crawled up the walls, working its way into cracked open windows. Whatever the yard had once been, it had been unoccupied for years. A feeble, crooked tree had forced aside a loose cobble, exhausting itself in the effort, leaning at an angle at one side of the yard. A narrow path wound through the weeds to the foot of steps that climbed to a high side door. A crow watched them from the roofline.

A pewter light still lit the sky but every shadow was dark and growing. The windows were blank with the backs of curtains or a glimpsed ceiling; none were lit.

'She said to come after dark and don't be seen,' Lil said, repeating herself for the fifth time that day. The wait until evening had been excruciating; Lil was on edge and kept reassuring Nancy that she could change her mind, that tramping wasn't so bad. They might even like it, get lucky, find some good places to stop. Pigeon had picked up on Lil's anxiety and was fractious and fidgety.

Lil looked back at the empty side street; she was as sure as she could be that no one had seen them coming into the yard.

'Look, Nance,' Lil said, 'I'm not happy about this. I wish I hadn't told you.'

'I've got to, Lil. I can't leave it as if he did nothing.'

'I know, I know. You're a stubborn one. Just listen.'

Nancy had opened her mouth to argue and snapped it shut.

'I've changed my mind: I'm going to stick around for a few weeks longer. I won't set off until after Christmas at least, and I'll come and say goodbye before I go, if you've not come back to me by then.'

Nancy threw her arms around Lil's neck and hugged tightly. Lil patted her back awkwardly. 'I just can't leave you in there without a friend out here. God only knows what could happen.'

'Thanks, Lil,' Nancy murmured into her friend's shoulder.

'But listen.' Lil took her by the shoulders and looked into her face. 'I don't know this woman. I don't know if she's telling the truth about anything. Don't trust her just because I led you here, for God's sake, Nance. Keep an eye out and be wary.'

'I always am.'

'Good girl.' Lil began rummaging in her clothes and brought out a folded red shawl. 'Just to remember me by.' She passed it to Nancy.

Nancy opened it, the warm red just visible in the gloom. 'But you could get two bob for this.' It was soft against her fingers, finer than anything Lil usually had.

'Yeah, well, think of it as a comfort in the cold. And insurance if you really need the two bob.'

'I'd never sell it.'

'Never say never, my girl. There's nothing I won't sell if it comes to it.' She cackled and nudged Nancy. 'Nothing anyone wants to buy anyhow. Right, I wanna get off so are you going in or what?'

Nancy threw the new shawl around her shoulders, passed her old one to Lil who held it open and eyed it appraisingly, before throwing it around her shoulders.

Nancy took Pigeon by the hand. She looked up the stairs to the side door. It was the only door that looked as though it had been opened in a very long time, and seemed to lead directly into the main house rather than the warehouse. She approached the steps, old ragwort plants crumbling against her skirt as she walked. Lil drew back into the alley and lurked as a deeper shadow. A full moon was rising, dusting everything with silver. Nancy shivered and Pigeon clung to her hand.

When she reached the top step and looked at the door, her belly squirmed. What was she doing here? She glanced back at the dark lump that was Old Lil, the only real friend they had. The urge to give it up and walk away was so strong that she paused. Then she remembered the smile on Darner's face, the one that said he'd deliberately sent her father out onto the streets to die in order to punish her, and she stepped up to the door.

As she raised her fist to knock, she heard a rustle from behind it. Someone was there, listening, maybe even peering at them through a hole. Not that they'd see anything in the dark, but Nancy's courage grew at the idea of someone sly and mean watching her, and she knocked sharply with her pointed knuckles.

The sound disappeared into the wood and Nancy waited, unsure. She was about to knock again when the lock crunched and a bolt slid back slowly, with great effort.

The door opened just a crack; a candle was thrust out into the night and an eye appeared in the gap.

'Yes?'

Nancy put her arm around her sister. 'Lil sent me,' she said, throwing as much fearlessness into her voice as she could muster. 'Lil sent me.' She said it more boldly this time, set her jaw and tightened her grip on her sister; Pigeon gave a squeak of protest. 'She said that if I wanted vengeance, I'd find it here.'

The eye stayed in the gap and a silence stretched out.

'And do you want vengeance?' the eye asked, eventually.

'I'd give my soul for it,' Nancy said fiercely, the words scoring the back of her throat. 'I'd do it now, myself, if I didn't have to keep my sister safe.' Her voice trembled, but not with the cold.

The eye moved, as the person it belonged to nodded.

The door opened wide and Nancy and Pigeon stepped over the threshold.

Chapter Twelve
Watcher

Spider pressed her eye to the knothole. The grain of the wood was rough against her forehead and her own breath huffed back into her face, warm and damp.

In the room on the other side of the wall, a girl sat at a scrubbed table before a giant black range, an open fire glowing at its centre. Her clothes were rubbed to fragility by the coarse dirt in them and she clutched a scarlet shawl around her shoulders, a flash of bright warmth among so much dullness. A small child huddled against her. The younger girl was, perhaps, around six years old, had thin hair the colour of straw and a simple brown dress and white cap, grubby with recent dirt. Her older sister's arm was a barricade around her shoulders.

Spider had caught the girl. Quiet in the kitchen, so different from the creature of stretched tendons and pointed blade she had seen in the street. The smaller girl was a complication, but she might prove useful since the older one was so clearly devoted to her. Nancy and Pigeon.

The small girl's eyes, wide and pink with tiredness, took in the kitchen with its hooks dangling bunches of herbs and cooking implements that spoke of a once busy house. The large copper pots were brown; only the smallest gleamed bright in the dim light which came from the oil lamps.

Nancy looked around with keen eyes, but Spider could tell that her attention was fixed on the figure by the range. Patience was stirring a pot, and behind the wall the smell of eggs was just noticeable above the scent of dust. Patience had said nothing since Spider had started watching. She stood at the range with her back to the girls, and gave the mixture another brisk stir. Then she emptied the mess into two bowls, turned and placed them on the table, a shining spoon in each.

Nancy held the spoon to the light, turned it, catching a gleam of dusty light in its bowl before scooping a small amount of egg and sniffing it. She ate a morsel carefully before swallowing and then eating the rest hungrily.

When they had finished, Patience placed a piece of buttered bread in each bowl and gestured that they should wipe up any remaining egg and eat it. The girls did as they were told. Spider's eyes were on them, as hungry for the small details of their faces and expressions as they were for each crumb of bread and each smear of butter.

'That'll do,' Patience said. 'Mistress said you were to be fed and cleaned and now one's done, we'll see to the other. I'll get the bath… and some fresh clothes.' She hefted an enormous kettle onto the heat from where it had been warming gently on the side and then she walked out, closing the door behind her.

The girls sat and looked at each other. Spider waited, hoping they would talk. She wanted to hear the bright tones of their voices ringing out into the kitchen that had been near-silent for years. There would be something in the echoes, as well as interest in the words.

'It's warm at least, Nancy,' the smaller girl said this as though it were surprising, as if she hadn't been warm for some time.

Nancy made a sound in agreement, but she sounded troubled.

Spider frowned, pressed her eye closer, hands either side of the spyhole.

'What's the matter? This is nice. Like a fairy tale. Are we going to be rich ladies?' The girl swung her legs.

'Lil said I'd find vengeance here, that this lady is as crazy to demolish Darner as I am. Well, we'll see, won't we? But nothing comes for free, Pigeon. We might have to get out quick if it goes wrong. I might have to get you out. To Lil. Maybe I shouldn't have brought you.' Nancy stroked the girl's head with short nervous movements.

Spider smiled. Sensible girl, to fear. Then Spider found she was also afraid, deep inside, somewhere underneath the awakened desire for vengeance. Here was a girl with a miasma of rage hanging around her, a girl who might be the one to bring a spark into a mine.

Nancy continued, pulling her hands back from her sister, tucking them both between her knees. 'But if it's safe, I can leave you here while I do what I need to do. Safer here than on the street with Lil. Maybe. Depends on who these people are. I can't leave him be. We can't go until after.' After what she didn't specify, but Spider could guess.

She was so single-minded. She was crying out for what she needed, ravenous. Strange in one so young. She said 'him' with a capital. Him.

'You're not going to leave me!' The smaller girl's voice cracked.

Nancy took her sister's hands and looked in her face. 'I promise I'll always come back for you. Didn't I come back for you?' A tear ran down the small girl's face. She nodded and Nancy took her sleeve and scrubbed at the tears. 'I promise.'

Promises, promises, Spider thought to herself and hugged the words in her mind. Promises and possibility and possession. Untouchable nothing shapes in the dark.

Pigeon nodded and wiped at her own face with her grubby sleeve, smearing the tears through the dirt.

In the distance there was an echo of a crash. Then a dragging clattering sound which got louder, closer. Nancy leapt to her feet, pulling her sister behind her. She darted to the range and grabbed a toasting fork. She stood, brandishing it towards the door. The noise got louder and then the door banged back.

Patience dragged a tin bath in and set it in front of the range. She looked up at the girls, who had frozen. She ignored their pale faces and the fork, and took a bundle of clothing out of the bath. She placed it on the table with a bar of soap and a scrubbing brush on top.

Spider repressed amusement at the sight of the scrawny girl waving a toasting fork at the oblivious housekeeper.

'Right, girls. This is not going to be much fun I'm afraid, but you've got to be clean if you're going to stay here.'

The girls exchanged a look.

'Why are you doing this?' Nancy asked, the question bursting out. The toasting fork quivered in her hand, still held up as if it were a sword.

This was it. This was what Spider wanted. This girl ripe with anger and willing to fight with anything. With her teeth and nails. With a toasting fork. If only she could be controlled, directed. She might be of use. Though she might also be a danger.

'Because the mistress said so.' The tin bath rang along the stone floor as Patience moved it close to the range. 'I reckon we can fit both of you in at once, get this over with quick. Then we can all get a good night's sleep.'

Spider stepped away from the wall for a moment, repulsed by the idea of watching them bathe. The filth and the skin. The water lapping at them.

'What's your real name, child?' Patience asked of Pigeon. 'I refuse to call you something as downright daft as Pigeon.'

Pigeon answered, her voice disappearing into the high ceiling, 'Polly.'

Patience tutted. 'Well, get all those nasty clothes off. We'll have to burn them; I can't see anything worth saving here, except perhaps your shawl.'

Nancy clutched the bright fabric tightly at the suggestion of burning it. 'But they're ours!' Nancy said. 'What about when we leave?'

Behind the wall, Spider stopped breathing. The girl thought she would leave. She couldn't leave, couldn't be allowed to leave. She was necessary and if she were loose, who knew what she might do? But that kind of vehemence was exactly what was needed and so a fine balance was required. She must be kept afire, but not allowed to burn free.

'What if you leave here? Well, these are yours now.' Patience laid a hand on the pile of clothes. 'And if you ever have to leave, you can take them. We wouldn't send you out naked. Does that reassure you?'

Nancy didn't say anything, but started to remove her clothes. She slid her hatpin from its seam and put it carefully to one side with her red shawl. The bodice ripped away where it had been mended with a sound that hurt Spider's ear. A sleeve flapped open at the armpit.

Patience hefted the kettle and poured out a stream of gently steaming water. 'Hop in.' She refilled the kettle from a bucket on the side and put it back on the heat. The girls stepped into the bath, grubby knees up by their noses, legs mixed together. 'Get scrubbing,' Patience instructed and she gave them each a lump of soap and threw a brush into the water. 'I'll do your hair while you scrub the rest.'

Nancy started to soap her arms. Pigeon stared at her sister, wide-eyed, and then jumped as water flowed over her head and down her face. She yelped. Patience put down the jug, having used it to douse the girl, and began to work the soap into a lather.

Spider twitched with impatience. How long would it take to remove the filth? She tried to distract herself with amusement at Patience's acquisition of a caring tone. An unanticipated motherliness, almost. She'd have to be careful of that. It could be dangerous. Divided loyalty, gentleness. Weakness.

'Sit still.' Patience began soaping the girl's head. Moments later, Pigeon was crying because the soap had got in her eyes. 'Shush you, the quicker this is done, the better.' Patience rubbed the lather through the girl's hair and worked her fingers into the scalp. The girls' skin began to shine through the dirt and their hair squeaked.

'Right, time for fresh water and then we'll have a scrub at the last bits,' Patience said. 'Though you're not so bad.' She nodded at Pigeon. 'I can see you've been clean more recently than your sister.'

Pigeon looked at her hands and Nancy answered for her. 'Some people had her. A church. Took her for a while.'

'Oh, is that so?'

'Claimed they had a right, that my dad would have wanted it,' Nancy said in a rush. 'But now he's gone, I'm in charge. It's my job to keep her safe.'

The girls stood, shivering by the range, as Patience dragged the tub to a drain in the middle of the floor and tipped it up. The water was the same grey-brown as the Thames.

Once the second bath of water had been dumped, less foul than the first, Nancy stood wrapped in a cloth, looking at the little hairs on her arm standing upright in the chilly air.

'Here you go.' Patience passed her some clothes. 'Put the night-gown on. The rest are for the morning. I'll help your sister.'

Good. Soon, perhaps, Spider could meet the child properly, look into her eyes and see if what she needed was there. She thought it would be; she thought the girl had the power to change things. Fear slipped in at the back of her mind and she tried to dismiss it. A girl, nothing but a girl with a hatred. A vital hatred. Why had she appeared just here at just this moment after all these years? Well, that was the thing, wasn't it? The exciting thing. A change. She had thought nothing would ever change again.

Nancy stared at the clothes in front of her.

She fingered the black woollen dress and fine linen petticoat; there was broderie anglaise around its bottom edge and she held it up. 'This is swell gear.'

'Oh, it's not,' Patience scoffed. 'If you think that's fine my girl, you haven't seen much finery. But you're right that it's good quality, plain and strong.' Nancy raised an eyebrow and Patience continued. 'It's what we had in your size.'

At one point, when Patience was busy with her back turned, Nancy took the hat pin and slid it into a seam.

Soon the sisters stood in the kitchen staring at each other; they both wore long nightgowns trimmed with touches of ribbon around the neck, their hair in plaits.

'You look like a lady, Nancy.' Pigeon smiled.

Nancy fidgeted at the ribbon. 'No, I don't,' she said gruffly.

Spider tightened, knuckles bone white, arms like stone. Her eyes were fixed on Nancy, dark hair now pulled back from her face. The clean white gown sat on her strangely, her watchful, pointed face looking out like a wary animal. Her eyes swept the room, taking in everything for a second time as if now she was clean, she could see better. And then, to Spider's horror, the girl's eyes met hers. She stared, boldly, right back into the watcher's own gaze.

Spider stepped back, stumbled. Her breath balled in her throat like an impassable wedge of putty. In the dark, the air was drawn out of her and, her fingers skittering along the walls of the tight passage, she hurried, scrambling back to her room, a sense of panic rising in her. The girl, the girl. Her eyes had carried death and yet this was what Spider wanted, this fire and fear. She recognised something in the girl. Death. Whose death?

Spider opened the door to her own rooms and hurried into her sanctuary. She moved among the clutter, pushing aside the leaves of her plants, leaning on the edge of the table, careful to avoid upsetting her instruments, touching a book for the comfort of its smooth leather cover. She sank into the chair and her eyes found the window, and there it was. Before the dim and dusty pane of glass hung a bird's skull, delicate lines and curves, the light of her lamp seeping through the frail tissue bone. It turned gently, spinning in a slow and deadly circle and she could not breathe, afraid that now it was here, now the time had come, would she have the strength to bring it to its end? She watched the skull spin and her head twisted with it, feeling herself tip back, until blackness came in and all she could see were the empty orbits of the skull's eyes and the curve of its beak.

Chapter Thirteen
Carrion

Her mother's heels span in the air above her, around and around, which wasn't right because at some point the rope would turn her back the other way but she just turned and turned.

Sara couldn't remember why she had come into the warehouse or why her mother was still spinning there after all these years. Corbeau, sitting on the stair rail, expressed his opinion in a solemn caw and flew across the space, landing on the asylum carriage which was parked where the carts always waited for their loads. Its horses were carved out of wood, still and lifeless.

She looked back up at her mother and thought she would cut her down with the knife she was holding. Her feet were soft on the cold iron of the stairs and she went up, but somehow when she got to the next level her mother was still as far above her as before. So, she went up the next set of steps and it happened again. She had just put her foot on the step for the third time when Corbeau gave a cry of anger and flapped across the space. Above her, beside the crane her mother dangled from, stood Darner. He held his own knife and he began sawing at the rope.

'But she'll fall!' Sara cried, the words drifting away from her lips as if made of smoke. He continued to cut the rope. Corbeau flapped at Darner's head with his wings and his claws outstretched but Darner continued as if he weren't there. Sara began to run up the steps, running, running, the iron steps cold beneath her bare feet, always finding herself at the bottom of the stair with each step.

The last strand of the rope frayed, stretched and snapped. Her mother fell.

She woke.

The old dream again. The addition of Darner and the asylum carriage were new. Sara thought, next time, she ought to try to use the dream-knife on him, rather than on the rope, if only dream Sara would remember. The bruises on her arms from her admittance had faded to yellow smudges and she allowed herself to fade as they did, into the background, watching and listening. Now they were gone and she was used to the rhythm of the asylum. She saw the way the life of the asylum swirled around Darner, further eddying around some of the attendants who seemed favoured in some way: Sullivan, a thin man with invasive eyes called Carey, and a woman who was quick to slap and shout, among others. The patients avoided, quieted, hid. The unfavoured members of staff turned their eyes aside, winced, walked away.

Lying in her bed, she could see up to the beginnings of the oracle mobile she was making. The construction had developed from those childhood treasures hung beneath the stairs above her bed and, along with her bone sticks, helped her to see the currents of the world. She could look through it and see. The dances and patterns the chosen treasures made conveyed so much. Here, she was rather restricted in her creation.

A stick from the garden had started it, then a fragment of an old green glass bottle found in a flowerbed; a feather; a stem of last year's snap-dragon plant, its seed pods looking like a string of miniature distorted skulls; a cup handle with an alluring curve – all hung from threads from the rag rugs. That was all for now. The doctor had seen it and, once he had checked that edge of the old glass was long since worn away and snap-dragon was not poisonous, he had allowed her to keep it for as long as she was in a single room. She had kept its purpose a secret; it was just a pretty mobile to him, and therefore harmless. Not the strangest thing his patients wanted.

As with all of Sara's constructions, it was carefully balanced so that any breeze from the window would catch the feather, making it turn in slow, graceful movements that would create eddies in her mind, spiralling images and thoughts. Now that she was without her bone oracle sticks, she struggled to detach the strands of her thoughts and dreams from the currents of the world and distinguish what was merely her own mood from the reality of events. A dark fog entangled it all.

She noticed a large dead spider lying under the chair that stood in the corner of the room, its legs curled in a complicated knot of limbs. She threw back her covers and drew the spider out to examine it. A house spider, a big one. It would have made Jenny scream back at Hangcorner House. Sara pulled a piece of thread from her small stash of rags under the mattress, drew her chair over and carefully hung the dead spider from a corner of her mobile, its weight so slight it didn't change the balance. Death, contraction, the idea of webs. It span.

A key was put in the lock of her door and it was opened before she could get down from the chair. Darner stalked into the room, his face gaunt. With one hand he gripped her arm and pulled her down off the chair, she landed badly, stumbled and cried out as she fell against the wall. Ignoring her, he ripped the mobile down. The bright green glass swung and smashed against the wall. Shards sprayed across the floorboards.

'This,' he shouted, waving a fistful of string and feathers in her face, 'is witchcraft and idolatry.' He pushed her away from him and she fell sideways into the corner, scrabbling against the wall, her feet cut by the glass shards, traces of blood smearing over the floor. He strode forwards, the glass crunching under his shoes and, again, shook the remains of the mobile in her face. 'Devilry,' he hissed.

'I don't know what you're talking about,' she said, trying to keep her voice calm, shamed by the way it fractured at the edges. Her feet hurt, small slices of pain from the glass fragments.

'Don't play innocent, girl.'

Sara found her attention caught by his hand. Blood was oozing up between his fingers. A drop ran, slow and thick, down a dangling thread, and crept into the tiny hairs on the dead spider's legs. For a moment she was confused. Why was her blood on his hand? He hadn't touched her feet.

'You're hurt.' She pointed.

He looked down at his hand, just as a drop of blood fell to the floor to mingle with her blood and the glass. He opened his hand in shock and dropped the remains of the mobile. The cup handle, bloody and jagged where it had broken from the cup, tinkled to the floor.

He inhaled deeply, nostrils flaring. He straightened. His hands reached for her, the right smeared and dripping with his own blood, grasped handfuls of her dress and lifted her so that he could stare into her face.

'What's going on here, Mr Darner?'

Darner's head snapped around.

Dr Whitehead stood in the doorway, looking from one to the other of them in bewilderment, settling on Darner, looking for an answer.

'I was informed of this blasphemous article and I came to destroy it.' Darner released Sara and pointed to the mess on the floor. 'And it seems Miss Atherton had constructed her infernal device in such a way that it would injure any who might remove it.'

Sara burst into laughter at the ridiculousness of this assertion but trailed into silence when she realised the doctor was looking at her sternly, as if he were taking the suggestion seriously. 'But you said I could have it,' she said, hating the petulance she could hear in her voice. She wiped at the blood on her dress from Darner's hands, smearing it.

'I said you could have the mobile if every part of it was carefully checked by a nurse.'

'She was praying to it!' Darner burst out. 'You allowed that blasphemy.'

'She said that watching the turning of the mobile allowed her to find the right frame of mind for prayer, which certainly seemed harmless,' the doctor said opening his palms apologetically. 'I'm most concerned about the fact unsafe items were added to it against my strict instructions.' He waved a hand to indicate the spattered and smeared blood, as if demonstrating the fact was self-evident. 'Your suggestion that this was a deliberate attempt to injure any staff who might interfere with the thing is concerning.'

Darner stared down at Sara, eyes wide with repressed rage. 'Why else would it be made of so many sharp things if not to injure anyone interfering with her blasphemous magic?'

Dr Whitehead appeared to wait for an answer and so Sara protested, 'I didn't realise the cup handle was sharp, and the glass wasn't sharp until it was broken. You saw to that yourself, Doctor. I couldn't predict someone would remove it by snatching it down.'

'Rubbish!' Darner cupped his right hand. The cut was still oozing blood. 'This is what comes from your slackness over discipline, Whitehead. All your blather about making the patients feel at home. Kindness.' He spat out the last word as if it tasted bitter.

Doctor Whitehead seemed unable to meet his chaplain's eyes and sighed. 'Well, we will speak further about it this evening. Perhaps we can increase chapel services.'

'Now we've got past your ridiculous assertion that attendance should be voluntary—'

'Other asylums do not insist—'

'Other asylums are sending their patients to hell without a backwards glance.'

'Yes, well, we agreed that services should be mandatory. And we'll talk later. Leave Miss Atherton to clear up.' He looked at Sara. 'I'll send an attendant to see to your feet and then you can tidy this mess. We prefer our patients to maintain their own space where possible.' His eyes dropped to Darner's hand. 'You ought to go and see my wife. She'll bind the injury for you.'

The glass crunched angrily underfoot as Darner marched from the room spitting angrily, 'We'll see about this, Whitehead.'

Sara woke as her arm was jerked behind her and her face pushed into the pillow. She tried to scream but all that emerged was a muffled whine. A hand in her hair pulled her head up and as she gasped for air, a cloth was shoved into her mouth. It tasted of dirt and lamp oil. Another cloth was tied over it, knotted roughly behind her head, tugging at her hair.

'I'll stretch her arm out.' The voice was Sullivan's. Her arm was wrenched to one side. She struggled but couldn't get any leverage. Air coming panicked and thin through her nose, not enough of it, she could do little more than wriggle. Rough canvas scratched up her arm and she realised what was happening. They were putting her into the restraint jacket they had used to bring her to the asylum in the first place. She redoubled her efforts to struggle but she felt a knee in her back, a man's weight on it.

'Penance,' Darner's voice hissed in her ear.

Sullivan dragged her to her feet. 'She don't like me.' He grinned as he pushed the other sleeve onto her left arm. 'Pity.' His fingers on the skin of her arm felt like they should leave dirty smudges.

He strapped her arms around her and fury and humiliation flowed through her, threatening to overwhelm her breathing. She pulled away from the hand holding her and was jerked backwards. The movement made her head spin and she tried to plant her feet firmly.

'There,' Sullivan said as he closed the last buckle. 'Wrapped up neat as a parcel.' He chucked her under the chin with a forefinger that smelt of tobacco and something worse and she glared at him. Through her confusion and dizziness, she could hardly focus her eyes.

He laughed and tugged the back of the jacket so that she nearly lost her balance.

'Excellent work, Sullivan. Whitehead couldn't run this place without you. Let's go,' said Darner, as he led them out into the passage. They hurried along the dimly lit corridors. Occasionally they would hear a patient calling and once they passed the murmur of voices from the open door of an office. Sara tried to shout but the sound in her throat squeezed back around the cloth in her mouth and made her gag. Sullivan shoved her between the shoulder blades; someone out of sight closed the door and she staggered on.

Once an assistant turned into the corridor ahead of them and walked towards them. Sara felt relief; surely he would see this and ask what was going on but, as they got closer, her hope died. He smirked. He wasn't going to ask what was happening, why they were taking a female patient away in the middle of the night. As they passed him, he turned and watched until they were out of sight.

Darner pushed open the doors to the chapel and they walked up the dark aisle. The tiles were cold under Sara's bare feet and, as they approached the altar steps, Sullivan pressed down on her shoulders and said, 'Kneel.' She resisted for a moment but then collapsed, hitting the tiles with a thud, pain shooting up through her knees.

The doors opened behind them and when Sara tried to twist to look behind her, she was pushed back into place by Sullivan. Footsteps shuffled up the aisle and then, with a thud-thud, two patients landed on their knees on either side of her. The man to her left was gagged like Sara and tears streamed down his face. His gaze met hers and his eyes seemed to plead with her before he bent double, sobbing and half-choking into his gag. The woman was not wearing a gag; she stared straight ahead, her face rigid.

Sara could feel that they each had an attendant behind them. Darner looked down the aisle behind them as more footsteps approached. A man passed the three kneeling figures and stood in front of Darner with his head bowed. He was wearing an attendant's uniform. Darner gave him a kneeler from one of the pews and the man carefully placed it on the floor so that it aligned with the steps in front of him; then he knelt.

Darner stood on the top step, looming above them. Sullivan reached around and forced her chin up so that she was looking at him.

'You are going to pray, all of you. All night. Carey,' he addressed the kneeling attendant, 'you will pray until midnight.' The man nodded, his head bowed.

'You are here because of your sins. Because you need to do penance for the good of your souls. Carey, you are here because of your incontinent behaviour with the female patients.' Carey nodded and raised his folded hands as if he was already praying. 'Simons.' The woman patient twitched. 'Because you allowed Carey's behaviour. Keeley, because you took the Lord's name in vain multiple times in my hearing. Atherton, because you must learn I will not tolerate witchcraft here and I will not allow you to pollute this place of healing. You all have sins for which you must atone and I urge you to pray, aloud, those of you who can. We will start with the Lord's Prayer.'

His face was dimly lit by their lantern and she could feel the warmth of Sullivan standing right behind her. When she shifted, he put out a hand and gripped her by the back of the collar until she was still.

Darner began to pray aloud.

'Our Father, who art in heaven...' The rich tones of his voice rolled around the empty chapel. Dark blue squares of night sky showed through the plain windows, no stained glass here. Her nightgown had risen up when she was forced to the ground, so that her knees were bare against the tiles. They were bitterly cold, even in June.

'...Give us this day our daily bread...'

The tiles were hard against her bruised knees, already uncomfortable by the time he finished the first prayer. After Carey and Simons said 'Amen' and even Keeley made a wailing noise in approximation of the word through his gag, Darner paused. Sullivan gripped her hair roughly and said, 'Amen. Say it with the others.' The only sound she could make was a groaning sound in her throat but it seemed to satisfy them.

Half an hour later, the pain was unbearable. Her knees felt as though they were on cold fire and she couldn't stop herself shifting in an attempt to relieve them. Every time she did Sullivan would grab her and force her back into the same position. Her thighs and back were burning with the effort of holding herself up. Simons was still as a statue and Sara wondered how that was possible. To her left, Keeley kept collapsing back onto his legs and whoever was standing behind him would just haul him upright time after time. After a little while she saw that they had placed their knee behind Keeley's back to keep him up – less for the man's comfort, she thought, than to prevent the repeated effort of hauling him upright.

'Lord Jesus Christ, our only solace…' Darner began another prayer. Sara felt her breath coming hard through the gag and she struggled to breathe slowly and get enough air.

At the end of that prayer, she was too engrossed in her pain to notice the approaching 'Amen', and when she failed to make the faint noise they demanded as her attempt at the word, Sullivan boxed her on the side of the head. She fell sideways against Keeley. For a moment she was glad, because her knees were off the unforgiving tiles, but the man began to wail as loudly as possible behind his gag. She straightened her legs for a fraction of a second of blessed relief before Sullivan pulled her up onto her knees once again. Keeley was boxed hard about the head and set upright again.

'Almighty God,' Darner started another prayer and Sara began to sob as the pain seared again in her knees. After a while Carey rose at the end of a prayer and stepped towards Darner who placed a hand on his head in blessing. As he left, with his back to Darner, he leered at Simons but, from what Sara could see, her eyes were glazed and hard as she resolutely looked directly ahead at the altar.

By the time the dawn had silvered the sky, brightened and dressed the church in the faint yellow of a June early morning, Sara was hallucinating dark enemies in the pew corners and Darner's eyes, reddened from a sleepless night, seemed almost to glow with his glee at their pain.

Sullivan had to half-carry Sara back to her room, as her legs wouldn't reliably support her. He dumped her on her bed, still shivering from the cold of the tiles against her skin for so long.

'Get the nurse,' Darner said.

Sullivan left, looking over his shoulder at her. Sara looked at Darner, her vision blurry with exhaustion. He said, 'You might be considering telling the doctor about your penance tonight. He has a very weak approach to the religious wellbeing of his patients, which is why he leaves the discipline of both patients and staff to me. He prefers not to be bothered by it and to pretend it is unnecessary under his so-called moral regime. You will find him unwilling to listen.'

Sullivan walked in followed by a young nurse with a rigid face.

'Nurse, you are a witness to be relied upon,' Darner said. 'Did this patient leave her room at any point in the night?'

The nurse looked at Sara, contempt flickering across her face. 'No, Mr Darner, she did not.' She was eager to please, consciously smart and attentive.

'How can you be sure?'

'I looked in on her twice, as requested by the doctor, on my midnight round and at three in the morning. She was praying on her knees on both occasions. I tried to persuade her to go to bed but when she refused, I let her continue; I didn't see any harm in her praying.' She pressed her lips together, her eyes fixed on Darner

Sara shook her head and tried to blink away the tears that were filling her eyes. She tried to speak against the gag but all that emerged was a desperate moan.

The nurse glanced at her and was gone.

Chapter Fourteen
Guide

Patience set off into the house, holding a candle high, leading Nancy and Pigeon into the dark. Each of the girls carried a bundle of the clothing they were to wear tomorrow when, it was promised, Nancy would meet the mistress.

'Why not tonight?' Nancy asked. 'It ain't late.' She pulled her shawl tight around her shoulders.

'Firstly, the mistress said the morning and this is her house, so morning it shall be. Secondly, she has delicate health and sometimes she just cannot do things and therefore must delay.'

So far, they had only seen the servants' quarters, following a route of narrow stairs and twisted corridors to the kitchen, past unused pantries and laundry rooms; most were empty and dusty but one was badly clogged up with vines and an earthy fungal odour. Now they went into 'the mistress's side of the house', as Patience called it.

The large hall was tiled in black and white, and shone in the flickering candlelight. A huge tiger's head hung on the wall facing the front door. Nancy was transfixed by the animal's long yellow teeth and the golden gleam of the fur. Corners and crevices were occupied by plants, dull green in the dark, some in pots, others sprouting between the floorboards. Pale mushrooms gleamed in the corners of skirting boards and underneath furniture. As they passed various doors, Patience named them: dining room, library, parlour. She gradually stopped pointing them out as the girls followed her away from the ground floor and the front of the house.

The room they were to sleep in was distant from the more used parts of the house; they had to walk up three staircases and down another to reach it. Occasionally they passed a window that showed a scattering of rooftops and chimney silhouettes; once, they walked past a window looking down onto the street and the gleam of gaslight streamed across the ceiling before they walked back into the dark. At another window a crow on the ledge looked in at Nancy and she looked back out at it before they turned and mounted another staircase. Streaks of white down the newel post suggested the crow did not always stay outside.

The inside of the house was confusing; almost every staircase turned on itself and many of the doorways had a step or two, so that no two rooms were at the same level and they were constantly changing direction. Dark panelled walls alternated with richly coloured but peeling paint or faded wallpaper torn away in patches to reveal greying plaster. There were plants everywhere, twisting around bannisters and growing in pots on once-fine tables, veneers peeling, black fingers of rot stretching out, its scent reaching everywhere. The walls were hung with odd pictures and one entire staircase was lined in masks, blank eyes that shifted as the candlelight passed. One cabinet held exotic curved knives, another a slumped puppet. Mirrors waited in odd corners to catch the movement of a passing skirt and transform it into the flicker of a ghost from the corner of an eye.

As they passed a cabinet full of pinned moths, their still wings sent a wistful fluttering into Nancy's imagination and she exclaimed in dismay. 'My mistress's family used to collect things,' Patience said.

When they reached their room, it was high-ceilinged and almost bare, with two beds, two chairs and a small table. Three botanical pictures hung on one wall, the paper peppered by the dark marks of dead insects inside the frame. The floor had once had a carpet in the middle and the boards had been painted around it, so that a large unvarnished square of grey wood was surrounded by faded green paint. The air smelled of dust and old plaster. A large window looked out onto the city and yet, for the moment, Nancy couldn't orientate herself. In its emptiness, it felt strange after the dark clutter of the rest of the house.

'It's clean,' Nancy said. Despite the smell of dust, Nancy couldn't see any. The place had been swept, but not polished. A pitcher and ewer stood on the table next to a brass candlestick and a small matchbox. A chamber pot squatted under one of the beds.

'Yes.' Patience patted a pillow. 'I gave it a brush out just the other day. By chance.' She rubbed at one of the brass knobs on the nearest bedstead.

For some reason the cleanness of the room made Nancy uneasy. It made her feel as though their presence had been expected, anticipated. It made her feel afraid.

Pigeon sat on one of the beds, wide-eyed. 'Nice to be just you and me, not like the dormitory or the doss house.' She pulled a face.

Nancy nodded and stroked the linen pillowcase. It was cold to the touch.

'It gets chilly of course,' said Patience. 'I told the mistress that a smaller room with a smaller window might be cosier, but she...' her voice trailed away.

Nancy turned to her. 'She what?'

'Well, she said this room was good for dreams. She has some funny ideas, the mistress.'

A fireplace with a cold-looking iron grate stood in the panelled wall; there was no coal bucket or poker. 'Can we light the fire?'

'We haven't had the chimney swept in a while,' Patience said, doubtfully. 'I think it's better not to. I'll get you a couple of extra blankets.' She bustled out of the room.

Nancy walked over to the botanical pictures. They were not paintings as she'd first thought, but pressed flowers, carefully labelled. A faded blue hooded flower was labelled 'Monkshood' and the next one she recognised: the pink trumpets of foxglove. The last looked a lot like cow parsley and was labelled 'Hemlock'.

Patience walked in carrying two thick wool blankets. Following Nancy's gaze, she said, 'The mistress's favourite flowers, you'll find, not that it's the season now, of course.'

Nancy went to the window and opened and closed the shutter. It creaked loudly and she slipped the small brass hook into its loop to fasten it. The bare wooden floor and the narrow beds didn't make for the most welcoming of rooms, but it certainly wasn't the worst place she'd ever slept. She only had to share with Pigeon, for a start. There would be no press of warm bodies with disembodied hands in it. No smell of sweat, stale piss and booze.

'Now, I wonder if we have a small rug somewhere,' Patience mused. 'Just so your toes aren't quite so cold when you get up in the morning. I'll have a look tomorrow.'

'Thank you, Patience,' Pigeon said primly, apparently remembering her lessons in manners from somewhere.

Nancy walked up to the door. There were three dark holes in it above her eye height. She stood on tiptoe but couldn't see if it was possible to look through any of the holes. One of them seemed to go all the way through. It gave her a dark, creeping feeling.

'There used to be a coat hook there, I think,' Patience said. She went to the door.

'Wait here in the morning. I'll come for you and we can have breakfast and then you'll see the mistress.'

Pigeon fell into sleep quickly and smoothly. Nancy wondered if she really understood they'd lost their father forever and that they'd left the Brethren for good. As she herself tried to sleep, she skimmed shallowly and surfaced often. The room was in near total darkness; a thin line of deepest blue outlined the shutters but she couldn't even tell the white sheet from the dark red blanket. Once, as she lay floating on the surface of sleep, she heard a sound outside the door. The soft hushing of skirts. And then it was gone.

There had been more food at breakfast than Nancy had ever eaten at a single meal before. She felt full and heavy as she stood by the warmth of the fireplace. The flames had burnt low and threw out a dim glow. A candelabra stood on the end of the table, its light sucked up by the dark wood, the rich carpets, the thick velvet of the curtains shut tight against the morning. The room smelled of coal and polish and underneath there was a hint of something warm and dirty.

Nancy stood on the hearth rug, unsure if she were alone. The faint warmth on the back of her legs prickled.

From the gloom at the back of the room something rustled, a shadow shifted.

'Hello?' Nancy said, 'Excuse me, ma'am, are you there? Patience told me to come.'

The rustling stopped and then after a few moments came a cawing sound. A strange thing to hear in a dining room. Then a clicking and rustling moved towards her. She stepped backwards and her foot nudged the poker which clattered into the hearth.

A harsh caw came out of the darkness. A large crow hopped angrily along the table towards her, emerging into the light with the candle flames gleaming in his black eyes and his beak pointing at her.

'Sorry,' she said instinctively to the crow who glared at her and then, as if relieving his feelings, pecked at the table. A chip of wood flew out, leaving a small, bright scar in the polished surface. A long-fingered hand reached out towards her and she turned with a gasp. The leaves of a fern on a table trembled. It was just a fern. A fern and a crow.

A low laugh came from the dark at the other end of the room.

'You've offended Corbeau,' a voice said.

'Corbeau?'

'The crow.'

'Oh.'

'He's getting elderly and rather irritable. Don't mind him, he's an old friend.'

Nancy felt that she was being mocked and she stared at the place the voice was coming from. She picked up the candelabra and walked up the room.

An indrawn breath came from the darkness ahead of her and then a flapping. A shape came out of the dark: wings and a smell of dry earth and death and the candelabra was snuffed out. Nancy took a step back. Slowly her senses pieced together what had happened. The crow had flown at her and the air from its wings had blown out the candles.

'You see,' said the voice, 'you might think Corbeau doesn't like you. But I think he does. He'd have gone straight for your eyes if he didn't.'

Behind her, Nancy could hear the crow moving and scratching. She heard the scrape of a match and a flame burst into existence at the far end of the room. It moved to a chamber stick and lit the candle, then the match was shaken out. The person who had held it leant forwards into the small light.

'Come here.'

Nancy took a step towards the voice. A pale face surrounded by swept-back hair. The eyes pinned her down. The woman rose and walked into the light. At first Nancy thought she was dressed in black but, as she came past the candle, she saw the dress was deep-green velvet, a little out of fashion. She didn't look like a person who couldn't afford a new gown — after all the velvet was rich and there was fine black lace at the sleeves. No, it was rather more as if she had been caught in place years ago, or had acquired clothes she liked and had never seen the need to change.

'You saw me? In the kitchen?'

'I saw what?' asked Nancy, utterly confused.

'Never mind.' The woman turned away. On the table, beside an empty pewter plate, lay a pile of sticks made of ivory perhaps, or bone. 'Pick one.' The woman waved a hand at the pile and Nancy approached it cautiously. As she reached out and touched them, they fell across one another with a clattering sigh and one of them slid across the table surface. Nancy stopped its movement by placing her finger on it firmly. It clicked.

She picked up the stick and passed it to the woman, who was watching her with an intensity that Nancy found uncomfortable.

The woman took the stick and looked down at it. She swayed slightly and reached out a hand to grip the back of one of the dining chairs. Her knuckles were ivory-yellow through her skin, like the stick she held.

'Of course,' she said, 'of course it would be this one.'

'What are they made of?' Nancy picked up another of the sticks and held it up to the flame, turning it in the light. She squinted at the carving and realised it was actually a word. *Despair*.

'None of your business.' The woman snatched it from her, gathered the sticks and carefully examined the one Nancy had touched. Finally, she put them in a pocket in her dress and then she put her hand in the pocket; Nancy could just hear the rustle and click as she moved the sticks between her fingers.

'I came for vengeance,' Nancy said bluntly, frustrated with waiting, wanting to have answers. 'Lil said I could get vengeance here. Was she right?' She looked at the woman who took a step back, face even paler.

'Yes, yes. I know why you came. I am Spider. I always knew. I knew you were coming.'

'You spoke to Lil.'

'Yes, but I knew. Even before I saw you, I think I knew.' She waved her left hand through the air. 'The way I always know things. The oracle, the birds, the currents in the air.'

Nancy clenched her hands. This sounded like cheap fortune teller's nonsense and she felt ridiculous for having been drawn in by the darkness and the crow, for being afraid and awed.

Spider waved her hands again. 'It might sound like fortune teller's nonsense to you…'

The way the words almost matched those in her mind made Nancy jump. She clenched her hands so that her nails dug into her palms, held herself tight against the urge to go out into the streets and run to where she understood everything, where even if all that waited for them was hunger and mud, at least she knew the shape of it.

'… but you'll note I had the room prepared before you arrived. I knew you would come.'

Nancy swallowed. 'I came because Lil told me you wanted Darner too and I'm telling you, Miss Whoever-you-are, he near as dammit murdered my dad. Not that the law could get him, but he did it deliberate.'

Spider smiled. A crooked little smile that caught on itself. 'Why do you say that he near murdered your father? Why nearly?'

'He threw a sick man out into an icy night without enough clothes.'

'Is that all?'

Nancy stared at her.

Spider continued, 'I can tell you it is not all because I saw—'

'In oracles and dreams?' Nancy said scornfully.

'No. With my own eyes. Just feet from where I lurked unseen and concealed, I saw Darner order that a man, whom I presume was your father, should be drenched in ice-cold water and then beaten before he was thrown onto the streets. The man who beat him, Bevel, admitted bluntly that the intention was that he should die.'

'I knew it!' Nancy spun on her heel and paced in front of the fire, the crow hopping out of her way, watching her warily. 'How did you see this?'

'From the gate in the corner of the yard.'

'You say he was thrown out? He didn't leave of his own accord?'

'Darner watched him go.'

The idea of her father in that state brought horrified tears to Nancy's eyes. Rejected, bruised and sick, dragging himself into the cold night, not knowing where she was or where to find warmth. He must have despaired. And when he did find her, it was too late. She angrily swept away a tear. 'He calls himself a prophet, but he's closer to the devil.'

'Prophet? He might call himself that. He believes it?'

Nancy thought for a moment, raised her eyes and squinted. 'Yes, I think he does.' She was a little surprised. Until now, she'd assumed he was a fraud, a charlatan, rather than a true believer. But now she found herself thinking that he really did believe. 'He thinks he's acting for God.'

'That sounds like the Darner I knew.' The fire flared and spat out an ember. Spider pressed it out with her foot.

'How do you know him? What's he done to you?'

'Around a decade ago he killed me.'

Nancy raised a sceptical eyebrow. 'Pretty lively for a dead person, aren't you?'

Spider ignored her comment. 'What is he doing with this Charitable Brethren?'

Nancy shrugged, 'He says he's doing the Lord's work, whatever that means. Wants to lift the poor out of their spiritual poverty as well as their material poverty, he says. Tend to their bodies and minds.'

'How many people?'

'There's about six families who live in. My father lived in. That's about thirty people. Then there's about another twenty or so who live out and just come in for the services, in the process of being gathered in. They're all supposed to commit to joining properly, though. They're only living out while they prepare themselves and their affairs. Seems to me that he gathers people into his group mostly to enjoy their worship of him, to have them where he wants them.

'I looked for him for so long. He disappeared into a mission to Africa for years and then suddenly here he is, reappearing on my very doorstep.'

'I wish he had died out there,' Nancy said. 'Then my father might still be alive. Prophet!' She said with a mouth full of spit and scorn.

'What's this about, this Charitable Brethren?'

'Well, it's not about money anyhow. He's set up here of all places, where no one has two pennies to rub together. Though since they give him all they have, it must add up a bit. '

'He gathers people to judge. And to punish,' Spider added and ground her teeth together. In her pocket, her hand moved through her oracle sticks. She drew one out and looked at it.

'Oh yeah,' Nancy gave a bitter laugh. 'He likes to punish.'

Spider nodded, satisfied and replaced the stick in her pocket. 'Are you willing to help me destroy Darner?'

Nancy stared at her for a moment. 'Isn't that why I came here in the first place?'

Spider paced. 'We need to get to him and I can't do that without knowing everything. You can tell me what I need to know.'

'Can I? I've never been inside his rooms and I don't know his comings and goings.'

'His meals?'

'Mostly from the same pot as the rest of us.'

'Only mostly?'

Nancy shrugged. 'Sometimes there's special visitors. And he often sets himself aside before a big service. You could join the Brethren. I'm sure he'd welcome a wealthy donor. He's not set up just to get money from rich ladies like some of his sort, but he certainly wouldn't turn it down.'

Spider shook her head, 'If he sees me, he'll recognise me, I'm sure. Or he'll suspect.'

'After all this time?'

'One thing you can say for Mr Darner is that however much of a religious lunatic he might be, he's neither stupid nor unobservant.'

'That's true,' said Nancy. 'And he knows me far too well, too recently.'

'You are *persona non grata* at the Brethren?'

'What?'

'They won't let you in?'

'Oh, they'd let me in. It eats him up that I left of my own accord. He wants to punish me for that. Thinks he hasn't done enough yet. And for the others, there's all that forgiveness and soul-saving they have to do. They'd enjoy my humiliation.'

'Humiliation?'

'It's a thing they do. Like confession, only not private. Once a week, you write a letter to Christ with all your failings, only Christ doesn't read it, one of Darner's nasty cronies does. Then Darner picks the juiciest and gets whoever's written them up on stage at a special ceremony. Berates them in front of everyone. It's supposed to make us humble. So me turning up and wanting to return would make them all excited for me to be humiliated.'

'They'd be pleased to see you?'

'Yes. But Darner would be watching me like a hawk. They'd suspect me if anything bad happened.'

'But you could get in?'

'I could.'

'And from there, once you're in... Well, we can find our opportunity. Once you can see a way to do it, you can come and tell me. We'll do it together.'

Nancy sat and stared into space, thinking. Eventually she said, 'Yeah, I could. I could get him. We could get him.' She looked at Spider. 'Pigeon would have to stay here. I ain't letting her anywhere near that place again.'

'Of course. Patience can look after her.'

'He killed you, you say?'

Spider sighed, a long exhalation that made the candle flame stutter. 'A part of me. The most alive part of me. She stepped forwards and held out her thin hand. 'Do we have an arrangement?'

Nancy shook it. 'We do.'

The girls had a day to lose in Hangcorner House. The Brethren humiliations service was not until the next afternoon and Patience said they were not to get in the way in the meantime. Doors were locked for a reason and they ought not to go in the warehouse which was long unused and likely to be unsafe; apart from that, no one cared where they went as long as they didn't damage anything or make a fuss.

'Let's go have a peek about,' Nancy said.

Pigeon nodded happily and rearranged her grip on her sister's hand. Their palms together felt strangely smooth and dry now that they were so clean. Holding Pigeon's hand, Nancy sometimes felt her father's there instead: weak with the tendons standing high in the thin skin. But then it would be gone and Pigeon's warm, little fingers would squeeze her hand gently.

Out in the hall outside their bedroom they looked up and down. There were two doors and a dead end in the direction they hadn't explored yet. One of the doors was locked and Nancy peered through the keyhole. 'Like ours,' she said, 'only a bit smaller and without the big window.' The other door swung inwards to reveal a darkened room, its curtains closed and its furniture covered in dust sheets.

Against the back wall leant a portrait of a man in old fashioned clothes. He stood on a dock in front of a ship busy with the tiny forms of sailors and dockworkers. The nameplate read 'Mr Nathaniel Blackwell'. The gilt frame was dull and chipped.

'I wonder if the mistress is related to him.'

'Mistress is a funny name,' Pigeon stated.

'Hmm, but so's Pigeon.' Nancy grinned and her sister stuck her tongue out at her. 'Careful, I'll cut it off.'

Pigeon gave a high-pitched squeal of laughter and then shushed herself with her hand over her mouth. Then she gave a yelp and pointed. Nancy turned and felt the hairs on her arms stand up.

Behind them was an armchair covered in a sheet and under the sheet was a form, touched and hinted at by the drape of the fabric. A domed head, a thin shoulder.

'It must be a mannequin.' Nancy said.

'I don't like it. Someone's hiding. Can we go?' Pigeon pulled her sleeve towards the door.

Nancy reached out to the sheet, caught it in her fingers and pulled it away.

Pigeon screamed and Nancy gasped.

Yellowed bones glistened in the dim light and the skull grinned at them. Then Nancy laughed and her sister looked at her as if she were going mad. She reached out and slipped a finger into the hook screwed into the skull, and shifted it from one side to another with a crunching sound. She laughed again.

'What are you doing?' said Pigeon, horrified.

'It's just a doctor's skeleton. Look.' She picked up the wired articulated arm and waved it at her sister who made a noise that was part scream, part laugh.

'Don't, Nancy!'

Nancy took the other arm and moved them both. 'May I have a dance, madam?' she said, putting on a posh voice.

Pigeon laughed, and choked on it, and then kept laughing. One of the hands detached from the skeleton, causing Nancy to swear and this set Pigeon off into reams of giggles, while Nancy struggled to keep a straight face. In the end, Pigeon was rolling on the floor and Nancy bent double clutching the hand as their hilarity gradually petered out. Nancy put the hand in the skeleton's lap and, with a guilty grin, threw the sheet back over their morbid find.

'That was so funny,' Pigeon said.

'You should have seen your face when that sheet came off.' Nancy grinned.

'What's it made of, the doctor's skeleton?'

'Oh, it will be a real skeleton.' Nancy moved towards a narrow door in the corner of the room, wondering if it went somewhere interesting or was just a cupboard.

'A real…' Pigeon stood in the middle of the room, looking at the shape beneath the sheet. 'You mean? That was a real person once?'

'Yeah, they clean them up, give 'em a polish. Probably a criminal.'

'It might be the skeleton of a murderer?' Pigeon backed away and, seeing the fear on her face, Nancy berated herself for not lying and saying it was just plaster.

'It's all right, Pidge, it can't do you any harm.'

'But you touched it. You broke its hand.' The last word rose into a wail and Nancy hurried forwards. 'What if it's cursed and you die?'

Nancy dropped to her knees and hugged her sister tightly. 'I ain't going anywhere, Pigeon. No dead old criminal can hurt me, don't you worry. No way. We're more than a match for any old collection of bones.'

'But it might come and get us,' Pigeon said.

'Look, would it be better if it was further from our room? I can move it to a loft or a cellar or something.'

Pigeon nodded and smeared away her tears.

'And we can chop its legs off so it can't move.'

Pigeon gave a little cough of laughter and nodded again.

'So, let's keep having a look around and we can find somewhere to stash muggins here.' She helped her sister up. 'Look, I wonder where that door goes.'

The narrow door wouldn't open at first and Pigeon pulled at Nancy's sleeve. Nancy gave it another jiggle, tried the latch again and the door opened.

'Was it locked?' Pigeon asked, anxious not to disobey Patience.

'No, just stiff.'

Beyond the door was a very narrow passage that led to the foot of a steep staircase. 'The attics,' Nancy said.

They walked through three attic rooms full of boxes, trunks and broken furniture. In one place, a gap under the eaves had let birds in and a grey pile of droppings and feathers sat beneath a scruffy collection of sticks balanced on a roof brace.

'We could leave Mr Bony in one of these rooms,' Nancy suggested.

Pigeon gave a tight little shake of the head.

'Too close to our room?' Nancy guessed and her sister nodded. 'What about that trunk? We could pile stuff on top of it. Shut him up good and safe.'

While Pigeon went to examine the trunk, Nancy looked over at the door into the next room. It had a heavier door than most of the others, almost as if it were the external door to a house. She could see a darker mark on the wood where it had once had a knocker.

Pigeon threw back the lid of the trunk. 'Blankets.' She started rummaging down into the fabric, her feet barely on the ground. Nancy grasped the handle of the thick door. For some reason she expected it to be locked but it swung open on silent hinges at her lightest touch.

A chill settled on her shoulders and she felt the big empty house around her, the loneliness. Only Lil knew they were here, and who would believe Lil if she told a tale of two missing girls? The quietness seemed to echo.

The room the door opened into was dark, lit only by a few shifting skeins of greyness from the edges of the closed shutters. Still figures dangled from the ceiling. People, five or six people, were hanging in there. A rope creaked and the one nearest the door began to gently turn.

Nancy screamed.

Chapter Fifteen
Webs

Spider sat at the table in her turret room. She shuffled her bone sticks in front of her. Corbeau perched on the back of a narrow chair, watching the sticks and hopping from foot to foot, waiting for the moment to play his role.

'Pick,' said Spider and the crow leant forwards and carefully extracted a single narrow stick. He dropped it in front of her and cawed, one eye turned up towards her, like a tiny crystal ball, reflecting the room, her own reflection in its glossy sphere. She bent towards it, stared for a moment, caught in its round gleam and then turned her attention to the stick.

Despair.

The word was carved in angular letters, like a crude whaler's scrimshaw, but this was not whalebone. Nor was it ivory that had seen the sun in a distant place, scavenged by empire.

'Despair,' Spider said. This was not new, this was the background shade to life – to all life as far as she could see, not only her own. 'How predictable. Tell me something new.'

She gestured at the crow again. 'Pick.' He lifted his feet one after the other, as if irritated that his first attempt had been rejected. He shuffled and kicked at the sticks. *Light. Hunger. Dreams.*

Then he picked.

Opportunity.

Spider breathed in.

The Antagonist had come, and then Darner had reappeared. Now Nancy was here and opportunity showed itself again.

A distant scream echoed through the house – real fear, a child. She jerked her head up, gathered her sticks hurriedly, put them in a pocket and went to the door. Putting her head out into the passage she listened again. Silence but not an empty silence. The silence that comes of small sounds that don't quite reach all the way. After a short while came high-pitched laughter.

Her own laughter had never rung through the house that way. She wrinkled her nose and glanced back at the crow, but he had flown out of the open window to do crow things among the chimneys and alleys.

She pulled a stick out of her pocket and read the inscription.

Carrion.

She gave a short laugh. 'Quite,' she said aloud, and then walked quietly upstairs and along the corridors. She paused once to pick a mushroom from beneath the corner of a dresser. She slipped it into her pocket and continued walking until she stood outside the room she had told Patience to use for the sisters. A rummaging and shuffling came from the room at the end of the hall; she assumed the girls were exploring in there, giving rein to their natural curiosity. Well, there could be no harm in that. Unless they could pick locks; not an entirely unlikely skill for street urchins to possess, she supposed. Well, that she'd leave to chance. She opened the door to their room.

It was quiet, the light slanting onto the floor, exactly as it had a few days ago. Nothing. They had brought nothing with them. No personal effects at all. No clothes across a chair, no box, no favoured toy however ragged. She lifted the pillow on one bed and was puzzled to see a crust of bread carefully stowed there. She made a sound of irritation and went to remove it but then stopped herself and carefully replaced the pillow as it had been.

They were here for a reason. They meant something. The small engravings of their lives were messages for her, they would bring something, change something. Their heartbeats in her house as full of hidden meaning as a telegram's clattering. *Opportunity.*

Standing in the hall, she could hear small footsteps overhead. She felt strangely angry, disturbed. Vengeance. She knew that particular desire and she had almost forgotten it. Almost. A memory of hatred, a shadow across her youth as she slipped further into darkness and quiet.

Soon they would be among her dolls. She smiled at the idea, wondered what they would make of them. She wanted them to have to face the dolls, to see. Feeling a keen lightness, she slowly and deliberately turned the key in the lock of the door at the end of the hall.

Chapter Sixteen
Transformation

Sara was hot and humiliated and so tired she could barely gather those facts together into anger, and so they simmered in resentment.

The earth was a grey-brown dust that threw the heat back in their faces; the sweat trickled in small rivulets down the back of their necks. Sara's group of patients had been assigned, for some indecipherable reason, to make scarecrows for the garden. Perhaps it had seemed like a good task for the women on a lovely sunny summer's day. At the other end of the garden, a group of male patients weeded the cabbages, watched by Lambert.

Sara could imagine the doctor having such an idea; he might even be watching from a distant window, thinking it a pleasant sight: the women at the end of the rows of vegetables, with piles of straw and sacking and old clothes. From that distance, he would not be able to see the sweat or the sun-reddened skin. However, she couldn't help but note that the patients chosen were those who had displeased Darner recently.

Darner had not forgotten the oracle mobile and recently his sermons had run long on the iniquity of fortune telling and witchcraft. A Jewish patient was with them and another woman who was prone to fits and vehemently refused attendance at chapel. One woman's madness had come on after childbirth and she still, even though her child would now be ten years old, constantly pleaded to see her baby. Miss Hawthorn, who would usually have enjoyed such a task and welcomed it with glee, was tired under a sheen of sweat. Sara didn't know how Miss Hawthorn had displeased Darner but her sad eyes and sore knees suggested that, somehow, she had.

Miss Gavins suffered under an umbrella which allowed her just enough freedom from the heat to maintain a narrow stream of admonitions. 'No, I'll cut the string, Miss Hawthorn.' 'Don't leave that there, someone will trip.' 'I've already said five times, ask Mr Sullivan to put it in place if it's finished.' 'No, you can't see your baby.'

Sullivan sweated and swore and emerged from the shade to erect their handiwork. 'Bet you're looking forward to hydrotherapy for once, eh, Hawthorn.'

Sara now knew why Miss Hawthorn was so averse to hydrotherapy. The water treatment given to her was one intended to cool an overheated mind and so she was subjected to cold showers while restrained in the chair. 'The water sprays in my face,' she had told Sara, with disgust. 'The doctor says I should be grateful because it does make me quieter and persuades me to behave more properly, but I'm only quiet afterward because I'm so cold!' After she had said this, the parrot had immediately started shrieking, 'Be quiet! Be quiet! Be quiet!' punctuated with ear-splitting screams.

Miss Hawthorn had covered her ears and laughed and laughed until she had fallen off her chair, drawing a sour look of disapproval from Miss Gavins, who had been hunting for a blanket to throw over Herman's cage.

The situation was made all the more unbearable because Mr Darner kept coming out from his chapel, bringing a tantalising drift of cooler air from within, though perhaps that was just Sara's imagination. Her knees were no longer bruised from kneeling on the tiled chapel floor, but they still pained her if they were bent for any length of time at all and they clicked when she straightened them. The rough asylum stockings were damp with her sweat; they rubbed at the small cuts in her feet. Sullivan saw her rising awkwardly and said, 'Well, well, Miss Atherton, surely you're a little young for housemaid's knee?'

Miss Gavins said, drily, 'No doubt she's above a mere housemaid's knee.'

Sara ignored the jibes. She shoved another prickling handful of straw into the body of a ridiculous man-thing. She stood sweating, looking down at her scarecrow. An unformed doll. Miss Gavins had taken her umbrella to the shade of a tree and was talking reluctantly to Sullivan. The other patients were confined within their own orbits of misery.

The dark forms of rooks twisted in the sky, clattering around their rookery in the trees at the edge of the asylum garden. They chattered, angry. Above them hung two buzzards, lazily sweeping the blue until a detachment of rooks burst out from the trees to nag and harass them. The high-pitched cries of the buzzards pierced the air. The sun crept round the top of the building. Miss Gavins made a comment about the afternoon moving on.

Sara had made this scarecrow tall and thin, at first by happenstance, but once she realised the resemblance, she developed it.

Now she had to dress it and she rummaged in the pile of old clothes. Sara pulled out all the black men's clothes and repurposed an old white shawl as a cravat; she gave the scarecrow scraps of dark wool for glowering eyebrows and dark hair.

After Sullivan had placed the scarecrow upright tied to his post he stepped back, squinted at it and gave a guffaw.

Miss Gavins laughed and said, 'It looks a little like the chaplain, Miss Atherton. You might want to change him a little.'

Sara eyed the scarecrow critically. 'Do you think so, Miss Gavins?'

'Well, in as much as any scarecrow looks like anyone in particular.'

'It does! It does. Just like him!' Sullivan said. 'You'll get in trouble with him, Atherton. Tell you what, I'll get you something to finish the effect.' He walked off laughing to himself and in a minute, he returned with what was recognisably the chaplain's black felt hat.

'Won't come to any harm, just for a moment.' He darted forwards and placed the hat on the scarecrow's head. 'It's eerie.' He laughed, a laugh that caught on itself and wasn't quite free. The nearby patients straightened from their work and looked over, shading eyes, rubbing sweat away. Miss Hawthorn laughed, a single high laugh that went up into the blue sky.

Sullivan was right, the effect *was* eerie. Sara had given the scarecrow Darner's deep hollow cheeks and shadowed burning eyes with some careful use of charcoal. It ought to have been comic, ridiculous, but the twig fingers sticking out from the sleeves looked like a skeleton's.

'Hang on, he'd better see this, then he can have his hat back.' Sullivan went off to find Darner. Sara smiled to herself.

Miss Gavins leant back against her tree and closed her eyes, and everyone went back to their work except for Miss Hawthorn, who stood staring at Scarecrow Darner with a smile on her face. Sara bent down to the scarecrow's feet, adjusting something, her hands cupped. In the still air, the heat wavered and the press of it spoke of thunder. The shard of glass she held was razor-edged and curved. The spot of brightness on the sacking of the scarecrow darkened in its centre as Sullivan walked out of the chapel laughing, with Darner stiff-backed behind him.

A thin trail of smoke trickled up between Sara's hands and the men got closer. A flame.

'What in the Lord's name?' Darner said, eyes widening and nose flaring as he recognised what stood before him.

'Hey, that's not—' Sullivan stopped dead as flames rippled up the leg of the scarecrow, burning the straw and scorching the wool trousers. They touched the bottom of the cotton shirt which lit and burned quickly, lighting the straw within and blackening the woollen coat on the outside.

The male patients weeding the cabbage beds stood up to watch. One whooped and another cheered. Lambert made a futile attempt to get them back to work. Miss Hawthorn started to laugh again.

Sullivan, seeing the danger to the hat, darted forwards and tried to snatch it, just as the bulk of the straw in the torso gave a loud crackle and ignited; flames engulfed the head, hat and all. Sullivan snatched his hand back with an oath and crushed out a flame on his sleeve.

The nearby patients laughed and cheered. Someone shouted, 'Bit of a preview, Mr Darner!' and set off another cheer.

Sara laughed with them. She laughed at the fury on Darner's face. She laughed at his hate and his burnt-up hat. She laughed at the way he stamped out the last flying embers, drifting about the dry garden.

She laughed still as he pointed a finger in her face and said to Sullivan, 'Bring her!', turned on his heel and strode back to his cool haven. The laughter of the other patients died away behind her as Sullivan dragged her through the door into the chapel.

She had been kneeling for two hours with Sullivan's fist in the back of her collar keeping her upright and Darner standing over her reading prayers. Her knees were hot with agony. The cool tiles had been a relief only for a few minutes. Sweat ran down her back and her mouth was parched. A headache pounded through her left eye and across the whole of her skull.

Thunder started to rumble in the distance.

The door to the chapel creaked open and Darner looked up.

'What's this?' A man's voice, unknown, authoritative.

Darner paused halfway through his prayer, a furious look on his face. Sara's back was towards the door.

'A patient in need of penance, sir,' Sullivan said and then, in an undertone to Darner, 'It's Riverton, one of the Lunacy Commission's legal men.'

Darner hissed in reply, 'I know, fool.'

'Mr Riverton.' Whitehead's voice, hurried. 'This is the Reverend Mr Darner, our chaplain.' There was a clatter of footsteps as a group came in.

'The archbishop seems most pleased with you, Mr Darner.' A new voice spoke. 'He called you a powerful believer and a masterful speaker.'

Darner bowed his head in acknowledgement. 'Thank you, sir. He has been a most generous benefactor.'

The voices advanced on them until Sara could see a tall, well-dressed man standing next to Dr Whitehead and his wife. Lambert trailed behind them. On seeing Sara, Mrs Whitehead exclaimed and dashed forwards, laying a cool hand on her head. Sara swayed on her knees and Mrs Whitehead supported her to sit.

'Mr Darner! This is most unfortunate, but Atherton here is not well.'

The doctor hurried forwards. 'They were working outdoors earlier. Perhaps a little too much sun and heat.'

'Patients working outdoors on the hottest day of the year, Whitehead? Is that wise? Do the benefits of occupation stretch so far?' Riverton asked.

The Whiteheads were lowering Sara to the cool tiles and feeling her skin's heat. The relief made Sara gasp and tears came to her eyes. Lambert arranged her skirts to cover her legs.

Whitehead looked up. 'For most of our patients, it's what their lives have been. Especially the pauper idiots. Perhaps the middle-class patients ought to be spared it. They're less used to the labour.'

'Indolence is corrosive to the moral fibre,' Darner said and stepped back, allowing the doctor and his wife space.

Sara swallowed and gasped. Her throat was dry and her lips cracked. She looked up at the tall man at the back of the group. He looked down at her with some concern and a little revulsion. She saw herself through his eyes for a moment: a dirty, sweat-stained lunatic woman sprawled on the ground, dazed and unwell. 'Sir.' She spoke, forcing the words through her dry throat. He looked at her, surprised to be addressed.

Darner spoke. 'Perhaps Atherton's penance should wait.'

'Sir.' Sara tried again, pain making her clutch her head and curl around herself; she forced herself to straighten and look at him. 'Please.' Riverton looked at her with annoyance.

'Perhaps I should leave you to take care of the patient,' Darner said to Whitehead, crushing her voice beneath his own and giving her a venomous look. Riverton showed no sign of having heard her plea. 'I could show Mr Riverton the new works until you can join us.'

'Yes, I think that would be best, Darner,' Whitehead said shortly.

Darner walked towards the door, an arm out, guiding the Lunacy Commissioner away. They were followed by Sullivan but Whitehead said, 'Sullivan, Lambert, fetch a stretcher.' Sullivan looked at Darner who nodded and the two assistants hurried off towards the wards.

Whitehead was staring into Sara's eyes, lifting her lids. Then he checked her pulse. The door banged shut behind Darner and Riverton as he counted to himself.

'Just the heat, I think, and then this penance of Darner's on top. Perhaps a little excessive, but well-meant I'm sure,' Whitehead said to his wife, relief in his voice.

She pressed her lips together and shook her head a little.

'Yes, yes, dear,' he answered her look. 'Well-meant I am sure. A cool bath and plenty to drink, that's what's needed here. In fact, if she shows no sign of vomiting, give Miss Atherton the hydrotherapy treatment she was due to have tomorrow, using cooler water at first of course. You can see to that can't you, dear?'

'And then to her own bed?'

'I should think so, no need to take up space in the infirmary. Call me if there are any alarming symptoms.'

'Ah, here they come with the stretcher. My girls and I will soon have you in a cool bath.' Mrs Whitehead patted Sara's hand.

Sara had not come to enjoy the hydrotherapy as Doctor Whitehead had promised. She had, however, grown to tolerate it. Her hands were not buckled in now that she took the treatment calmly. But every part of her, except her face, was still trapped beneath the canvas, almost as effectively restrained as she had been on her first time in the bath. But it was time alone, at least. Time to think, interrupted only by the checks on her and the nurse's occasional provision of water to drink.

Sara watched the spider that had made its web across the obscured glass of the window. Her headache receded as she cooled down and reduced to a dull throb and a heat in her left eye. She let her mind drift into plans that were mostly fairy tale. She wondered if Corbeau would still be her friend when she returned to Hangcorner House or whether he would have reverted to a distant savagery. Here, there were only rooks in the distant trees, a couple of cages of budgerigars and Herman, whose ear-piercing screams made him unpleasant company even when her head was not aching. When it was, he was unendurable.

When she eventually returned to London, what would she do and how would she do it? She could expand her collection of medicines and herbs, order new seeds, experiment, find unusual ones, ones of different tastes and effects, different speeds of action. Blend them. Find different methods of application. Observe the effects on the inmates of the house. She would have to be careful not to go too far, so as not to raise suspicions again.

She turned over possible projects: a series of distressing intestinal issues for Mrs Nichols, an unsightly and painful rash for Bristow. She would leave Jenny out of this; she was so feeble that one nasty bout of indigestion could be fatal. Besides, Jenny had never done anything to warrant it, whereas the housekeeper and manservant had been rather too obviously entertained by her detention on that last day at Hangcorner House; they deserved to suffer. She had better steer clear of her uncle until she were ready for him. Other subjects were safer.

With these thoughts floating around her mind, she drifted off to sleep, into a dream of corridors and crows. A conversation with her uncle in which she couldn't hear what he said and he got angrier and angrier. The flap and scuffle of feathers, a wing across her vision and the smell of crow.

Cold water sprayed into her face. She sputtered, struggled against the hammock that held her below and the canvas sheet that held her above. She scraped her knuckles uselessly against the taut canvas. Water went in her eyes and up her nose, it sluiced into her ears, and ran down the sides of her face and into the bath; little shivers of cold stealing into the warmth.

Over the gushing and splashing she became aware that someone was talking. A loud droning voice. She tried to open her eyes but all she could see was a tall, dark shape. A man. Was it Sullivan?

The shape got nearer and then ducked below the line of her vision. The water stopped. She shook her head, blinked her eyes and called out wordlessly, a cry of panic and confusion. The rim of the bath and her canvas covering stopped her seeing what the man was doing – a rummaging beside the bath, a clink.

'Ask your saviour for help, witch!' a voice said, and fear swept her. It was not Sullivan. It was Darner.

'You must be punished, you must repent your sins. Then you must be baptised and reborn in God, or die and meet him to be judged.'

There was one last clink and, to Sara's horror, she felt the hammock give way beneath her. She grasped at the edge of the bath but the canvas was tight against the rim, and she couldn't gain purchase. She gave a desperate scream that ended in a gurgle as her upper body sank. If she slipped beneath the canvas, she would be unable to find the opening and she would drown. Fear bubbled around her in the water. She sank, rose up again, her face pushing against wet canvas, lips reaching for a fragment of air. She sank again.

A hand grabbed her hair and pulled her up, yanked her face into the air. She breathed a great water-infested gasp and coughed. Darner stood bending over her, the stale smell of him wafting across her as she gasped in a snatch of air. She coughed again. She could feel foam at the corners of her mouth, water in her throat.

'Do you know of ducking stools, witch?' he hissed in her ear.

She scrabbled with her hands at the underside of the canvas, but before she could answer his question, he plunged her beneath the water again. A swirl and rush, the grey canvas, a mess of her hair and clothes, her nose painfully full of bubbles. He was going to kill her. She kept her mouth tight shut and then she was hauled out again by her hair, her scalp, agony. She coughed the thin air and a few of his words broke through as a plug of water rushed from one ear.

'...the waters of the River Jordan...'

And then, in again she was plunged, the tight rock of his hand scraping her hairline. She didn't manage to close her mouth in time and panicked as she drew in water. She was going to die here. Then she was out again, coughing the water over the canvas into the air.

'…cleansed in the water of life…'

As she was thrust under, she heard a bang. The water swirled around her hair, twisting; she felt it moving around her like fate, like time. Down here in the swirling dark, Sara knew she would die. There was no air, no hope. And yet Death had not touched her dreams and visions. That Sara, the Sara of poisons and whispers could die here was impossible even as the Sara of weakness and hope drowned, helpless at the bottom of a gritty asylum bath.

PART III

Chapter Seventeen
Strife

Nancy ran back the way they had come, Pigeon's hand sweaty in her own. When they reached the skeleton, Pigeon pulled back on Nancy's hand and made her give it a wide berth.

As they reached the door that led onto their corridor, Nancy grabbed the handle and turned. But it wouldn't budge. She rattled it and still nothing.

'Is it stuck?' Pigeon asked. 'Like the other door?'

Nancy bent down and looked between the door and the jamb. The lock was firmly home.

'It's locked!'

She tried to find a reason the door was now locked to reassure her sister. 'Someone must have come to get something from this room and just locked it behind them, that's all,' she said, recognising the look of panic spreading across Pigeon's face, and forcing the tremble from her voice. 'It will be all right, love. Worst comes to worst, we'll have to shout until Patience hears.'

She calmed her breathing and tried to think. She really couldn't have seen what she thought she saw upstairs. Hanging people. There had been no smell. If it really had been a room of dangling corpses the smell would have been overpowering. Now this door was locked. She needed to have a closer look.

'We'll try the other door upstairs.'

'The door you ran away from?'

'It was just a bit spooky. I let myself get scared, it was daft.'

Pigeon looked at her dubiously. She glanced at the shrouded figure. 'I can't go past him again, Nancy,' Pigeon whispered. 'I know it's silly, but I can't.' She closed her eyes. Her voice rose to a whispered squeak. 'He'll come for me, I know he will.'

'It's all right, I'll deal with it. You wait here.'

Pigeon slid down into a crouching position by the door and, her eyes fixed on the shape beneath the sheet, nodded.

Nancy lifted the sheet, holding it so that Pigeon couldn't see what was beneath, and took a closer look at the skeleton. Several of the wires were rusty and fragile and, with a twist, Nancy removed its left leg, then its right. It made a rasping sound and Pigeon said, 'What are you doing?'

'Just putting the bones together,' Nancy said. She threw the sheet back over the skeleton and gathered it up in her arms, careful not to let any of the bones show or fall out. She shuffled back into the narrow passage with her burden and struggled up the stairs.

When she had deposited the skeleton in the trunk, she returned downstairs. At first she couldn't see her sister but then a bulge in the curtains sniffed and wobbled. Nancy avoided the distorted body of a spider hanging in a mess of cobwebs and slipped behind the faded velvet curtain. The space was cold and smelt of mildew. Pigeon was drawing on the window in the mist of her own breath. 'It's the main street,' she said, pointing down.

Nancy looked over her shoulder at the busy world below. People were walking up and down, going about their business; there were handcarts, cabs, large drays with their enormous horses; people, people, people. Two ragged children ran up the road tossing something from one to the other; an apple, she thought. A shopkeeper came running after them, raising his fist and puffing. People turned to watch but no one helped, not for an apple and some hungry kids.

'That might be us. If we end up back out there.'

'It isn't us,' Nancy said resting a hand on her sister's shoulder.

'No, I mean, I know. That was two other children, but it might be us. And we might have to go back like before.' She looked out of the window again. 'Ow, Nancy, you're hurting me.'

'Sorry, love.' Nancy let go of the girl's shoulder quickly. She hadn't realised she was gripping it so hard. 'Well, we won't need to go back to the Brethren.'

Pigeon was leaning her forehead against the glass, her breath fogging it. She said something quietly as she put her finger against the cold surface. A droplet ran down from it and pooled against the rotting wood of the frame.

'What?'

'I said, I meant back on the streets, not back with the Brethren. Going back there would be better than that.'

'Than what?' Nancy asked.

Pigeon swiped her breath from the glass and put her finger against it, pointing at a small girl in rags. 'Better than *that*.'

A cold gush swirled through Nancy. 'Would you rather I'd left you there?' Her voice rose, defensive.

'No, 'cause we'd have never come here then.'

'Better to be anywhere than with the Brethren.'

Pigeon shook her head. 'It was warm and there was always food.'

'They killed Dad. Darner deliberately kicked him out knowing he would die, soaked to the skin and without enough clothes. They beat us and they did the bell thing to me. Sometimes there's still ringing in my head.'

Pigeon looked down at her feet and nodded. 'Yes, Nancy.'

'Better to be free and starve.'

Pigeon looked dubious, as if she wanted to shake her head again, but Nancy's voice had an edge to it. 'Yes, Nancy.'

Nancy threw the curtain over her head, feeling tight and hot and like she might scream at any moment. She tried to do the best for them, always. The idea that Pigeon's ideas about 'best' might differ from her own took her by surprise.

'Come on,' she said, roughly, and Pigeon scuffled with the curtain to escape it. Feeling slightly malicious in withholding her help, Nancy left her sister to sort herself out. She was just about to give in and untangle Pigeon when she looked towards the locked door and her breath caught. A movement. The light and shadow at the bottom edge of the door shifted. Someone was there.

'Help me, Nancy,' Pigeon squeaked, flapping at the curtain. Nancy turned towards her sister and when she looked back towards the door, the shadow was gone.

With a couple of brisk movements, she freed her sister and while Pigeon was still huffing and flattening her disordered hair and clothes, Nancy ushered her out of the room and up into the attics.

The door to the room of hanging figures was slightly ajar and Nancy approached it cautiously. She was sure she'd heard it slam shut behind her when they'd fled.

'Wait here,' she told Pigeon.

The hanging figures were still as she slipped through the door, trying to block the sight from her sister. They hung so that their feet were about waist high; she would have to walk among them to move across the room. There was the pale outline of a white-painted door on the other wall and she stepped towards it. The air from her movement or some vibration in the room caused the nearest figure to gently rotate towards her and Nancy suppressed a scream. An empty face stared down at her from the gloom. A mask. It was just a mask. The figures were not real people. Of course they were not real people.

She had once seen a public hanging, back before the family had joined the Brethren, and the man's contorted face and the weird twisting jerks of his last movements had stayed with her for a long time. They had leapt back into her memory when she had first seen the hanging figures. Now she could see they were fabric, stuffed and dressed.

Perhaps she could persuade Pigeon they were only dolls. Her scalp prickled as she looked around. In the dim light they were frightening and she could feel her breath shallow in her chest. She couldn't shake off the feeling that someone was creeping between them, just out of sight. Pigeon would be terrified. More light would help.

The shutters on the windows folded open with a creak and when she turned back to the room of dolls, she caught her breath. Her passage to the window must have nudged them because now they were all swaying slightly on their long ropes, tied to the rafters. Turning and swinging. She swallowed. The one nearest her had black clothes and a white cravat, a skull-like face. Darner. It was a figure of Darner.

Another had grey sideburns and cold blue eyes. One seemed almost like it could be intended for Spider; thin, in dark women's clothes, with hair in a bun. One wore an elaborate nightgown with ribbons and lace and had disordered hair made of torn wool. There were smaller figures too. One in a grey dress looked like it might be intended for Patience. Its hands were tied together and this gave Nancy a creeping feeling up her back.

She opened the other door and then went back to get Pigeon.

'There's dolls, Pigeon, that's all,' Nancy said and led Pigeon into the room. Pigeon looked around interested, but not at all frightened to Nancy's surprise and relief.

'Very strange dolls. Oh, Nancy, look! This one is you!' She dropped Nancy's hand and ran to one of the dolls. Its noose hung slack about its neck as she held it.

Nancy slowly approached, feeling sick. She saw that Pigeon was right; it was her in her Brethren clothes, her plait dangling behind.

'Why's there a doll of you?' Pigeon asked.

'I don't know,' Nancy said, 'but it gives me the creeps, let's get out of here.' She hurried through the rest of the room, closed the door firmly behind them and gave a great huffing breath out. Spider had been watching her before, when she was with the Brethren. How long had Spider been watching them? And yet Darner was still alive. Did she really want him dead? Could she really want it and yet not have done it?

The door opened into a passage that immediately bent to the right. From out of sight they heard a strange scraping sound. Nancy steeled herself to face another unknown and peered around the corner.

She found herself looking down onto a small landing with two sets of stairs leading down in different directions. A tiny window opened onto a patch of roof covered in fern and moss and in the windowsill sat the crow, head hunched into his neck, happy with himself. He carried a white stick in his beak, which he threw down onto the wooden floor below, apparently enjoying the clatter. He hopped after it, picked it up and began scraping it back and forth along the floorboards, marching along in a very self-satisfied manner.

'It's just a crow!' Nancy said, and the crow cocked his head at her as if disputing the word 'just'; then, with a flapping that almost filled the small space, he flew up to the window and departed, leaving the stick in the middle of the floor.

Nancy bent to pick it up. One of Spider's word-sticks. When she turned it over, she found that the scratches on one side resolved themselves into a word. *Antagonist*.

That seemed a strange word to scratch on a stick. She thought she knew what it meant but she wasn't certain. Something like enemy.

She peered out from the small window. The crow flew into her sight and then disappeared out of the edge of the window frame, as if disappearing from the world. The curve of an awkward turret poked out from a corner but that was all she could see of it. She thought she might be looking towards the yard but was unsure.

From this window she could see several others. She stared at one from a room that seemed made of all windows; twisted shadows of brown and green were all that could be seen within. A dark figure appeared, a face like a smear of paint against wet glass. The figure was just far enough away and obscured by the glass, so that it was impossible to see if they were looking in the girls' direction.

'Is it her? The mistress?' Pigeon said, leaning her weight on Nancy, trying to see out of the window too.

'I don't know.'

The figure stood still and unmoving until she lifted her hand, touched the neckline of her dress, held her hand there as if she needed air.

'She can't see us,' Nancy said, but she couldn't shake the feeling that the woman could see them perfectly well. 'Come on,' she said, pushing against Pigeon who was still leaning on her. 'I'm tired of this now.'

She looked at the two staircases and tried to decide which was likely to head back to the part of the house that held their rooms; she was thoroughly sick of exploring. She'd prefer to wait safely in their room until she could return to the Brethren. She had much to think about and she had to warn Pigeon, now that she'd seen something of the house, not to wander, to stick to Patience, who at least seemed kind and sane. There might be other rooms like the doll room but worse, places that would frighten her. Other skeletons.

'She's gone,' Pigeon said and turned away from the window. She looked at the staircases and said, 'This one.'

Nancy shrugged and followed.

They were greeted by locked door after locked door. Once they found they were accidentally retracing their steps somehow. Finally, they emerged into the large hall; a balcony ran around the top floor and they peered down to the tile, past the faded old tiger and the creeping ivy leaves.

'How do we get down, Nancy?' Pigeon said.

'The main stairs must be nearby.'

Nancy went around to the other side of the hall and opened a door at random. It led onto a passage and she started down it. Around a corner she was relieved to find herself standing at the top of a staircase and Pigeon followed her, hopping down two steps at a time. A few moments later they were both staring in disbelief at yet more stairs upwards, a blank door at the top.

Nancy was about to turn back when Pigeon skipped up the steps and pushed open the door.

Greenish light spilled into the doorway, bringing a smell of old leaves and mould.

The greenhouse was cold; several panes of glass were broken and a sheen of algae covered the roof. A strange mobile hung from a central beam: a mess of string and stones, feathers and bones. Large troughs of earth sat on either side of the long, thin room. The turret was just visible through the dirty glass, closer than Nancy had seen it yet. Pots were precariously balanced on rotten wooden benches. All the plants seemed to be dead except for green searching tendrils of ivy, which stretched across the ground, and mushrooms that pushed themselves out of heaps of soil in the corners and edges. A leafless rose sketched a thorny ascent into the roof, a single red flower falling apart, moisture dripping from its petals.

'Winter is never a good season for my greenhouse.' Spider stood in the doorway at the other end of the room and gestured at the blackened leaves. 'These will all spring back into life in a few months, I can promise you. Beautiful flowers: tall spires of foxglove and the rich blue of aconite.' She touched a small grey-leaved shrub, 'Even lavender. The greenhouse used to be warm and smelt of jasmine back in my mother's day, before he stopped her heating it and before—' She cut herself off and reached up to touch the rose, which disintegrated, falling at her feet, the damp petals sticking to her skirt.

'You were exploring?' she asked and, seeing the white stick in Nancy's hand, stepped forwards and took it. She looked at it and then looked back at Nancy. 'Where did you get this?'

'The crow had it.'

Spider nodded as if that was an expected answer. She turned. 'This way.' She led them through the far door in the greenhouse and down passages, through twists and turns. 'This stair leads to the kitchen, where you'll want to go for meals.'

She stopped in the middle of a blank passage and opened a door in the panelling that was almost invisible when closed. They passed through and were soon standing outside their bedroom.

As they walked past her into the room, Spider said, 'You found my dolls.'

Pigeon nodded enthusiastically. 'Lots of dolls, big ones and small ones. And one of Nancy.'

Spider smiled and the blank humourlessness of it chilled Nancy. 'Oh good. I did so want you to see my dolls.'

She closed the door and Nancy jerked towards it, not wanting to be shut in, dreading the sound of a key. But the sound never came and when, after a few breaths, Nancy opened the door to look out into the passage, she found it empty and still.

When Nancy walked into the meeting hall of the Charitable Brethren the next day, no one noticed her. They were riveted by the spectacle on the stage. The people at the back had risen from the benches to have a better view and the lectern was placed to one side.

Darner stood, tall and stern, above Mrs Aldridge. She lay face down with her arms spread wide and, judging by the shaking of her shoulders, she was crying violently.

'Becoming humble is one of the most important parts of our work for Our Lord,' Darner was saying. Always the same opening address during the humiliations. Some of the Brethren knew it by heart and would mutter along with him, their voices rising up to join his at the important moments. 'We give our pride...' (*our pride*, the Brethren murmured) '...as we give our bodies, our bodies and souls that always belong to him...' (*belong to him*) '...and are never ours,' (*never ours*). 'The humiliations might seem a cruelty to outsiders, but they do not understand the vital work...' (*vital work*) '...we are doing here. The word humiliation coming, as it does, from the Latin *humiliare*: to humble.'

Nancy had always wondered how a group that consisted of carpenters and street sweepers and overburdened mothers could need to be further humbled. Yet there was something in this public penitence that left the members elated afterwards. They felt cleansed, their spirits winging upwards to heaven. Not humbled at all. She thought it might be an effect of the crying; she'd noticed how a really violent sobbing cry could leave you feeling as if a stiff, cold breeze had run through your soul.

Nancy slid onto a bench near the back of the room. A woman further along looked at her and nudged her neighbour. A ripple of whispers ran through the nearby Brethren. Nancy fixed her eyes ahead of her.

On the stage, Darner was reading from the prostrated woman's letter to Christ from the previous Sunday. Mrs Aldridge coughed a few quiet sobs into the floorboards. Mr Bevel stood with folded arms at the side of the stage, scowling at nothing in particular.

'*I spoke at a little length to a man who was neither a brother in our family in Christ nor my own husband. The man brought materials for my husband who is a cabinet maker and when he stayed to talk, I did not turn him away.* Well, sister,' Darner said, 'this is not how we expect our sisters to behave, is it Brethren?'

He turned towards the group and everyone in the room chanted, 'It is anathema'.

'What are you?' He shouted and stamped his foot, which echoed loud on the wooden stage.

Mrs Aldridge muttered something.

'Say it louder!' He stamped again. Nancy knew from experience how that stamp travelled through the wood.

'A sinner. An awful sinner,' the woman said.

'A sinner!' cried Darner and the congregation together in a roar of disapproval. 'What will you do?' He shouted. 'How will you atone?'

'I'll pray that I might sin no more.'

'Sinner!' called the congregation.

'You will pray on your knees. Here,' he stamped, 'for the whole night, tonight.'

'Amen!' the congregation shouted, arms raised.

All of them had done this penance at some point, felt the pain of the hard floor and the stretching out of the night.

'And what must we all do?' Darner turned to the whole audience.

They responded. 'We must seek to raise ourselves up in the Lord's sight.'

'Blessed be the Brethren.'

'Blessed be the Brethren!'

Darner now addressed Mrs Aldridge again. 'Rise! And go forth! Be humbled and improved.'

She gathered herself up, slowly rising to her knees and then her feet. Her hands clutched her wooden cross. Almost everyone, once humiliated, took their time to stand afterwards, as if they had been physically knocked down by the words Darner had spoken above them. She curtsied to Darner and he placed a hand on her head in blessing, looking deep into her eyes. She left the stage, head up, joining her family who patted her arm and whispered to her.

Someone passed her a handkerchief and she wiped her tears away, folding her hands in front of her skirt, bright eyed, waiting for Darner to recommence.

Darner turned to the room and spread his arms. 'And next we will seek to humble—'

Nancy stood. 'Me. If you please, Mr Darner.'

A ripple of whispers and shuffling dresses ran around the room and the Brethren all turned to look at her.

She stepped into the aisle.

Darner, skin pale and eyes wide, stared at her.

'You. What are you doing here?'

'I've been called to repent. To be humbled.' She stepped forwards and he took a step back as if she had threatened him.

'Repent?'

She nodded and tried her best to look meek.

'Oh, good girl,' Mrs Aldridge said and clapped, cheeks glowing with pleasure, smiling widely. People nearby took up the clapping and it began to spread.

'Quiet,' said Darner, calmly but with a force to his voice and the clapping fell away into silence as if cut off.

The whole room seemed to hold its breath.

'Tells us your sins, tell us what you seek redemption for and then maybe you can come up here and be humbled. Speak!'

'In my sin and my grief after my father's death, I blamed you. I am very sorry.' She bowed her head. 'I'm sure you did what you thought was best.' There was nodding and a murmur of sympathy. Someone expressed surprise in a whisper and murmured explanations hummed. 'It was a sin. I understand that now and I can only beg that you will show forgiveness.'

'I watched her on the street. There was an incident. She had just cursed two boys and I witnessed their subsequent demise under the wheels of a dray.' Darner's deep voice filled the room, every word clear and powerful.

One of the children gave a small scream and then cried out, 'It's true, then. She's a witch.'

Nancy, baffled, shook her head. 'I didn't do anything to make that happen.'

'You wished it, you know you wished it. I saw it in your face. And then they died!'

'I can't make things happen by wishing.' Exasperation came into her voice and then a fragment of doubt. Matchsticks breaking like small frail bones, a fire roaring up behind Darner. She shook her head.

'Ill-wishing an enemy with hatred and revenge in your heart is tantamount to witchcraft.' Darner pointed at her. 'Sin-ridden woman! The worm in your heart will damn you.'

Nancy swallowed something in her throat. 'I've always had a rebellious heart, Prophet. But I hope that I am redeemable by your faith and holiness.' Something inside her winced at these words and she continued. 'Didn't Jesus sacrifice himself for worse sinners even than me? So, I ask that you forgive me, give me one last chance and allow me to rejoin you.'

A few moments of silence made her fear that she had overdone it, but a few people standing nearby broke into loud and spontaneous applause at this little speech and the applause quickly spread until almost everyone was clapping. Even Bevel reluctantly joined in.

Darner narrowed his eyes and watched Nancy. He smiled. 'This is a difficult decision. Here we have the opportunity to save a soul from the depths: a young woman who wishes to blame others for her own faults. For if you, Nancy,' he gestured towards her as if displaying her to the other Brethren, a piece of evidence before them, 'if you had not treated Mr Bevel so badly, if you had simply taken your punishment and learnt from it as you should, would your father have suffered and died? Or would he still be here among us?' He spread his arms wide and looked around, sad to find a congregation lacking one Nigel Ratcliffe. 'If you cannot humble yourself by seeing your own faults, what hope is there for you?'

Nancy dug her nails into her palms, squeezed down her hatred and anger.

He continued. 'It is a great risk. Will I be allowing the viper among us? Damning others to fall with her? Inflicting a bad influence on our impressionable children? She has already taken her sister away and I note that Polly is not returned with her. For someone who pretends to care so much about her sibling, she has not brought her here, where she can be safe and well fed. Tell us, Nancy, where is little Polly, whom many among us remember with such fondness?'

The rage that had flared up at the suggestion she might not care sufficiently for her sister threatened to break out. She clenched her fists and breathed hard until she could trust herself to speak.

'She is with a trusted friend. Safe and well.' Doubt suddenly swept over Nancy. Was this true? Could she trust Patience and her mistress? They were nearly total strangers – she had known them for only two days and had left her sister there with them, alone. She pushed away the fear.

'Why not bring her with you?'

'She's with a friend and she'd rather be with that friend. I'm sorry for it, it's my fault, but I'm sure I can bring her round eventually, bring her back.'

Mr Darner gave her a look that clearly said that he didn't believe her, but he let it pass. 'So, to return to my question – to risk readmitting the viper in the hopes of saving her soul, or deny her entry in order to protect you all?' His eyes swept the room. 'I will pray on this. I request silence as I do so.'

He folded his hands, turned his back to them all and sunk to his knees, head bowed.

Silence fell on the room. A silence that consisted of people looking to their neighbour with raised eyebrows, a shrug, a scowl, a shaken head.

She stared at the back of Darner's head, careful to keep her face neutral. After a little while he stirred and everyone in the room straightened their backs and raised their heads. He turned to face them all.

He focused his gaze on Nancy, spread his arms wide and said, 'Come, child. Never let it be said that the Charitable Brethren turned a soul away. Come and be held to account.'

A few minutes later she lay face down on the stage, the smell of sawdust in her nose and the wood against her cheek. Her father had built this stage and she felt his hands slotting the planks into place, tapping the nails in: one, two and a small third tap that nestled the head of the nail flat and neat. Explaining to her each small thing as she sat and watched him work.

Darner's lecture on her shortcomings became a rant, his feet stamped and the congregation shouted but she found she could ignore it. It became a loud ringing noise in her ears, swinging like the bell and she smiled into her father's woodwork because everything was going according to plan.

Chapter Eighteen
Despair

Pigeon was sitting alone on her sister's bed, a few trinkets spread on the blanket in front of her.

Spider's eye was to the hole in the door, long fingers spread either side of her head, peering. She had not been able to settle since Nancy had gone. Since she could not be with Nancy, watching Darner directly, she had intended to watch the Hall from the shop. Instead, she found she was drawn to Pigeon; Pigeon was the key to Nancy, and Nancy was both opportunity and threat in Spider's crusade against Darner. What did that make Pigeon? Another opportunity, perhaps?

The girl had returned to the room of dolls and taken down the doll that looked like Nancy. The Nancy doll now lay on the bed playing with the trinkets, according to Pigeon's game.

Seeing it there prickled and itched at Spider's mind. She wanted to reclaim it but that would frighten and alarm the child, and she wanted to avoid doing that. She would have to choose her moment. If only the child wouldn't cling to it and drag it everywhere.

The other things lying on the blanket were a pair of masks taken from one of the wall displays and two feathers. One was a crow feather, which the child might have found anywhere. Corbeau might even have given it willingly. The other was a peacock feather, which Pigeon must have taken from the vase on the table in the library. The peacock feather's eye waved above the girl's head as she passed it to and fro, watching the edges flutter.

The evil eye, bad luck – that was what the peacock feather was supposed to bring. But bad lack for whom? Whose eye, and whose luck?

Pigeon clambered off the bed, clutching the doll and Spider's breath quickened. What was the girl going to do? The girl hugged the doll with one hand and peeled back the bedsheets with the other. She laid the Nancy doll in the bed and carefully tucked her in. Her thin voice was just audible through the door. 'There you go, Nancy. We've got to go to bed, Patience said. Now I've got to blow the candle out myself because you can't. I'll be brave.' She pulled back the sheets of her bed in preparation and approached the candle. Spider watched with amusement. She did not remember ever being afraid of the dark.

Pigeon blew the candle out and, in the darkness, came the scuffling of her feet as she hurried back to the bed. She must have run into it as there was a small bang and an 'oof'. After a few moments silence she said. 'I did it, Nancy. I did it. Sleep well.'

For a little while the darkness beyond the door was filled with small rustlings and sniffings, but they gradually faded away. The girl was likely asleep. Spider sought out a candle and placed it on a small table a little way from the door so that the light would trickle into the room.

She opened the door and listened to Pigeon's gentle snores. She had planned to simply take the doll and leave but now, somehow, she wanted to linger. Pigeon's cheek was lit with a gentle sweep of orange candlelight and her eyelashes rested there, an infinite softness. Spider stood looking at the bundled girl for a little while. She could just smell the warm sweetness of the child's breath in the air around her, disappearing into the cold of the room. A thick feeling rose in her throat and she turned away. She took the doll from under the sheets on Nancy's bed, and without looking at Pigeon again, head bowed, she slipped from the room and closed the door quietly behind her.

Chapter Nineteen
Justice

Spider drifted in and out of sleep. She slipped between moments of memory and dreams.

An attendant's voice: 'Shall I pull her all the way out, sir?' Whitehead, frantic. 'Is she breathing?'

The world, foggy and nonsensical. Anger in her stomach burning something away. Darner banished by Whitehead.

The attendant again: 'Surely this is a police matter, sir?' His hands trembling, he lifted her, water cascading from her. The Sara part of her was left behind in the water like discarded clothes. Weakness.

When she found herself in the infirmary, Mrs Whitehead's hands had been tense, her fingers trembling, her instructions abrupt. 'Lift your legs', 'Sit forwards so I can prop you with this pillow', 'Use this if you need to vomit', as a pan was held up to her. The coughing seemed to have passed now which was a relief, though there were bruises dark against her skin where Darner's hands had pushed her down. Her knuckles were lightly bandaged, scraped raw against the canvas. Seeing her hands gave her a strangely heightened feeling. Unable to grip. Nothing to hold. She held the sides of the bed.

Although outdoors it was bright and sunny, in this room with its pale light and open windows there was a chill breeze. She pulled the bedclothes up to her chin.

In the next room, she could hear the murmur of the doctor's voice as he spoke to his wife, who, as matron of the whole asylum, was in particularly close control of the infirmary ward. It was she that was so insistent that windows should be open whenever possible, and held that it was almost always possible.

The door opened and Doctor Whitehead came in. He looked far from his usual neat self. His hair was sticking up from where he had absent-mindedly been running his hands through it and his collar sat awry where one of the studs had fallen out.

'Morning, Miss Atherton.' His eyes flicked around the room but wouldn't rest on her. He checked her over, touching her as little as possible. 'I hope you are feeling well?' He barely gave her an opportunity to mutter an answer before he was hurrying away. 'Well, can't linger I'm afraid, good morning.'

Spider drifted into a white sleep and woke when the door opened. She was astonished to see Lambert shuffle in sideways, glancing over his shoulder as if trying to avoid being seen. There was only one other patient in the room, who was asleep facing the wall. Lambert looked at Spider nervously. He approached the bed, his cap in his hands.

'Hello there, miss.' The cap circled around in his twitching fingers.

'Morning. Or is it afternoon?'

'It's a quarter past two, miss.'

'Thank you.'

He shifted from one foot to the other and glanced over his shoulder again.

'Well, what is it?'

'I was there, miss, when it happened.' Spider recognised his voice now. He had been the attendant lifting her out of the water. So that hadn't been a dream. He came close to the bed and leant over, speaking quietly. 'He's not going to get rid of him.'

Spider guessed that the first 'he' was Doctor Whitehead and the second, Darner.

'It's a disgrace!' Lambert's hands were trembling and his face flushed.

Spider sat up a little.

'What he lets people get away with,' the man's eyes were wet, 'it makes a man ashamed. I got this job to help poor people like my little Ellie and now look.' He waved a hand indicating her lying in the bed but the gesture widened and took in the whole asylum.

'Ellie?'

'My little girl. She was never in her right mind, not from the start and…' his voice crumbled at the edges. 'Well. It ended badly.'

'Until I'm allowed out of this bed there's nothing I can do.'

'I'm going to write. To the Justice of the Peace who gave Doctor Whitehead his license. Will you tell him what happened when he comes to look into it? He might get the Lunacy Commission involved.' The poor man looked terrified. His eyes were red. He looked as though he hadn't slept.

He continued. 'I'm going to go, I can't stand working in a place like this, not any longer. God knows what I'll do instead, but I can't…' He sniffed. 'Well.' He calmed. 'So I might as well do the honest thing on my way out. But will you tell?'

'I can assure you I'd never tell a lie to protect Darner. Or Whitehead, or any of the others. But will they believe me? I'm just a lunatic.' She smiled. An angry smile.

'But there's my testimony, too.'

She needed Darner to be here in the asylum, within reach, to exact her revenge, but if this man was bracing himself to do something about the conditions at Lansdowne Asylum, she could not bring herself to stand in his way. But she could delay him, just by a few days, in the hope she could find a way to reach Darner herself.

'They'll never believe you, Mr Lambert. Just a few lines of malevolence from a disgruntled member of staff, that's what they'll think. Even if they do come, who will they believe? A bunch of respectable men, or one attendant and a lunatic woman.'

Lambert wrung his hands. 'No, miss, no. Surely they'll come and look? Talk to you. And I think, if it all comes out, Whitehead will have to admit to it. He's pretended not to see the worst of it but if it was there in his face, and a commissioner was asking him in a stern voice, I think he'd let it all go.'

Spider considered this. Whitehead was a weak man. She guessed that when he started out he'd been a well-meaning, honest physician. But he'd allowed Darner's influence to grow and then, when he found where that led, he was not able to face the consequences, nor brave enough to expose it. Lambert was right: if he were exposed, he would not be able to withstand questioning. She wanted Darner to face the full consequences of his actions, to die writhing in pain, but the asylum as a whole needed to be purged; she could not do that herself with merely a few foxglove plants from the garden. Not quickly. There was also the consideration that she had survived this incident. She might not survive another.

'Once I'm out of the infirmary I'll write too,' she said. 'You'll have to enclose my letter with yours. If I try to send it directly to them, it'll be read.'

There were voices in the outer office. 'Yes. I can work it.'

The door opened and Lambert jumped. He stood upright and turned to leave.

'What are you doing here, Lambert?' Mrs Whitehead asked, surprised as he made for the door. Darner stood behind her.

'Just wanted to give my best wishes to Miss Atherton, ma'am. See she was all right. I was worried she was quite bad, but I'm glad to see she's much better now.' His eyes slid away from Darner and he scuttled out past the matron and the chaplain who looked down at him as if he were a cockroach.

Several days later, Spider was sitting in the day room with several other patients and a couple of attendants. The patients were supposed to be mending a pile of torn and damaged asylum clothing as Miss Gavins read to them from the Bible, but several had stopped to listen, or were pretending to listen while they gazed out of the window. No one seemed to have noticed that they were a group not usually allowed sharp things.

Miss Dutton sat with a needle in one hand and stared at it.

Every member of staff Spider had seen since her return from the infirmary seemed distracted. They stood in corners and whispered, some would not meet the others' eyes, and Spider had heard one woman say loudly, 'What a scandalous accusation!' as another attendant scurried out of a room, head bowed. Their eyes followed Spider as she walked about, and she heard them turn to talk to each other after she passed.

Miss Hawthorn looked up from a patch she was sewing and then she laughed, the sound bursting into the fractured silence of the room as if a tray of tea things had been dropped. She pointed out of the window. Sullivan was sprinting across the fine lawn, face red, mud kicking up from his feet. A gardener shouted 'Oi!' as he went past.

'What's Mr Sullivan doing? Where's he going like that?' Hawthorn said. 'He looks so silly.'

Miss Gavins and the other attendant exchanged a look and then the other woman slipped quietly out of the room.

'I'm sure everything is fine, Miss Hawthorn,' Miss Gavins said. 'Come now, get on with your sewing. Your stitches are very fine and we must make good use of you.'

Miss Hawthorn beamed at the compliment and sat down, Sullivan forgotten.

In the distance two smart carriages drove through the lodge gate, up the drive, then out of sight. Spider thought one of them had a crest on its door.

'Maybe we're getting a private patient from a good family,' one of the patients said. 'That was a fancy carriage.'

'That certainly could be it,' Miss Gavins said, and gestured to the patient who'd spoken to carry on with her work.

'We've already got a Lord's son and a baronet,' Hawthorn said.

'There are no Lord's offspring here unless we've got some bastards,' Miss Gavins said drily, 'but the baronet is true enough.'

Miss Hawthorn objected about the Lord's son and Miss Gavins set about telling her that the so-called Lord's son suffered from delusions and his word could not be trusted. They were still arguing when Sullivan walked back across the lawn, mopping his brow with a handkerchief.

The other attendant came back into the room and whispered in Miss Gavins' ear. She paled and exclaimed, 'Oh!' Then she looked at Spider and Spider understood that Sullivan's sprint and the carriages must both be the result of Lambert's letter. The disturbance had to be an inspection from the Justice of the Peace or the Lunacy Commission. Too soon. She had not reached Darner yet, and now she realised where Sullivan had been running to.

'What have you done?' Miss Gavins asked her, acidic and pointed.

'Shush!' the other woman said. 'You don't know it was her. Lord knows there's enough.'

'Nonsense. It's just good discipline.'

'Is it?' the woman asked firmly, and put the Bible back into Miss Gavins hands. 'I think reading and sewing quietly would be a good idea.'

Spider watched Sullivan enter a side door and she knew. Darner had been warned. What would he do?

The next day the staff table at breakfast was nearly empty with neither the Whiteheads nor Darner anywhere to be seen.

As Spider rose from the table, Miss Gavins, pale and agitated, approached her. 'Dr Whitehead would like to see you in his study please, Miss Atherton.' The rumour the Lunacy Commission were in the asylum had spread rapidly the previous day and the staff were both distracted and officious, liable to tell you to do something, then berate you for doing it. The doors to all the padded rooms were firmly shut, presumably upon the most disruptive of patients, who were nowhere to be seen.

Miss Gavins led Spider through the gardens towards a house that stood apart from the main building within its own grounds. They walked between beds of roses and lavender, the smell almost sickly in the bright sun. A woman opened a side door to them.

'Mrs Whitehead asked me to bring Miss Atherton to the doctor's study.'

The house seemed dark after the bright light outside but, as her eyes adjusted, Spider saw that it was comfortably furnished. Each wooden object gleamed with polish. Paintings hung on every wall, depicting gentle landscapes or hunting scenes of hounds and horses running through gentle landscapes. Rivers lined with poplars seemed to be the doctor's preferred view.

'Here we are,' said the housekeeper, grasping the door handle and swinging it brusquely inwards.

'Miss Atherton, sir,' she said.

'Come in, come in.' Mr Whitehead's voice drifted out of the room, quiet and sad.

Spider found Mr Riverton, the Lunacy Commissioner, sitting behind what must have been Dr Whitehead's desk with an authoritative presence. Dr Whitehead stood to one side and polished his glasses. He sagged at the shoulder as if weighed down by a heavy pack. In one corner a young man perched on a stool over a paper-strewn folding table, a pen eager in his ink-stained fingers.

'You are Miss Atherton?' Riverton spoke, his voice filling the room as if it belonged in every crevice. The scratching of the young man's pen began.

'Yes, sir. We have met before.'

The man's chin shifted back a little as if being addressed by a lunatic who seemed to be expecting the politeness of an introduction was rather an affront. He peered at her.

'Ah yes, the penitent.'

'Mr Riverton,' Whitehead said, 'is a Lunacy Commissioner. Please answer him as best you can. There have been some rather distressing incidents and he is here to look into them.' He gripped the wing of an armchair that was placed to look out of the window and swayed slightly. He pulled a handkerchief from his pocket and mopped his brow. The window looked out towards the front of the asylum. The new building work going on in the rear of the site was invisible: Doctor Whitehead's great works to take the asylum into the future, to take a greater number of county patients, paupers and criminals, as well as private. But from this house, it seemed almost like the country home of a minor peer. He saw her looking out of the window and turned to look at the view himself. He said, 'I often used to read here, so that I could see my asylum. I was so very proud of it. I modelled the regime on all the best thinkers, visited Connolly at Hanwell, took on all the principles of a moral regime. And that is why I am so very troubled by what happened to you the other day. Such a thing should never have happened at Lansdowne Asylum. And the other…' his voice trailed away, 'the other things.' He closed his eyed for a moment and then, waving a hand in the direction of Mr Riverton, he muttered, 'Please,' and perched on the edge of the armchair. His hopes, his dreams for his work were all that seemed to concern him.

Riverton cleared his throat and said, 'Miss Atherton. I wish you to tell me, in your own words, what happened with Mr Darner in the hydrotherapy room. Mr Lambert has already given us his account, as has Dr Whitehead here, so we will be able to check your accuracy of recall.'

The young man in the corner sat up and readied his pen.

Spider said, 'I asked for help but you ignored me.'

Riverton flushed and Whitehead hurried to speak, 'Well, well, dear, he's here now. Don't fret.'

This Riverton already thought of her as an unreliable witness at best, probably a liar, an embroiderer of facts. Did he even believe truth was possible from the mouth of a madwoman? She wanted to scream at him all that had happened but it wouldn't matter. She remembered Lambert, sacrificing his job to bring this man here. She couldn't waste the chance, however tainted.

'Mr Darner tried to kill me by drowning me in the hydrotherapy bath. That's all there is to it.'

Whitehead started and fidgeted, shaking his head.

Riverton scoffed. 'Dr Whitehead is of the opinion the man was trying to baptise you or possibly submerge you as they did the witches of old. That being surrounded by lunatics he had himself succumbed to a religious mania and that, for some reason, you were its focus.'

'He did have a particular dislike of Miss Atherton,' Whitehead interjected. 'Because of the witchcraft in her case.'

'He mistreated me from the start,' she said, 'and made nonsensical accusations.'

'Accusations of witchcraft are always nonsensical given the non-existence of witchcraft,' Mr Riverton said. 'But that does not mean a lunatic cannot believe in it and act upon such a belief.' He eyed Spider.

'A half-finished sewing project and some botanical preparations, that is all. My uncle's evidence for locking me away.'

'Evidence of what?'

'My witchcraft, my murderous intent, my lunacy.'

'Your behaviour is not in question here, Miss Atherton. We are looking into the reprehensible and potentially criminal behaviour of the missing chaplain, Mr Darner, and several of the attendants.'

A wire of cold ran down her spine to her legs and she stumbled, leaned on a chair.

'So he has gone.' Her eyes flicked between Whitehead and Mr Riverton.

'He has not been seen since we arrived on the premises.' Riverton's lips were thin and compressed.

'He's probably with the archbishop,' Whitehead said miserably.

'Possibly, but the archbishop is not God,' Mr Riverton answered.

Spider didn't much care what happened to the attendants, the asylum or Whitehead, but if she were to find Darner, she needed to be free. She pulled her attention away from her anger.

'Doctor Whitehead. My uncle showed you, I believe, my bottles of foxglove, poppy and wormwood? Did he also show you my harmless tinctures and preparations? Extractions from lavender and tansy and rose? Do you look with suspicion on every pharmacist handling arsenic or every gardener planting foxgloves?"

'Are you suggesting that your uncle was lying? To… what? Have you locked up?'

'My uncle was genuinely concerned, I am sure. He had an illness recently which has obviously made him suspicious.'

'He said that his health improved when he stopped drinking the cordial you gave him.'

Mr Riverton looked impatiently from one to the other of them. 'This is not the question. We must take Miss Atherton's account of the incident.'

Spider ignored him and addressed Whitehead. 'Perhaps there was indeed something in the preparation that disagreed with him. I don't know, I'm not a doctor. All I know is that he didn't fall ill because of any addition that I made to the drink. You are a medical man, you must see patients that occasionally sicken or improve for no discernible reason?'

'Well, that's a truth that every doctor must face, though some of my colleagues in medicine would like to pretend it never happens,' Whitehead said reluctantly.

'I know very well what a state of poverty I would be reduced to, if not for my uncle's kindness. Why should I seek to harm him?'

'I'm sorry to be so blunt, Miss Atherton, but are you not his next of kin?' Whitehead said.

'I don't believe so. There is a male cousin who will inherit first.' Cousin Franklin, subject of her mother's laments.

'All I know is that your uncle said that you would inherit his property, and that you knew it.'

Spider stilled, careful to hide her reaction to this news. 'I did not know it.'

Riverton slammed the flat of his hand down on his papers. 'This is not the question at hand here! We are getting away from the point of this interview.'

Spider turned on him. 'What is the point of this interview? Your job is to make sure these places are not disgusting pits of cruelty. You seem to have failed.'

'How dare you!' Riverton rose.

'Wait, wait. Both of you.' Whitehead interjected palms out. 'Mr Riverton, I am starting to wonder if I may not have made a mistake here. And given the experiences this poor young lady has endured, and the uncertain future of this institution, I do wonder if we might not consider the question.'

'It would be one mistake among many,' Mr Riverton sneered at Whitehead.. 'Your failures, your mistakes.' He looked angrily at Spider.

Whitehead swallowed and looked down at his hands. 'Indeed, and I am trying to make amends now. My poor asylum.'

'If this gets out, it will be an enormous scandal, Whitehead. Your "poor asylum"! If only–' He suddenly recollected that he was speaking in front of a patient and closed his mouth.

Mr Whitehead rubbed his forehead, 'Miss Atherton, I understand your anger. If I promise to review your case with Mr Riverton here before he leaves, will you please tell him your version of the incident? Not what you think Darner's intentions were, just the bare facts of what he did?'

Spider looked searchingly at the man. Behind his glasses, his eyes were moist and his hand trembled a little but he met her gaze. She nodded and seated herself opposite the commissioner. The clerk dipped his pen again and she began.

Chapter Twenty
Cataclysm

Nancy spent the first few days watching Darner and the others. She already knew the general day-to-day routine of the Brethren of course, but exactly when and where and how Darner and his cronies moved through the Hall was not something she had ever needed to take notice of. Mr Herbert always went to the chapel to pray at a quarter to four. Mr Bevel's daily chastisement of one or other of the boys always took place at precisely four o'clock (and one of them always seemed to have deserved it). Mr Darner had a cold bath on the Saturday night before the most important weekly service on Sunday and must not be disturbed that evening; she had seen Robbie Johnson and his father, who generally acted as Mr Darner's manservant, carrying buckets of water up to Darner's room. Robbie was saying, 'Why cold? That's what I don't understand,' and was quickly shushed and told it was a sign of the Prophet's holiness.

There was also the laudanum, but she had known about that for some time. No one else in the Brethren knew, of that she was sure, but her father had let slip something he had discovered when working in the Prophet's private rooms. It had been the first small break in his faith. Nancy wondered if it was enough, whether she ought to take it back to Spider yet. She had already drawn Spider the layout of the Hall, showing where his rooms were and she suspected the Saturday evening seclusion was more about the drug than the bath.

Nancy stood on the stone floor under the bell tower. She looked up at the ceiling, the floor of the ringing chamber above her, white-washed and grey in the corners with the rags of old spider webs. Above that she imagined the open mouths of the big bells, heavy and still. She could still see the bells in her mind's eye; she could still hear them, feel the weight of them, the way the whole tower had shifted slightly as they had swung. Her head spun and she brought it down, stood for a few moments as the swirling stopped, a high chiming in her ears.

She felt him behind her before he spoke. 'What are you doing here?' She turned to see Darner, his eyes hard on her.

'Just passing,' Nancy said, 'and I looked up at the tower, which made me dizzy.' The truth.

'Come,' he commanded and stalked off in the direction of his rooms. She followed along, reminding herself that she was to seem calm and repentant. *Seem*. She didn't have to mean it; he just had to believe it.

The Hall was silent – everyone seemed to be out or busy in some quiet fashion elsewhere. As she followed in Darner's wake, Nancy began to feel afraid. What if he'd guessed? What if he knew? She looked over her shoulder. No one was around at all.

Long green velvet curtains hung either side of the tall window that looked out onto the rear yard of the Brethren Hall; it was getting dark outside. The room was higher than the yard so that anyone outside would need to climb up to look in at the window.

It was a hard-edged room. The chair by the desk was straight and high-backed, the rug of a thin style. The books, packed tight and upright on the shelves, did not lounge and lean. Not many of the Brethren had seen inside this room. Fewer had seen beyond it into his private sitting room and bedroom.

She took the opportunity to memorise the layout of the room and wished she could see his adjoining rooms.

Darner stood behind his wide desk, his back to the window, and stared at her. 'I do not believe you actually repent your behaviour, Miss Ratcliffe, yet I'm glad to see you've realised you need the Brethren. I have no doubt your return is about self-interest rather than faith.' A muscle in his cheek jumped as he clenched his jaw around his words. 'You need a strong hand, and without your parents and until you marry, I'm your only hope of discipline and salvation though you may not know it. Providence returns you to me that I might do what needs to be done. It pleases me that God gives you this choice; it is me or disgrace and the workhouse.'

'I could go to my mother,' Nancy blurted out and immediately regretted it.

'Your mother! You could run to your mama, could you, little girl?'

'She lives in a village near Whitby. I could find her.' She stood firm, chin jutted out.

Darner laughed. A genuine laugh and it chilled Nancy; it was the first time she had ever heard him give a real laugh of amusement, not just some satirical bark or scornful sneer.

'You wonder why I laugh. Let me show you.' He rose and went to a line of drawers labelled with the alphabet. He opened the one labelled 'R' and flipped through the envelopes within. 'Here we are.' He retrieved a letter and threw it on the desk with a slap.

Nancy could read but not easily and she eyed the envelope with concern. Darner watched her, a cruel twist at the corner of his mouth.

She took a deep breath and examined the address. Mr Ratcliffe, c/o the Charitable Brethren. A letter to her father.

'Why do you have his letter?' Her father could puzzle out a few words but he was no reader and a letter would have been a challenge he might have brought to her. He never had. 'Did he ask you to read it for him?'

'No. Your father never saw it.'

'You stole it.'

'I sought to spare him.'

She looked up at him, her eyes expressing the disbelief at a charitable motive. Then she drew the letter from the envelope. With relief, she saw the copperplate handwriting was neat and readable. She would not have to ask Darner to read for her. Her thumb stroked her father's name as she worked out the next words.

Dear Mr Ratcliffe,
It is my sad duty to write to you and inform you of your wife's death.

Nancy felt it like a blow to her chest. Her eyes wouldn't focus. She squeezed them shut and when she opened them, she found Darner was watching her, mouth tight against a smile he was holding back. She hated him. Pure hatred at his cruel superiority, his pleasure in her pain. She knew he had smiled as he had thrown her father on the streets to die, just as he smiled now watching the letter do its work.

'You didn't tell him?'

'No. He was a sick man. Weak in mind and body.'

'Not too sick to turn out on to the streets.' Nancy spat out the words and forced her eyes back to the paper. Darner did not answer but continued to watch her.

> I understand your wife returned here alone in an attempt to escape the demon temptations so prevalent in the city. I am afraid she could not escape them even here and they finally claimed her life. She would not allow me to write to you while she was alive, but I have considered it my duty now that she has passed away. She will receive a pauper's burial and if you or your children are ever in a position to visit her grave, I will provide any information you require.

The writer identified himself as the vicar of the parish and signed his name followed by a string of letters that meant nothing to her.

Dead.

The word clear in her mind as if it was on one of Spider's bone sticks.

Dead.

The hope that one day she and Pigeon might travel to Yorkshire with Lil and find their mother was futile. That hope that they might get there and find her cheerful and healthy was like a picture drawn in dust on a window; Darner had swept it away with a contemptuous flick. It was just her and Pigeon. She ought to have known.

'I never met your mother,' Darner said. 'But that letter makes it clear she was a degenerate. Your father was a good man on the whole, though weak. He could never bring you, or apparently his wife, to behave properly.'

'You knew this and you kept it from him. You knew!' Anger soured in her belly as she tried to keep it contained.

Nancy made a move to tuck the letter into her pocket and Darner lunged forwards and grabbed her wrist.

'Oh no, you don't. I'll keep that,' he said, grabbing for the letter.

'What use is it to you?' She stretched it away from him and he snatched at it. She held on hard and the paper tore. She was left only with a small corner of the envelope. Darner kept hold of her and threw the paper into his fire. It crackled and burnt. Then he turned and, grabbing her shoulder, threw her face down on the rug.

She cried out and tried to get her hands under her. He put his foot on her back and pressed her down.

'Well, Nancy,' he said. 'I think we might need a daily humiliation, here in my office to help you reach a more genuine repentance. Shall we start now? One must take opportunities as the Lord offers them.'

She wriggled. 'Let go!' He pressed down harder.

'Your mother was a sinner, weak and unworthy and I fear you are too much in her mould, but never let it be said that we don't try.' He pushed down against her attempts to rise and her cheek slammed against the rug.

He continued. 'Of course you abandoned your father. Selfish to leave him when he needed a daughter's love in his illness.'

'I was going to come back for him.' She tried to push up. 'I did come back for Pigeon.'

'I don't believe you. You were going to go off and sin, and enjoy sinning. He left to find you and make you return. Foolish to do it immediately after his penance, perhaps, but we do not need to pretend your father was any kind of genius.'

She saw now what the story had been to the rest of the Brethren.

Nigel Ratcliffe had foolishly run off into the freezing night to look for his wayward daughter, still wet from his penance and had met his fate through his own fault.

'You…' Darner bent and, with his hand flat on the back of her head, pushed her face into the carpet so she couldn't talk. Frustrated rage swelled through her, tears running down her face. He was lying. But the vision of her father choosing to seek her out when he was unfit to be out in the cold still hurt her.

Nancy scrabbled and bucked against his restraint. Her fingers caught the leg of the small chair. She stretched and tugged and the chair toppled. He stepped back to avoid it, letting go of her head and she twisted, grabbed the chair and flung it at him, scrabbling to her feet. He laughed as the chair clattered feebly across the floor. She grabbed a paperweight and when it cracked against his shoulder his laughter stopped dead. Shock and then fury came into his eyes. She followed it with an inkwell which smashed against the wall, a spider mess of black ink against the yellow paint.

She ran.

Nancy pelted along the passage away from Darner's room. She didn't know where she was going. She bolted around a corner and ran dead into someone's chest.

They said, 'Oof!' as she stumbled sideways. Before she could right herself, a hand grabbed her arm and then her throat, and she was slammed against the wall.

Bevel leered down into her face. 'Now, where are we going in such a hurry, little miss?'

She dragged at his hand and he gave a laugh, tightening his grip a little. She choked and clawed at his hand around her throat. Her ears were ringing again. She put her foot against the wall and tried to push away, but that just made the pressure against her throat worse.

'Bevel! Keep a hold of her,' Darner swept along the passage, rage flooding his face so that his nose and eyes seemed outlined in blood rising to the skin. He grabbed Nancy's arm and pulled her towards him. Bevel changed his grip to the back of her collar, tight against her throat and between them they propelled her forwards. They seemed to know where they were going and Nancy quickly realised too. To the bell tower.

'What did she do?' Bevel asked as if she weren't there.

'She had the temerity to throw things at me because I told her the truth.'

Bevel grunted and gave her an extra shove. 'Little cat.'

She had failed. They would throw her out and that would be an end to it. She wouldn't be able to return to Spider with any information that could help them. She would have to return to her original thoughts: direct attack; blood under her fingernails. In some ways it was what she wanted, but what Lil had said that day on the road out front with the knife was true. If she were in gaol or, worse, was hung for a murderess, what would happen to Pigeon? Lil would do her best, no doubt, but Nancy wanted something more stable than Lil's life for Pidge, where she wouldn't know where her next meal was coming from or where her night's bed would be.

The two men pulled her into the entrance hall. Two Brethren members stopped to watch, open mouthed, until Bevel snarled, 'Get on.' They scurried into the chapel hall. Darner dropped Nancy's arm to fling open the door to the stairs, trusting Bevel to follow behind. Nancy pulled against his grip, but he just tightened it even further. Bevel walked past her, twisting her collar and dragging her, her feet tripping on the narrow steps of the spiral staircase, her breath cut off by her collar, then released, then cut off again, her hands trying to find the wall or steps for balance. If she fell, she would surely die, strangled by her own dress.

At the door to the ringing chamber, they paused. The door was open. This room's name made it sound elaborate and important, but it was just a small round room with two bell ropes at its centre, whitewashed and empty. She gasped for breath as Bevel shifted his grip to her arm, leaving her throat free.

Darner ran up the stairs to the belfry door. 'Bring her up.' His voice called down.

'I think—' Nancy tried to stop them.

'No thinking,' said Bevel, and pulled her up the first stairs.

'I'll do the humiliations. Like you said.' She stumbled up the stairs, looked up at Darner above her. 'In your room. I can listen.'

Bevel gave a short laugh. 'Too late, little witch.'

Darner said nothing. He pulled his cravat off. Bevel pushed her into the small space beside the bells and Darner shoved the cravat between her teeth. Behind the fabric she started to scream but it came out as a muffled whine. He tied it tightly behind her head, the knot pressing hard against her skull, fabric tight at the corners of her mouth, sound leeching up her throat, dammed up in her mouth. Then he tied her hands together and pushed her away. As she stumbled into the corner, tight under the eaves, the door slammed behind her and she heard a key in the lock. Their footsteps went down the stairs and shuffled into the room below.

Nancy turned to watch the bells. They'd left her free to move this time but taken her voice. Darner had not mentioned how long she was to stay up here but there was something in his face; something final and vicious that said he intended to leave her here until she were dead or broken.

The smaller bell started to swing. Then the larger.

They couldn't ring forever. They would have to stop at some point but she had to get through the ringing. The pain it caused her the last time, the way she still heard ringing at times, made her wonder if her ears would burst.

The first few notes of the bell hummed through her.

Quickly and clumsily with her tied hands she tore two small pieces of cloth from her dress and stuffed them into her ears.

Once the sound was dulled a little, its ringing blade of sound blunted, she tried to reach back to untie the knot of her gag but couldn't. The floor vibrated under her feet and she wondered how sturdy the bell tower truly was. The bells each swung hard against the braces holding them in place, the larger one shifting very slightly as it moved thanks to the broken part, a half-ton of bronze hefted back and forth to send its cry over the roofs.

She tried to hook her thumbs into the gag but it was too tight a fit over her jaw. She might be able to shift the knot down to her neck and that would give her the space to get it from her mouth. It was so tight and caught up in her hair that she felt a tearing as she pulled it down, scraping her mouth as she took it out. Now her mouth was free and her breathing clear of the wad of sweaty fabric, she turned her mind to freeing her hands.

The bells continued to swing and a pain was now pulsing in her right temple in time with the ringing bells. She screamed in her head for them to stop, to fall on the men below. Darner and Bevel were hauling at the ropes, knowing she was up here with the sound, each tug of the rope causing her pain. She wished the whole tower would fall on them, could feel it juddering under her feet; she pushed at it with her mind, a great mass of wood and brick. She wished it even if she would die, too.

She sat down and started to gnaw at the knots in the bootlaces Darner had used for her wrists. The vibration of the wooden floor under her transmitted up through her legs and into her pelvis, shaking her core. She tried to ignore it. There was something wrong in it. Last time the vibrations had been strong, painful and whole. This time there was a hitch in them, a shift, a difficulty. As she gnawed, she watched the wooden stay that was supposed to prevent the bell from rotating all the way over at the top of its swing. At each swing it touched its end point. A shift, a push – it hit the end stop harder than usual, then as it swung back the bell shifted in its seat slightly. Nancy's hands sighed open as the bootlace fell to the floor. There was a crack.

Half of the wooden stay was flung across the room as the bell fell over the top of its circle. Rope flew up through the hole in the floor, a cry and a thump coming from the men below. The rope end whipped towards her and she jerked away just in time. It narrowly missed her face and she stumbled back.

The larger bell spun wildly, the noise was chaotic, discordant and the other clanged. Something shifted in the supporting structure and the bell and its wheel fell through the floor with a crash. The smaller bell tottered for a moment before slamming after it, followed by a rain of smaller bangs and thuds until silence.

Nancy pulled the cloth fragments from her ears, her mind still humming. She crawled to the edge of the hole and looked down. Beneath the broken bell mechanism, she could see blood, an elbow, rubble, hair. Then she realised Darner was seated against the wall, legs bent and arms braced as if he'd just fallen there. He turned his head and looked up at her, eyes blazing. Blood streamed down his face from a wound in his head. He slapped his hand to it and looked back to the mess in the middle of the floor.

The bells had crashed into the wooden planks of the floor, breaking into them, almost breaking through. Beneath them, between the metal and the broken floorboards, was what remained of Mr Bevel. Nancy was grateful that from her position she couldn't see much of him. An arm at an impossible angle. Legs splayed unmoving. Blood trailed across the floor in a thread and then dripped through the boards to disappear below. Someone on the ground floor began to scream.

Sounds were still dim and thick to Nancy's ears but through it she heard a shout. 'Prophet?' Mr Herbert stood in the doorway of the room below. He circled around by the wall, staying away from the damaged floor and Bevel's body.

'I'm alive,' Darner said, putting the power of his voice into the proclamation so that it was clearly audible. The screaming stopped, replaced by concerned muttering and footsteps on the stairs. 'Get a policeman. And a doctor,' he instructed Herbert.

Herbert stared at Bevel's body. 'He's…'

'With our maker, certainly,' Darner said and crossed himself. He sent a last poisonous look up at Nancy and carefully got to his feet with Herbert's help. 'I will pray for him later. We must do something about this,' he gestured at the mess, 'and her. We must do something about her.'

Herbert looked up at her, eyes wide. He was grey with shock. Darner walked carefully towards the doorway, one hand on the wall, visibly trembling. Nancy stayed where she was, looking down on the bell and on Bevel. She waited.

CHAPTER TWENTY-ONE
HUNGER

Something was happening at the Brethren Hall. The bells were ringing at an unusual time of day, crows and pigeons throwing themselves up into the air in fright. Then the bells had stopped with a ringing crash. People began rushing towards the Hall. Fear roiled through Spider and although she had been torn between staying in her hiding place and getting closer, the need to know had won.

Some policemen went in and Spider heard raised voices. A doctor hurried through. She worked her way to the front of the crowd and waited, listening to the eager speculation around her. A policeman emerged, gripping Nancy by the arm. Spider swayed as her head spun. If Nancy had been arrested, had she killed Darner? Had she got there first? Had Spider assisted her in killing him, in making real the disaster of his early death?

Nancy was saying something indignant and the policeman muttered to her and started to lead her off towards a small group of his colleagues talking to one side.

Darner burst through a crowd of Brethren around the door and Spider felt a rush of relief, then fear that he would see her. She moved back in the crowd, away from his view. There were iodine stains on his face and blood on his collar. A doctor chased after him. 'Mr Darner, let me finish!' Darner ignored him, heading straight for Nancy and the policeman.

'That girl is a murderess! A witch!' Darner shouted.

The policeman turned. 'I'm sorry, sir?'

'You heard me. A witch. I've seen her kill three people now. Two boys and now Mr Bevel here.' He caught his breath.

'You are suggesting, sir, that this girl, this,' he looked Nancy up and down, 'this very young girl, somehow manoeuvred your bells, which must be a third of a ton each, I should say, and caused them to fall on Mr Bevel?'

'Not manoeuvred physically, but she caused them to fall, yes.'

So, the girl had tried. Failed, but she had tried. She could not be trusted.

A man shouted from the crowd. 'If you want to know who caused it, look to yourself, Reverend.' People shuffled apart to let him through. He spoke to the policeman. 'I was part of the crew that put those bells in and they was far too big for their place. Replaced a single bell a fraction the size. They've fallen, have they?'

The policeman nodded and Darner fixed his blazing eyes on the man.

'Yeah, well. I maybe wouldn't have thought they'd fall, but it's still not much of a surprise. I thought, given a few years, the tower would crack for sure. Said as much to the missus.'

The doctor put his hand on Darner's arm. 'Sir, I tell you, you must let me finish my work. Come inside and sit. You must rest for a while.' Darner shook the man's hand off but followed him back into the Hall, casting a last look after Nancy who was still firmly but gently held by the policeman.

A stretcher with a man-sized lump under a blanket was seen through the door and distracted the crowd. Spider needed to get to Nancy. The girl had to be restrained, kept in her hands so that she could be certain where she was. *Antagonist*. Not Darner this time, but the girl. She slipped around and approached the policeman.

'Excuse me.' Spider drew herself up and reached for her most authoritative tone. 'What are you doing with this girl? She's the sister to my new housemaid and I have some responsibility for the family.'

A weariness spread across the policeman's face. 'Nothing, ma'am, nothing at all.' He turned to Nancy. 'You're free to go, Miss Ratcliffe. I've got your name.'

'Really?' Nancy glanced at Spider and back at the policeman as if, just for a moment, she were afraid of Spider and reluctant to go with her.

'Yes. That man seemed determined to blame you, but it seems to me you can't possibly be any more than a witness to a horrible accident. You're probably a bit shook up. Let this lady take you away.' He looked dubiously at Spider. 'Go and have a nice cup of hot sweet tea, that's my advice.' He joined the small group of policemen gathered at the edge of the road.

Spider leant in as she started to lead Nancy away in the direction of her house, her fingers tight on Nancy's arm, her voice hissing through her teeth, 'His blood is mine to take, not yours.'

Chapter Twenty-Two
Thought

'So, you're back.' Jeremiah Blackwell leant back in his winged armchair and looked at Spider.

She stood demure and contrite and murmured, 'Yes, Uncle.' Her senses reached out in all directions and touched the edges of the house. She was back. Home. It was right. Almost right.

'Rather earlier than anticipated.'

She nodded.

'When I got the doctor's letter, I was surprised,' he continued. 'Especially given your mother's moral weakness. Of course, the incident was shocking; and now I'm seeing reports of a scandal in the papers. Perhaps it is best that you're out of there.' He eyed her, watching for her reaction, hands tight on the arms of his chair.

She bent her head further. For a moment, the sensation of swirling water threatened to swallow her. She focused her eyes on the carpet, forcing her mind to still.

'His conclusion was surprising.'

There was a long silence.

'However,' he continued, 'he's the medical expert, with experience of madness of all kinds and so, therefore, I suppose I must give his opinion its due weight, supported in his opinion by a Lunacy Commissioner, no less. He tells me that you did not know you are the heir to this.' He waved a hand to indicate the house surrounding him.

'Indeed.'

'But I told you.' His eyes narrowed and he watched her carefully.

'You said that I should be in an acceptable position after your death. I assumed that meant you had made some kind of provision, perhaps arranging a trust, a guardian, but not that I would inherit the whole.'

'I see.' He pressed his lips together.

'I am very grateful to you for taking me in and providing for me, Uncle. I am well aware of the dire situation in which I should have found myself, had you turned me away.'

'Hmm.' The sound came from the back of his throat. 'I believe in duty. I am not a soft-hearted fool who relies on familial connection, or *love*,' he said the word with a slight sneer, 'but I do fulfil my duties, even where they are unpleasant and inconvenient, as my duty to shelter your mother – and now you – has always been.'

Spider kept her face still. She heard her mother's bare footsteps along an uncarpeted passage, cold skin and creaking rope.

'I also do not believe in disinheriting family. One's fortune should follow one's line. One makes provision for servants and other dependants and then the rest goes to the next of kin, whoever that may be.'

'I always thought Cousin Franklin—'

He waved his hand to dismiss the cousin. 'A cousin by marriage only. The blood relative was his wife. Your mother latched onto the idea and it suited me not to correct her but there is no other claim.

I did think that you knew.' He brought his eyes back to her. 'So. You deny that you made any attempt on my life.'

'Certainly, Uncle.'

He humphed.

She cleared her throat and spoke. 'As I said, I'm grateful for your generosity. Neither of us is a very warm individual,' she risked looking at him, 'and so I can see how you might have been unaware of my gratitude. I will endeavour to make sure that you know it in future.'

'I will be hiring a female servant to be your particular companion. I can see how you have been kept outside wider society because of your lack of chaperone. I will see to it.'

Spider's heart sank. The last thing she wanted was some interfering old woman following her around everywhere, but she smiled. 'Thank you, Uncle. How kind.'

Her turret rooms were empty. She sought out the housekeeper to ask for her belongings.

'Your things are in the attics. I will ask Bristow to get them for you.'

'No, please don't, Mrs Nichols, I'll go.' The idea that they had handled all her things when they were put away made her skin crawl; she did not want them touched by anyone else again. Ever again.

She already had her 'ivory game pieces' as the doctor had referred to them. They had been in her pocket when she was taken to the asylum and, along with the clothes she had been wearing, they had been kept safely shut away while she had been there. She ran her fingers through them in her pocket and smiled. They were all there; she'd checked.

In the attic, she found that her best dress had been placed on a mannequin. It was the green velvet one that she wore for special occasions. Someone, probably Mrs Nichols, had carefully placed it with all her best underpinnings on this mannequin. It must have taken some time. She unbuttoned and unlaced the garments, a tingling revulsion in her fingertips. When it was done, she hurried to her turret room and put the dress away where it had always lived.

She could have piled all her clothes in a single chest and asked Bristow to carry it down for her, but she took them down herself, in armfuls of fabric. She noticed that small repairs had been done before the garments had been stored and, again, this felt like an intrusion. Even though Mrs Nichols and Jenny would usually see to the cleaning and mending of her clothes, somehow the fact it had happened while she was not there, perhaps as they talked over whether she would ever return, felt as though her shroud had been sewn to her skin by someone indifferent.

The greenhouse was bare; the troughs held dead, dry soil but nothing else. A few more of the glass panes were cracked and a whole pane was missing. The scramble of jasmine was gone and the passion flower nothing more than a stump. She bent and looked closely and found a tiny beginning of a leaf against the stem. It would resurrect itself without any of her interference; it was stubborn like that. The rest she would have to work carefully towards: sending for seed, taking cuttings.

Her dried herbs and so-called herbal extractions were all gone and she would have to restart her collection. In fact, she felt a wider selection was required, reaching outside of simple botanical extractions and mixtures, though no doubt they would still be useful. She could take her time; there was no hurry. Her collection – of pressed flowers, feathers, seashells and sticks from particular trees, and the cleaned bones of small animals – was in the box it had always lived in, tucked in a corner of the attic. She imagined the housekeeper pulling a face and making a comment about dead things. The dolls were gone but the sewing kit and fabric were still there.

As she sorted through the box of twigs and bones, she began arranging them on her desk. A shadow flicked across the light and then she heard the flapping of wings. She looked up to find Corbeau in the window. He put his head on one side.

'I was taken away against my will,' she said, and offered him a small piece of cheese she had taken from the kitchen. He accepted the offering, ate it and then eyed the mess of objects on her desk. He stepped among them carefully, lifting and placing his clawed toes as gently as a ballet dancer. Then he stopped and lifted a small bird skull with his beak. It was a robin's skull, pale and translucent, light seeping through the fine bone and into its hollows and holes.

'That one, you think?'

He placed it before her and then hopped over to the window and watched as she picked it up.

'Who killed cock robin?' she said and picked up a thread.

Once she had dangled it from a horizontal stick, carefully balanced and feathered so that it would swing and dip in every slight breeze from the window, she hung it in front of the draft.

'Who killed cock robin?' she repeated as she watched the skull turn gently in the air. '"I," said the sparrow, "with my bow and arrow. I killed cock robin".'

The old doctor objected to Mr Blackwell's choice to keep his niece with him after her return. Spider watched the debate through the hole in the wall.

'I do not trust that girl's eyes,' the doctor said, pacing the rug in front of his patient.

Mr Blackwell pshawed this away.

The doctor tried again. 'Old Whitehead had an excellent reputation—'

'Indeed! You recommended him. And he had – *had*, mark you! – an excellent reputation until this scandal. All gone now, of course, but there's no reason to doubt his judgement on this.'

'Well, I think you're wrong. Mark my words you'll be dead in six months. Please listen to me. You know I'm retiring soon?'

'Retreating to the Scottish moors, I understand.'

'Certainly. My son will be continuing my practice. Please stay with him.'

'Dammit, no! I'll not have your interfering.'

The doctor nodded. 'Well, if that's your final word—'

'It is.'

'Then I will say goodbye. My best wishes for your health in the future, Mr Blackwell.'

He bowed, swept his hat from the sideboard and walked out of the room with a quick snapping stride.

Mr Bakewell advertised for a lady's companion. There were plenty of responses, but once they saw the house and the minimal staff, and had met Miss Atherton, they politely realised they were unsuited to the position. Eventually, however, Patience sent in her application.

An older woman, Patience had worked in service in her youth and then left to care for ailing parents. Finding herself an aged orphan with little hope of finding a husband, she had no way of supporting herself after the meagre inheritance had gone to her brother. A brother who, he regretted, simply didn't have the means to support his sister. His six living children and his wife, sick after her tenth laying-in, took precedence. So back into service Patience went.

Spider found that she was kind, grateful for a relatively easy berth in a world that might have seen her squinting herself to blindness over a sewing needle for fifteen hours a day. She was also sympathetic to the strange heir to the house and her unusual hobbies. She and Spider enjoyed visiting gardens together, a healthful activity that relieved Mr Blackwell's concerns about his strange niece. He did not take much notice of the way the greenhouse refilled.

Some time after the arrival of Patience, Mrs Nichols started to fall ill. A stomach complaint worsened until she took to her bed. Between Patience and Jenny, the work of the house continued to be done. Patience, it seemed, was a more than adequate cook.

When Mrs Nichols took a turn for the worse, young Doctor Fredericks arrived to attend to her. He was fresh from medical school, clumsily handling his hat and large bag and coat. Spider smiled politely. Doctor Fredericks blushed and hurried from her presence. He was perfect.

Doctor Fredericks could not save the housekeeper.

Patience took the great bunch of keys and made them her own.

A short while later, little Jenny left to marry an ostler. The next maid left because her nerves were bad and grew worse in the strange house. The final straw for the poor girl was when the tiger's head hanging in the great hall fell and narrowly missed her. A new maid would be hired eventually, Mr Blackwell said, but Patience managed without one for the time being. It was easier in some ways, she said, as she knew the job was done to her standards.

Mr Bristow left at the same time as the last maid, and if anyone had been left to gossip, they might have drawn conclusions.

When Mr Blackwell hired the next manservant, Mr Metcalfe, Spider noted that he had a drinker's nose and a smart manner; in his younger days, he had worked as a footman in the most exclusive of addresses.

Patience pressed her lips together. 'I can see I'll have to keep an eye on the brandy, ma'am.'

The household, already small for such a large house, had shrunk by one: one set of eyes, one set of ears. Already no one but Mr Blackwell and Spider herself knew she had ever been away from the house, or about the dolls and the small bottles of interesting substances.

Spider laid out her bone sticks on the table one by one and eavesdropped on a conversation happening in the next room. *Despair. Fortune. Antagonist.* She was laying them out to decide whether she needed any more, whether there was a thought or concept that they did not cover. She had some spare bone sticks; they just needed carving. That is, if she decided she needed more.

'Don't forget I don't like citrus peel in the pudding,' Mr Blackwell said to Patience.

Death. Justice. Strength. Spider laid the sticks quietly so that they didn't click and rattle and obscure the voices from the next room.

'It's long since made, sir, one without peel for you, and another one with, for Miss Atherton.'

'And you didn't do any of that nonsense with sixpences and such like?'

'No, sir, just as you asked. I got everyone to stir it though, for luck.'

'Luck!' he snorted. 'I note I wasn't required for this foolishness.'

Creation. Luck. (Spider smiled.) *The blank one.* There must always be a blank one to account for the unaccountable. She enjoyed its empty gleam in the light from the window.

'No, sir, I thought you wouldn't enjoy it. Just the household: Miss Atherton, Mr Metcalfe and me.'

Mr Blackwell barked out a laugh. 'We're not a very big household. It will be pudding for months no doubt.'

Patience agreed.

Ally.

On Christmas Day, they ventured out to a service and sat quietly at the back. Spider had suggested it and her uncle agreed and patted her arm, almost affectionately, and wondered aloud whether the doctor would like to come to dinner one evening. Back at Hangcorner House, they nearly approached a state of good cheer. Mr Blackwell's cheeks were pink with sherry before they sat down to eat.

Every minute felt like a grinding hour to Spider.

At the end of the meal, Spider was sitting with her pudding in front of her, complete with holly sprig and blazing brandy; she looked to the head of the table, at her uncle who smiled at his own pudding, blue light flickering in his glasses. Once the flames died away, he dug in with his spoon, served himself a dollop of brandy butter and began to eat.

Spider wanted to sit and watch him, but she forced herself to eat some of her own pudding, glancing at him every few seconds as she did so.

It was a shame he should die on Christmas Day, but when the doctor was called, exuding his own faint brandy fumes, he shook his head and said it wasn't uncommon. An old man, all the extra food and drink, the excitement, the strain, all combined to create a sad situation when all should be making merry, by rights. Mr Metcalfe nodded and mumbled a prayer for the old man's soul. Patience cleared the table, disposed of the uneaten pudding that no one would want and brought Spider a drink for the shock.

Spider dabbed her eyes with a handkerchief and said, 'Poor uncle. And we had been getting on so well recently.'

The old doctor had been wrong in one sense only. It took a little over a year, rather than six months, but Jeremiah Blackwell was dead all the same.

Spider sent an unusual number of letters at this time, her pen scratching the words 'seeking to trace a man called Darner who may be styling himself as a man of faith, a vicar or similar role', on page after page, writing to any it seemed might be able to find him. The negative answers poured in.

Then came a letter from Dr Whitehead. It was addressed to her uncle and Spider slit open the envelope.

Dear Mr Blackwell,

I am writing to tell you that I have news of Mr Darner's movements from Mr Riverton. You will be relieved to know that he has left the country and is leading a mission into southern Africa. He is understood to have no plans to return and expects to sacrifice his remaining years to the task. Mr Riverton would not approve of my writing to you; however, I felt I owed this much at least to you and your niece. I hope it brings you both some measure of peace.

Yours Sincerely, Dr Whitehead

The letter drifted from Spider's fingers to the floor and Patience, passing about the room, bent and picked it up. She saw her mistress's face and stopped, holding the letter out.

Tears were running down Spider's cheeks, one after the other as if, back in that nearly fatal water bath, she had taken on the fluid and now she must release it. A pressure began to build in her head and she stood, her legs trembling.

'I think I need to go to bed, Patience. I've had some bad news.'

The dark pain was starting to creep around Spider's head and she turned away, turned in.

Soon Mr Metcalfe was encouraged to seek another position, the pony and trap were sold and the house folded in around Spider and Patience. The outside world began to think the house was empty, haunted, a witch-ghost's home. In the darkness, Spider dreamt of Darner, beyond her reach, taunting her.

Chapter Twenty-Three
Light

Nancy hurried to keep up with Spider, caught within the scent of her – faded roses and crow. The hissing voice was hardly coherent but she gathered that Spider thought she had made a deliberate attempt to kill Darner, and regarded this as a sort of attempted theft. The words 'This is mine, I must have him' repeatedly surfaced from among the coils of sentences.

They reached the side door of Hangcorner House, and Spider stopped and turned to Nancy. 'Antagonist,' she said. 'Just who is the antagonist here? I assumed it was Darner, but is it you?' It was fully dark now and her eyes were hidden as she looked down at Nancy.

'Why is he yours? Why do you get him?' Nancy straightened her back and stared back.

Spider didn't answer but pulled Nancy into the house.

Nancy tried again. 'We were going to do this together. To help each other. Wasn't that the point?'

Spider stopped still, head tilted to one side.

'Wasn't it?'

Silence. The house creaked. In the distance, a murmur of Patience's voice. Spider set off towards it.

Pigeon was sitting at the kitchen table in front of a pile of oranges. Her tongue was between her lips as she grated an orange. Patience had flour up to her elbows, her hands in a mixing bowl. The room smelled of oranges and of something sweet baking in the oven. They looked up, surprised.

'Ma'am?'

'Nancy!' Pigeon shoved her chair back and stood up.

'Hands!' Patience thrust a cloth at the girl before she could go to her sister. Pigeon dutifully rubbed her hands clean before running to Nancy, the smell of oranges pouring from her.

'Bring the girl,' Spider said to Patience.

Patience frowned and cleaned off her own hands. She opened the oven and seemed satisfied at what she saw inside. 'What's going on?'

'Miss Ratcliffe made an attempt to kill Darner. Too early. The girls need to be kept in their room while I decide what to do next. I cannot risk Nancy rushing in there and crudely hacking at him before I have developed a coherent plan of action.'

'I didn't make any attempt!' Nancy said. 'That bastard locked me in the bell tower again and it's not my fault the bell fell and nearly killed him.'

Spider's eyes flicked sideways towards her, but she said nothing.

When they reached their room door Nancy asked, 'If you don't want my help any more, why not just let us go?'

'Because you'll do something rash.'

'I won't,' Nancy lied.

'Just until tomorrow. I just need time to think. Consult. Dream. And while I do that, I need to know you're not ruining everything with some bloodthirsty wildness.'

The door slammed and the turning of the key sounded loud and final.

After their footsteps had left, Pigeon flopped onto her bed. 'What did you do, Nancy? You're always being naughty.'

'I didn't do anything. Nothing but wishing really hard and then my wish came true but that's not doing anything, whatever she says.'

'Well, it is doing something. It's wishing.'

Nancy sighed. 'You know what I mean. I can't push you off a cliff just by wishing it.'

'Noooo…' Pigeon said, doubtfully.

'I can't. How hard did we wish for Mum to come back? I've spent my whole bloody life wishing things, or praying for them, but they only ever came true a couple of times.' Nancy looked at Pigeon and realised she would have to tell her about their mother. She pushed the thought to one side. Later.

'I suppose.'

'No, Spider believes in wishes because it means she can pretend that she's doing something. That she hasn't wasted the last few years doing nothing. Well, I'm not going to sit around and pretend to myself that I'm doing something just because I'm dreaming about it.'

'What are you going to do?'

'Get out of here for a start.'

An hour later, Nancy was sitting slumped against the door, trying to pick the lock. Her candle had guttered out a little while ago and she had not relit it. Pigeon was asleep. Nancy's eyes were closing, a dullness creeping up her. Her hand was loosely closed around her hat pin, the end of which was bent.

Spider said they'd be released the next day. There was nothing to fear. Her eyes could close for a little while. With her back against the door, she would know if anyone came in. They were safe, they really were. The warm darkness flooded through her, heavy and soft.

The bare boards stretched away from her and it seemed further to the opposite wall than usual. Strange but it must be because she had slipped down and lay with her cheek against the wood. Lines stretching away. Above her loomed the beds, square and tall. She could see nothing of Pigeon, just hear the gentle hush of her breath. And the creaking. What was the strange creaking? Not a floorboard nor the bedsprings under Pigeon – more like a rope.

She was in a large room with criss-crossing stairs. An enclosed carriage with barred windows stood where large doors would let it in and out. A small girl stared upwards. White nightgown and wide eyes. Nancy followed her gaze.

The body of a woman hung above them. Turning on the end of a rope.

The small girl vanished and a young woman, thin and intense, was trying to climb the staircase, but at each step the stairs drew back with a clank. She made no progress. She held a knife and somehow Nancy knew she wanted to cut the woman down. Her feet walked up and down and up and down and getting nowhere and suddenly there was Darner with a knife of his own. He sawed at the rope. The girl's mouth opened, crying, 'No!' but no sound emerged.

Nancy pushed her ear. Had she gone deaf again? Had the bells done it?

Darner's arm, back and forth across the rope, that look of triumph.

The body fell.

'Wake up and do something!' Lil's voice. Red shawl across her face.

She jerked upright as Lil's voice said, close to her ear, 'She'll get him first, you know, while you're locked away, and then what will she do with you?'

She looked wildly around her, but they were alone in the room as they always had been. The shutters were outlined in bright light; it was the next day, late. She drew the red shawl around her shoulders and shivered. She was stiff with lying on the floor.

She looked at the lock. There was no point trying to pick it again; her pin was bent and useless and she hadn't made any progress at all. The doorknob wobbled a little in her hand. She picked up the hair pin and, instead of attempting to pick the lock, she tried turning the screws on the lock with the bent tip. The point of the pin slipped and even when she got a good hold, the screw didn't budge. She tried a different screw and it shifted slightly. She pushed against it and turned harder. It freed and she span it, suppressing a cry of glee. Then the next and the next tinkled to the floor beside her. Only one left and it resisted but eventually, with bleeding fingers, she dropped it beside the others.

The handle on the other side of the door dropped to the floor with a bang as she pulled away the mechanism. She held the door closed and listened, hoping that no one had heard it. Behind her Pigeon watched her.

'What's going on, Nancy?'

'I've got to go. I've got to finish this. Once he's dead, we can get out of here and we can go with Lil.'

'To Yorkshire?'

Nancy stumbled on an answer. She still hadn't told Pigeon about their mother's death. A darkness spiralled inside her. There was nowhere to go, no home, and she had to look after Pigeon, just her. Lil might help but really it just came down to her. It was her job to find them a safe, warm place with enough to eat. She suddenly felt as if great tendrils of loneliness were trailing out from her and finding nothing to cling to.

'Yeah. Yorkshire. Look, Pigeon, there'll be a fuss when they realise I'm gone but you just tell them you slept through it all.' She looked down into the round, trusting face of her sister. She wanted to say goodbye, just in case she never came back but her throat was closed and dry. She bent and put the red shawl around Pigeon and then kissed her. She still smelled of oranges.

Nancy closed the door behind her and stood in the silent hall. Where should she go now? She didn't have any sort of plan. She could find a knife down in the kitchen, but a faint smell of baking suggested Patience would be there. The walls of this house were crowded with strange things, and she remembered a case of Indian knives, though she couldn't remember where it was. She set out to find it.

She had walked the passages for some time, recognising many but not all, lost as she and Pigeon had been a few days ago, until at the end of a narrow passage she tried a door and it swung inwards. It opened onto a circular room and she realised this was the strange turret visible from the yard. She had thought it was part of the warehouse – something about the brickwork made it look like it was allied to that part of the building – and yet this very definitely belonged to the house. This wasn't where the knives were. She was about to step back, when she saw Spider.

A cold chill rushed through her and she stood on the threshold looking in. In front of the curved window hung an elaborate mobile of twigs, glass and feathers and bird bones, like the one she had seen in the greenhouse. It spun slightly in the breeze from the open door. Around it candles had melted into pools of their own wax over hours, extinguishing themselves. A single flame guttered on. Ivy reached across the wall, and a pot of something green and fernlike balanced in a corner. Spider sat in a winged armchair, legs stretched out before her, gazing up into the glittering and moving shapes of the mobile. Behind her sat the crow, hunched, his eye half-open, catching the light.

Spider was so still that for a moment Nancy thought she was dead. She stepped into the room and saw her throat move and the rise and fall of her chest. Her eyes, with their small, distant pupils, remained fixed on the mobile. Nancy felt sure that Spider wasn't aware of her presence. The crow lifted his head and watched her. The light from the window was grey and weak; it wouldn't be long until it was dark.

She stood for a moment gazing at Spider, then her eyes fell on the small table at her left hand. On it stood a tiny green glass with a sticky residue in the bottom and a brown bottle.

Labelled glass jars of various sizes lined the shelves; some contained powders or dried herbs, others glistened with what looked like iridescent beads, until Nancy got closer and saw they were beetles: hundreds of shining green beetles in one jar, crimson ones in another, like clots of blood. Bunches of dried plants hung in front of the shelves; somehow Nancy knew they weren't for cooking. A few specimen jars held unidentifiable things that had once been animals or fish; in the corner, some chemistry equipment. Between and under and alongside these things were books: piles and piles of books, new and old. Books on religion and magic, and chemistry and botany.

Among the litter on one of the shelves was a large knife and, keeping her eyes on Spider, she reached for it. The crow opened his beak slightly as if considering whether to cry out a warning, but he contented himself with jabbing his beak half-heartedly towards her fingers as she took the knife.

Spider gasped and twitched. Nancy stood paralysed; her heart seemed to stop beating. Spider didn't wake. Spider had spent so much time watching and preparing that Nancy didn't believe that she would ever make Darner pay for what he'd done. Nancy couldn't bear the thought of that; she had to do it herself.

Nancy took a careful step back but her attention was caught. She paused. In the centre of one shelf stood a frame, holding a small picture. A blackened substance smeared across the image, a small pen knife blade thrust through the broken glass and into the picture beyond. Rust on the blade suggested it had been there some time. Just visible through the mess, Nancy could see that the sketch looked like a young Darner, standing in front of a large building, perhaps a stately home. The blackened substance seemed to have been smeared again and again. In places, it had gathered and crumbled away from the glass. Blood. Old blood.

The crack and flap of a bird's sudden flight, a blackness across her face and then Corbeau flew across the room and settled on the top of the door, passing the mobile, which span wildly in his wings' wind.

He cawed resentfully and flapped.

She sidled past him and out, the knife clutched in her hand.

Chapter Twenty-Four
Pursuit

Spider's hand twitched and the small green glass fell over. Wings spread across her vision and she flinched away, pushing back into the chair, but then her mind began to focus and she realised the wings were Corbeau's, that he had simply flown across the room. The mobile spun in the wind of his passing, the robin skull turned through her vision and then a wing that was no longer attached to a bird. A candle flame shifted and flickered.

Death.

'Choose,' she whispered through dry lips.

Corbeau hopped onto the table, stirred the ivory sticks with his claw and then darted, choosing one with a stab of his beak. He hopped over to her and, with trembling fingers, she took it from him.

Death.

She nodded. Whose? His? Her own? The girl's?

The sticks had never commented on the past, not in her years' long experience with them. Past deaths no longer concerned her; they were dark doorways through which she no longer had to look. Future deaths – those were questions yet to be answered. Or perhaps they were the answers. Death was so often an answer, she had found over the years. What else but an ending could create freedom? What else but a death could be a beginning?

He needed to die, and soon. Tonight. It was dark outside but still quite early in the long winter evening. Darner would soon be taking his laudanum and having his bath, if Nancy were right about his routine. If there were more time, if there were not an eager, bloodthirsty girl involved, she would replace that laudanum with her own creation. She had mixtures for dreams, for flying, for divining the future, and for death. Different deaths: a quiet, still death or a nightmare rictus death, screaming with cramps and the pincers of flesh-tearing demons. She sought out both bottles and slipped them in her pocket.

As she approached the girls' room to check on them, she heard a knocking sound. It came towards her from the stairs around the corner. She stopped. It stopped. She strode towards it and found Pigeon standing at the top of the stairs, holding a door knob. She was playing with it as if it were a ball, but turned, wide-eyed and silent at the sound of Spider's footsteps.

The girl pressed herself into the wall as Spider ran past her to the open door. The lock and its screws were scattered on the floor. She grasped the door frame, suddenly dizzy. Nancy was gone. She would get there first. She would see him die and Spider would not. A pain speared through Spider's left eye and she bent her head in her hands, squeezing herself against the pain.

She wrenched her head up and turned on Pigeon. 'Where is she?'

Pigeon looked down at her dress and shrugged. 'I don't know. She went while I was asleep.' The words thudded dully, learnt by heart. Lies.

'She's gone to the Brethren Hall, hasn't she?'

Pigeon glanced up, bright-eyed and afraid. 'I don't know.'

Where would she have gone but back to the Brethren Hall? And for what purpose but to kill Darner? If so, Spider needed to get there without wasting another moment. She dismissed Pigeon and through a haze of pain raced down the stairs, the sound of her feet clattering through the passages. Past the wall covered in masks, past the collections of insects. The dull eyes of the taxidermied creatures didn't follow her, though her reflection flitted through their gaze and it almost seemed as though they should. Patience came out into the hall, her mouth open with confusion.

'What on earth is going on, ma'am?'

'Nancy's gone.'

'What?'

'Nancy. Gone. She's gone and it must be her intention to go after Darner, because she's left her sister. I need to stop her.' She marched across the hall.

'She might be hurt or in trouble!'

Spider stopped, exasperated. 'That's not my concern. She knows the consequences, but I can't let her get to him first.'

'Oh, but she's so young.' Patience pulled at the ends of her shawl in distress.

'She's a bright glaring light in my eyes when I need darkness. If you feel so concerned for her, I give you leave to go and find that old beggar woman, Lil. She might be able to help in some way. She might be able to persuade her not to be so rash.'

She dashed past Patience and hauled the front door open. The hollow bang of it slammed behind her and she hurried up the street. The girl must not kill him first. She mustn't.

Chapter Twenty-Five
Commit

Nancy stood trembling in Darner's bedroom. She had waited until darkness fell, huddled against the wall below his window. She had heard Johnson's voice in the Prophet's rooms and known that his bath was being readied. Once there was silence, she scrambled up onto the brick ledge below his high windows and hauled herself up into his sparse bedroom.

With the door open a little, she could see that a tin bath was waiting in Darner's private sitting room. Although it was set in front of the fire, she knew that the water had not been warmed. The cold water was part of the ritual for him. The scouring of his body. A small square of soap and a rough bristled brush sat beside the bath. Voices came from Darner's office, two people, quiet and ordinary.

She silently took off her shoes and crept to the bedroom door, which stood slightly ajar. The private sitting room beyond was more comfortable; a large carpet covered almost the whole floor and bookshelves lined one wall.

She remembered the bookshelves. Her dad had built them for Darner in those first months after they had joined, when his enthusiasm for the Charitable Brethren had been untainted and whole, when his health had seemed as good as any other man's, although the disease was already lurking. She had not been allowed into the room, but she remembered the care he had taken with the detail, inlaying fine strips of mahogany decoration and ensuring all of his work was hidden and smoothed away before the shelves were carried out of the workshop. He had run his hand across the polish of the last one and said, 'That's a worthy piece.' Then he'd faltered. 'I hope he thinks it's a worthy piece.'

A comfortable winged armchair sat beside the fire, a small table at its side, on which stood a brown glass bottle and a spoon. Like his public office, the window was high; no one outdoors could look into it without a ladder and the curtains were closed, shutting out the night.

The voices in the other room stopped. The door opened and Darner came in, then locked the door behind himself. A frown folded his forehead. Nancy held her breath, hoping that he would not come into the bedroom. Her heart thumped and she looked behind her at the window. Her last chance to leave; she could go and fetch Pigeon and take Lil up on her offer, go looking for peace and warmth, and leave Darner to his fate, whatever that would be. Perhaps Spider would get him. But perhaps she never would.

Darner removed his clothes, placing them on a table, and carefully climbed into the bath. His long thin muscles moved under pale skin spread with sprouting hairs. The empty bag of his thin stomach wrinkled and, as he bent and turned, the hollow of his groin was like a tree cleft filled with moss and old fungus.

He began vigorously soaping and scrubbing himself. The brush left his skin pink and alive, his breath coming short with the cold.

He paid close attention to his ablutions as if each small motion, each rasp against cold skin, were a thing to be observed fully. He raised his foot and scoured every toe. He scrubbed behind his knees. He leant forwards and reached his back, his beard dipping in the water. Once he had cleaned every part of his body, he stood and dried himself, being careful to avoid splashing. Then he put on a robe and settled into his chair.

Soon, Nancy thought. Soon. She gripped the knife. She remembered the wiry strength in his fingers, the ease with which he had thrown her to the floor, and she put the knife in her other hand to wipe the sweat from her palm against her dress. It stuck to her. She had to get him before he had a chance to fight back. Then she had to get away quickly or she'd hang. She looked at the window again.

The little brown bottle glittered in the firelight as he poured a few droplets into the spoon. He took it and leant back in his chair. This was the reason he always locked the door, this illicit pleasure. Or perhaps there was pain to ease. The hollows in his cheeks softened as he drifted in the warmth of the fire and the drug. She shifted from the ball of one foot to the other, listening for sounds outside the door. The Brethren had been directed not to disturb him on these evenings, to keep away and to give him privacy. It had always been taboo for the children to disturb him at any time. The door opened into his office. She wondered if he had locked the outer door; she thought not. Whoever had been with him had left only a moment before Darner walked in.

Darner shifted so that his face was partly hidden by the wing of the armchair and no longer in her line of sight. She couldn't see if he were fully asleep. She cursed herself for not having thought of this sooner, though there was nothing she could have done. If she'd moved the chair he'd have noticed. She waited. His breaths lengthened and slowed. He sat still and quiet; his hand rested on the arm of the chair and then slipped off, dangling down, yellowed nails against the carpet.

Nancy pulled back the door, wishing hard for it to stay silent and stepped through into the room. She could feel her pulse in her throat, and the rush of it beating in time with the bells in her ears. She looked back at the protection of the small bed chamber, then turned to Darner. She looked down at him. His head lolled onto the wing of the chair; his pale eyelids were folded down like a puppet's and made his eyes seem large.

He shifted slightly and she jumped. His head tilted back in his sleep, his lips lightly sneering as if even in his dream he was berating someone. She gripped the knife harder, clenching her empty hand too. She held her breath, raised the knife and stabbed.

As she moved forwards, his eyes snapped open. He cried out in surprise and raised his arm. Under the knife, his arm gaped red. His hand closed around her wrist and she stumbled back. He stared at her and then at the blood gathering in the deep wound on his arm. Before he could gather himself, she pulled herself out of his grip and rushed at him again, knife held in both fists, aiming for his chest and she hit her mark, the knife point pierced the skin. But before she could drive the knife home, he threw her away from him. She staggered and fell. He reached for the knife and she slashed wildly. He gave a cry and kicked out as the knife sliced across his leg. The knife flew out of her hands and she lunged for it.

'What have we here?' He stepped towards her and grabbed her by the hair. 'A murderous young witch.' He kicked the knife away.

He swayed as he pulled her upright, staggering to keep his balance. His blood was running freely down his arm and chest, drops scattering. He seemed to neither notice nor feel it. He pulled her face into his and stared into it. Nancy felt as though he was not seeing her as she really was, but as a vision of hell through those distorted pupils, so small and intense. She struggled to get away.

He turned, still holding her and shoved her down into the bath. Water swirled around her, bubbles in her nose and mouth, and she tried to find something to push up on but there was nothing. She kicked out but her feet could get no purchase on the ground.

He was not going to win, he couldn't. Her anger at her father's cold death roared up through her. She writhed and the bath shifted slightly. She was pulled up out of the water; it poured from her as she was raised up, still gripped in Darner's hands. Spider stood behind him, one hand clenching his throat, her nails scoring the flesh, the other hauling him back by the hair.

'Mine!' Spider hissed. They struggled as a group. Darner dropped Nancy onto the floor to free his hands to claw at Spider's.

'No!' Nancy screamed and grabbed at him. Together they pushed him towards the bath; he staggered, weakened by the loss of blood running freely down his chest. He gave a roar of pain and anger, turned, eyes wide and desperate, and then the edge of the bath caught him behind the knees and with a shove from Spider he fell back into it.

Spider pushed Nancy away. Weak and shaking from her plunge under the water she slipped, staggered and fell. From the floor she watched as Spider pushed him under the water.

Chapter Twenty-Six
Death

Spider looked down at the man in the bath. He was wild-eyed, confused, spluttering water. His robe fell open. His wiry, naked body sprawled.

Nancy breathed hard, gave a coughing sob and got to her feet, leaning against the wall.

Spider pushed his head back under the water and his hands came up to grasp her wrists, clinging and tearing with a futile desperation. Coils of blood twisted from the wounds in his arm and chest. Spider's head pulsed darkly.

'He has to die,' Nancy panted.

'Prophet?' called a voice from outside.

Spider ignored it and dragged Darner's head up again. He was heavy and she braced herself. He coughed water into the air and blinked and kicked.

'Do you remember me, Mr Darner?' Spider asked.

He puffed and blinked and pulled at her arms. Eyes darting, he gave a shake of his head. 'Demon.' His voice trembled.

'Think back to your asylum days.'

'So many,' he moaned. 'So many witches there.'

'No, no there weren't. There were so many sad women, and there was me. You remember me.'

His eyes met hers and widened. 'You! God save me.'

As she pushed him back under the water, he clawed at her face. She ignored the pain. The bath water was a dull iron pink.

'Here, help me,' Spider said. Nancy heaved him up out of the water. Darner let out a bellow and at the same moment Spider uncorked one of her small bottles. Nancy held his jaw open and Spider upended it into his mouth. She flung the bottle into the corner and held his mouth shut, his cry cut short with a stifled choke. His eyes were wide as she pushed him under the water.

'What was that?' Nancy asked.

'Nightmares,' Spider said as footsteps hammered in the outer room and someone beat on the door. Nightmares spinning and death a relief at the end of them.

'Prophet! What's going on?' Someone beat on the door with weak fists.

Another voice said, 'We'll have to break down the door. Get Johnson. And send someone for the police.'

'We aren't going to get out of this, are we?' Nancy said. The girl looked frightened now, pale and holding herself tight against her trembling. She stared at the weakly struggling figure in the bath.

Spider didn't answer. A great calmness had fallen over her. The pain in her head retreated and left in its place a distant lightness.

Spider hauled Darner out again. He choked up a mix of bloody water and bitter brown fluid. It spattered across her face. Then he gave a heave, a twisting struggle. The whole bath fell sideways with a crash, a flood of water spreading across the room. Spider kept hold of him and Nancy reached for the knife, holding it out towards the great Prophet. The tip trembled but it was unnecessary. The heave had been a last desperate flailing and now he was exhausted. He lay gasping under Spider, who still held his hair. A pulse fluttered visibly in his neck.

His eyes looked up into hers, but the pupils were minuscule; points of darkness that he could not reach out from. He didn't seem to see anything. His breath sounded wet. She wiped her face on her sleeve. The bitter smell of her concoction joined in her nose with his blood. Iron and death.

A movement distracted her and she looked up to find Nancy was dragging a table to place it in front of the door. She kicked the doorstop under the bottom edge of the door, pushing it home as hard as she could and shoved the table against it. It occurred to Spider that any table that Nancy could drag alone could hardly weigh enough to constitute any real obstacle, but she said nothing.

Darner gave a ragged groan and she looked down at him. He looked past her and held up his hands, reaching weakly towards something she couldn't see. 'No,' he mouthed and tried feebly to pull away. The hollows in his cheeks and the lines in his face seemed to have deepened in his damp grey skin.

A voice outside the door called out again. 'Prophet!' Darner's eyes flickered and he tried to roll to one side. Spider stopped him.

Someone started beating on the door.

Spider pulled herself up into the armchair and, grabbing Darner by the hair and under his arm, she hauled him up so that his head was resting in her lap like a child's.

'I was an odd young lady, it must be admitted, when I was sent to the Lansdowne Asylum and we met for the first time. Do you remember it?'

Nancy watched with tired, flat eyes. She leant against the wall and slid down it. Spider interrupted herself. 'You should go.'

Nancy shook her head. 'I started this, it's my fault. I've got to stay to the end.'

Spider looked at her. 'No. You have Pigeon to look after.'

Nancy shifted uncomfortably and opened her mouth to protest. Spider leant forwards and hissed, 'We're going to hang, Nancy. The bite of hemp in your neck. Your sister truly alone. You'll jerk on the end of that rope and then turn and turn and turn with your blue distorted face and God only knows if your sister will ever forget it. I hope to God she doesn't see it.'

Nancy swallowed and then a stillness came over her.

'Go!' Spider said, flinging her arm out, finger outstretched towards the window of the small room.

The decision flashed across Nancy's face a moment before she bolted to her feet. Then she was gone, a thump as she landed and her footsteps hurtling away down the side alley.

Spider listened for a moment, hoping there would be no cry of pursuit, no trouble. There was none.

'I dreamt about my mother at the asylum.' She continued talking to the blank-faced man dying in her lap. 'I often dream of her but there it was constant, even without my herbs to take me to her. Her turning on her rope and you! You came into those dreams.' He was heavy against her legs. Her skirts clung to her, soaked with the water and his blood but it didn't matter. She had no need to move freely.

Darner raised his hand as if brushing away a cobweb. She slapped the hand away from her face. A taut breath hung. Spider watched, a small smile tugging her lips, waiting to see if there would be another breath. There was. She continued.

'I wonder if you remember the penance. I suspect it's still a favourite of yours and that I was just one of many. But then I defied you.'

The door shook and a crack came from the lock.

Spider was calm. Her temple throbbed but she was not in any great pain anymore; it seemed that murdering a man she had wanted to kill for many years caused her less agony than a bright sunlit day or a minor dispute with Patience. Her lips tingled. She smiled and licked them. They tasted bitter.

The doorstop was driven back as someone pushed hard and the table fell with a crash. As a man in a policeman's uniform squeezed through the gap, Darner coughed. A long drawn-out breath ground out of his throat and then he died.

She looked up at the men who stared back at her in horror. She followed their eyes. 'I do apologise for the mess.'

She pushed Darner's corpse off her lap. It slumped sideways on the floor and she rose. The policeman stepped back.

She held out her arm. At first the policeman took it as if he were about to walk her across the road but then, stiffly, he shifted and gripped her by the upper arm. The world was taking on a hazy aura and she felt happier than she ever had before. The policeman led her away.

Chapter Twenty-Seven
LOVE

Nancy pelted along the alley, her breath tight around her heart. When she reached the street, she almost fell over herself in coming to a halt, realising it would be better not to be seen running away from the scene of a murder. She looked down at her dress. Her upper body was soaked to the skin but the dark fabric meant that any blood spots were barely visible in the gaslight.

Policemen were gathering at the front of the Hall and the nearby pub had disgorged a curious crowd. Another policeman leant against the wall chatting to a costermonger. He looked at Nancy and then returned to his chat.

'There's some trouble with the barmy Brethren,' one man said to a friend, peering over his shoulder.

'Again? Have they dropped another bell on themselves? How many 'ave they got?' He gave a hoarse laugh.

Nancy slipped past them. She needed to get to a place where she could think, somewhere she could decide what to do next, somewhere she could sort through the swirl of things inside her. She needed to get off the street.

'Hey, Nance,' a hand gripped her arm. 'What the hell is going on?' Lil muttered harshly into her ear. Then the old woman stood back and looked Nancy over. 'You look like you've seen a ghost. And you're wet. Come here.' She pulled her into a doorway. Pigeon detached herself from Lil's hand and grabbed Nancy's. Pigeon's hand was warm and soft and Nancy felt so grateful for it that she almost cried. She pulled Pigeon against her for a hug and held her. Another figure hovered over Lil's shoulder and she realised that Patience was there too, staring at the Hall.

'Where's my mistress?' she asked.

Nancy looked at her feet, a sense of dread and guilt swinging through her. 'She told me to go.'

'Oh no.' Patience clasped her hands.

Nancy didn't want to tell Patience she'd left her mistress talking in an odd voice to a dying man. Someone called out from inside the building and all the policemen hurried inside.

'What happened?' Lil asked, her fists on her hips. 'Come on, girl, out with it.'

'I went at him.'

'Oh, Nance!' Lil exclaimed.

'I know, but it was my best chance. We had a tussle, then Spider came in,' she glanced at Patience, 'I don't think she expects to get out.'

'Quick, follow me,' said Patience.

Patience led them round the side of the building and unlocked the door. They followed her into an old empty shop, thick with dust, then up a staircase. Trails of footsteps led through the dust: one to a faded velvet armchair near the window and another to a plain high-backed chair against the back wall. A small work basket stood by the plain chair: Patience's station. One of Spider's strange mobiles dangled in the light of the candle. Bits of old rubbish twisting through the air. Lil touched it with a finger and shook her head.

Patience tore away a sheet of newspaper from the window so they could see out and Nancy stood beside her. In the street people milled about, craning their necks, asking each other what was going on.

Nancy started to shiver and Pigeon held out the red shawl. Nancy took it without argument.

They drifted into silence for a while until Lil asked suddenly, 'Why do you think he hated you and Spider so much? Why did he pick you out from the others?'

Nancy tore at the newspaper edge with her thumb. Words came tight from her mouth which trembled with the rest of her. 'I don't think he did. I don't think we were special to him. The difference is that we were the ones who fought back. He didn't choose us. We chose ourselves by standing up to him and he couldn't let that happen.'

'What next?' Patience said, stiff-backed, staring down at the people outside.

Nancy met Lil's eyes and shrugged. 'Tramping up to Yorkshire.'

'We'll go and live with mum,' Pigeon said.

'I think my mistress will want you to stay.'

Nancy said, 'I'm not so sure about that. And, Patience, I don't think your mistress is coming back.'

Patience looked back over her shoulder, her eyes sad and then turned again to watch the street. 'Well then, I'd like you to stay. If the worst… well, I'll be the mistress then I suppose. I'll be alone.'

Lil nudged Nancy and she knew what she meant by it. She meant, don't look a gift horse in the mouth, girl, you don't have to abide it forever.

'But we'll be going to mum.' Pigeon gripped Nancy's skirt.

'We can all go to Yorkshire together. God knows there'll be enough money.' Patience gave a small laugh.

In her mind's eye Nancy saw a country graveyard in summer, daisies in the grass dancing in a warm breeze. She would get a headstone for both of them: her mother and father together again. Pigeon would be sad but well fed and safe; she'd finally take her to the toyshop. If they tramped, they'd arrive at her mother's pauper's grave stinking of workhouses, half-starved with oakum under their fingernails, if they ever arrived at all.

This was what Spider had given her, she realised. An ongoing life, free from the deep distortion of ongoing hatred. The future, open like a flower. Nancy nodded.

Lil gripped her arm, gave it a reassuring shake. 'I'll still be around somewhere, love. You won't get rid of me,' she said in an undertone.

Outside in the street there was a clatter as a police van pulled by two sturdy greys trotted up to the Hall's door.

A group of policemen came out surrounding Spider who stood tall between them, her face pale under a smear of blood.

Patience gasped and ran out of the room, downstairs and out into the street. Nancy leant forwards and Lil gripped her shoulder. Patience elbowed her way through the people.

Spider walked towards the police van like a witch queen conveyed to her golden carriage. Even from this distance, it seemed the policemen had a wary, deferential attitude. One of them held the door open for her, and she turned on the top step to watch as a covered stretcher was brought out of the Hall. She smiled and, seeing Patience in the crowd, raised her hand as if in benediction, and then the doors closed her in.

Chapter Twenty-Eight
Dissolution

Spider sat in the van opposite a square-built policeman with lopsided eyes. A broken fragment of light came through the barred window and fell on her face. She lurched as the van pulled away and the policeman put out a hand as if to steady her. Where was she going? Gaol or Lansdowne Asylum? The light jerked away from her face and slipped to the floor as the van moved. Her lips tingled. *Antagonist. Death.* Of course the oracles had been right, they always were. *Ally.*

Patience would be better off without her; she'd have the girls now, and the house. Money.

A cramp spasmed across her stomach and she bent forwards with a groan. Her lips were no longer tingling so much as numb.

She fingered a small bottle in her pocket. The quiet death. But she couldn't swallow it with the policeman there watching her every movement. It didn't matter though; death was following the van swiftly and if nightmare came first, relief would not be far behind.

She and the policemen were not the only inhabitants of the carriage. Mr Darner dripped and bled in the corner; Mrs Nichols was propped on a bench like a broken doll. Her uncle would have liked to make a sardonic remark – she could tell by the way his glasses danced with the light of burning brandy. The creaking of the van sounded like the creaking of a rope. Eliza crooned a lullaby, invisible in the corner, the scent of jasmine enclosing Spider.

Her heart trembled and twisted and she laughed at the pain. It was whole. They had come to the end.

The van jerked in a pothole and Darner slid to the floor with a groan.

Spider put her hand in her pocket, the one without the poison, and ran her fingers through her oracle sticks, choosing one last fragment of future. The policeman shifted uneasily, watching closely.

She drew it out and she already knew what it would be, felt it in her fingers and did not need to hold it to the dim light. Her fingers spasmed and she dropped it. It lay on the floor in the dancing square of light from the window.

Blank.

The policeman bent, picked it up, turned it over and back. He held it out to her but she could no longer lift her arms and just stared at him.

The oracle had fallen silent and the numbness flowed up her limbs towards her heart, around her head. It felt as if she were being submerged in a fluid nothingness. She slipped from the bench and heard the policeman's cry of alarm as a distant crow's call on the wind. A feather hung in the crossed window light; a bird skull turned in the breeze; a fragment of glass glittered. A bitter herb on her tongue, a black wing across her vision, and then darkness.

ACKNOWLEDGEMENTS